BOLD
STROKES
BOOKS

LOVE &
HONOR

What Reviewers Say About BOLD STROKES' Authors

✌

KIM BALDWIN

"Her…crisply written action scenes, juxtaposition of plotlines, and smart dialogue make this a story the reader will absolutely enjoy and long remember." – **Arlene Germain**, book reviewer for the *Lambda Book Report* and the *Midwest Book Review*

✌

ROSE BEECHAM

"…a mystery writer with a delightful sense of humor, as well as an eye for an interesting array of characters…" – *MegaScene*

"…her characters seem fully capable of walking away from the particulars of whodunit and engaging the reader in other aspects of their lives." – *Lambda Book Report*

"…creates believable characters in compelling situations, with enough humor to provide effective counterpoint to the work of detecting." – *Bay Area Reporter*

✌

JANE FLETCHER

"…a natural gift for rich storytelling and world-building…one of the best fantasy writers at work today." – **Jean Stewart**, author of the *Isis* series

✌

RADCLY*f*fE

"Powerful characters, engrossing plot, and intelligent writing…" – **Cameron Abbott,** author of *To the Edge* and *An Inexpressible State of Grace*

"…well-honed storytelling skills…solid prose and sure-handedness of the narrative…" – **Elizabeth Flynn**, *Lambda Book Report*

"…well-plotted…lovely romance…I couldn't turn the pages fast enough!" – **Ann Bannon**, author of *The Beebo Brinker Chronicles.*

"…a consummate artist in crafting classic romance fiction…her numerous best selling works exemplify the splendor and power of Sapphic passion…" – **Yvette Murray, PhD**, *Reader's Raves*

LOVE &
HONOR

by

RADCLY*f*FE

2005

LOVE & HONOR

ISBN 1-933110-10-4

THIS TRADE PAPERBACK ORIGINAL IS PUBLISHED BY
BOLD STROKES BOOKS, INC.,
PHILADELPHIA, PA, USA

FIRST EDITION: MAY 2003
SECOND PRINTING: OCTOBER, 2004 BOLD STROKES BOOKS, INC.
THIRD PRINTING: MARCH, 2005 BOLD STROKES BOOKS, INC.

CREDITS
EXECUTIVE EDITOR: STACIA SEAMAN
EDITOR: LANEY ROBERTS
PRODUCTION DESIGN: J. BARRE GREYSTONE
COVER DESIGN BY SHERI (GRAPHICARTIST2020@HOTMAIL.COM

By the Author

Romances

Safe Harbor

Beyond the Breakwater

Innocent Hearts

Love's Melody Lost

Love's Tender Warriors

Tomorrow's Promise

Passion's Bright Fury

Love's Masquerade

shadowland

Fated Love

Honor Series

Above All, Honor

Honor Bound

Love & Honor

Honor Guards

Justice Series

A Matter of Trust (prequel)

Shield of Justice

In Pursuit of Justice

Justice in the Shadows

Change Of Pace: *Erotic Interludes*
(A Short Story Collection)

Acknowledgments

I once said that I didn't want to write sequels, especially to romances, because romances traditionally ended with the two main characters embracing their love and "riding off into the sunset." Where was there to go after that?

Romances have changed, and so have I. Now there is more of a demand to see what happens after the honeymoon, and romance sequels are more common. The Honor series is a bit of a hybrid, with an ongoing romance within an action framework. The third in the series has been both a challenge and a pleasure to write, and I am grateful to all of the readers who have followed along, encouraged me, and asked for more.

I am extremely grateful to Kathy Smith, my friend and colleague, for the assistance in producing all my books. Kathy's expertise, professionalism, and support are invaluable to me.

I am blessed with two superb editors, Laney Roberts and Stacia Seaman, who never fail to make me look good. Jane Chen proofed the final version and her assistance is much appreciated. They are innocent of any remaining errors, all of which I must claim as mine.

As always, many thanks to my friends and beta-readers, Athos, JB, JC, and Tomboy, and to HS and all the members of the Radlist, for their ongoing encouragement, support, and inspiration.

Sheri continually surpasses herself with each new cover, which says a lot. I love her work and am ever humbled by her talent.

Lee's presence in my life is the constant that allows me to dream. *Amo te.*

Dedication

For Lee,
Forever and Always

CHAPTER ONE

Fresh from the shower, Cameron Roberts walked naked across the carpeted living room to the bar. The floor-to-ceiling windows in her top-floor apartment afforded an unimpeded view of the night skyline of Washington, DC. The view was breathtaking.

She poured an inch of single malt scotch into a heavy crystal rock glass and leaned against the bar that edged one side of the room, staring at the city lights mingling with the midnight stars. There had been a time when this vision of piercing beauty had lost the power to move her—a time beyond loss when she had been convinced that nothing would ever stir her soul again. She had been wrong.

After drawing a gray silk robe from the back of a barstool, she slipped it on and then reached for the phone. She dialed a number from memory and waited expectantly for the only voice she had wanted to hear all day.

"Hello?"

Cam smiled. "How's San Francisco?"

A quick intake of breath, and then a throaty laugh. "How bad can it be? It's the city of beautiful men and handsome women. And it's August, so the sun shines more than it rains."

"Sounds pretty perfect."

"It is." Blair Powell sat down on the edge of the bed and glanced out the window of the guest room in a multilevel glass-and-cedar house tucked into a niche on the slope of Russian Hill. Visible over the tops of trees and rooftops, the expanse of San Francisco Bay below reflected the colors of the setting sun. It was achingly beautiful, and she wished her caller were by her side to share it. Her voice husky with emotions still new enough to be frightening, she added, "Almost."

"Almost?" Cam sipped her scotch, imagining deep blue eyes and wild golden curls. She edged a hip onto the arm of the leather sofa and watched the night. It was odd how a vista she had seen a thousand times suddenly made her long for company, when for so many months it had barely registered in her consciousness. She knew what had changed, and it hadn't been intended. Or wise. "Problem?"

"Mmm. I can't find a date to the reception."

"Ah..." Cam sighed. "I might not be able to help you there. I'm sorry."

"Really?" Blair teased, trying to hide her disappointment. They hadn't made any definite plans, but she'd hoped. "What's happening back there?"

"The usual bureaucratic maneuvering—too many opinions, too many section chiefs, too many people worried about their political careers." She drained the scotch, set the glass gently down on a carved stone coaster on the end table, and forced a lighter note into her voice. "Like I said, nothing out of the ordinary for the Hill."

"So this debriefing thing is likely to be a few more days?"

"I think so. Today was just the blow-by-blow review of events. The who was where, when, and did what analysis."

"And tomorrow?"

"Tomorrow it will get interesting." *Tomorrow will be the day someone gets hung.*

"You don't sound too worried." *But there's something—you're hiding something.*

"No, I'm not. Is everything all right there? Has the press caught up to you?"

"It's fine," Blair hastened to assure her. "Nothing out of the ordinary."

"Who's at the house?" She'd reviewed the details with Mac Phillips, her communications coordinator, earlier in the evening when she'd gotten a break between meetings, but being separated from her team made her uneasy. The tumultuous events of the last few weeks had left her on edge and had only served to remind her that anyone could get through the best-designed protection if they really wanted. It was not a thought she could tolerate, especially not when it concerned Blair.

"Stark is in the bedroom across the hall, and Davis is downstairs playing cards with Marcea and an extraordinarily handsome silver-haired gentleman with a devastating Italian accent."

"That would be Giancarlo." Cam laughed, picturing her mother entertaining a houseful of artists, foreign visitors, and Secret Service agents. "Sounds like it's all under control."

"Mac knows what he's doing, Cam. You don't need to worry."

"I'm not worried about a thing." Cam was glad that Blair couldn't see her face. The president's daughter seemed to be able to read the truth in her expression, when all anyone else ever saw was her neutral game face.

"You sound tired."

"I'm fine," Cam responded automatically. In truth, she still had a ferocious headache left over from the concussion she had sustained in an explosion two nights before, and she hadn't had much sleep since she'd left Blair Powell's bed the previous afternoon. Spending the entire day explaining how two federal agents under her command had ended up in the intensive care unit hadn't helped the pounding.

U.S. Treasury Assistant Director Stewart Carlisle closed the door behind him and regarded the first daughter's Secret Service crew chief expressionlessly. "You okay?"

"Bumps and bruises. Nothing serious." Cam sat in the chair on the right side of the head of the table where she knew Carlisle, her immediate supervisor, would be seated during the upcoming debriefing and after-action report. The FBI would take the other end while representatives from the National Security Council and the president's personal security adviser filled in the more or less neutral territory between. At the moment, she and Carlisle were the only two people in the room, but that would change in fifteen minutes when the others arrived to discuss the assassination attempt on the president's only child.

"If you're not ready for this, Roberts, tell me now."

"I'm fine, sir." He didn't need to know about the intermittent double vision or the persistent nausea or the dizziness.

He blew out a breath and took the chair at the end of the table. *"Okay, run it down for me. How did things get so goddamned fucked up?"*

"How do things ever get fucked up?" Cam rubbed the bridge of her nose and shook some of the tension out of her shoulders. *"The guy was good, a professional—he was familiar with protocol; he anticipated what we would do; he knew where we would deploy. He was always a little ahead of us the whole time. He got by us."*

"Why didn't you know about him?"

"Because I wasn't in the loop! None of us were—you know that. The FBI task force shut us out." She paused, clamped down on the anger. She'd known Stewart Carlisle for more than a dozen years. She liked him—she respected him as much as she respected any bureaucrat—but they weren't exactly on the same team. He was an administrator, and by definition, he had to play Beltway politics. He knew very well that she and her team had been kept in the dark about threats to Blair Powell's life, because he had agreed to the information blackout. Reluctantly, maybe, but he'd known. However unwillingly, he'd endangered the life of the woman she was charged to protect, and she'd never trust him completely again.

Shrugging, she said more quietly, *"Interdepartmental intelligence broke down—nothing out of the ordinary there, either. Someone should have picked up on his identity months ago, before he ever got close. We were lucky to get away with only the casualties we sustained."*

"I can't put that in a report to the security director."

"You asked me what happened. That's what happened—we got our asses kicked."

Carlisle stared at the ceiling. *"Give me an assessment of your team."*

"High marks all around." Cam sat up straight, her eyes suddenly sharp and intense. *"There are no fall guys on my detail, sir. If somebody swings for this, it will be me."*

"Let's hope it doesn't come to that."

"Cam?" Blair repeated. "You there?"

Cam jumped, disoriented for a second. "What? Yeah. I'm sorry."

"What aren't you telling me? Are you in trouble back there?" Blair stood up and reached under the bed for her suitcase. Something was wrong. Cameron Roberts did not lose focus. Not like this. Blair struggled not to panic, but the memory of the way Cam had looked after the blast was too fresh in her mind. "I can get the midnight flight back to DC—"

"No." Agitated, Cam rose abruptly and swayed with a sudden rush of light-headedness. Swearing under her breath, she was forced to sit down before she could continue. "For starters, I shouldn't even be discussing this with you."

"Don't start quoting protocol to me, Roberts." Blair dropped the suitcase. The thud echoed hollowly in the still air. *Not now; not after what we've all just been through.*

"Plus," Cam continued, smiling faintly as she imagined the fire leaping in Blair's eyes, "this is not the sort of thing you can be involved in. You need to stay above all of this—"

"I'm sorry? Above what—*life?*" The room suddenly felt cold; the sunset no longer seemed quite so welcoming. *When will you start seeing me as your lover first, and the president's daughter second?*

"You aren't supposed to know anything about the details of your security."

"Jesus, Cam. How can you say that now?" Blair crossed rapidly to the window, trying to imagine Cam in her apartment, needing more than her voice. *I've never even been there. She knows everything about me, and I know practically nothing about her.*

"You can't be seen as concerned about it—or about me," Cam said gently. "It will raise flags."

"Raise flags? Do you really think I care?" But even as she said it, Blair knew that she *had* to care. Leaning her shoulder against the window frame, she watched the sun die over the bay. It was hard to believe that only a little over a day had passed since they'd awakened together after enduring a nightmare. Cam and two of her agents had nearly been killed stopping a madman—a madman who had fixated on Blair, a madman who had been willing to kill if he couldn't possess her.

Blair lay naked beside her lover, one arm thrown across Cam's abdomen as she slept. For a few moments, she simply luxuriated in the feel of her, liking the quiet sense of belonging. When Cam stirred, Blair pressed a kiss to her bare shoulder, tasting the light tang of salt. Quietly, she asked, "Are we free now?"

"Yes."

But Blair knew that wasn't quite true. For her, freedom was relative—she would still need twenty-four hour a day protection— from the media, from overzealous admirers, and, in a world made increasingly smaller by global terrorism, from the nameless, faceless individuals who hoped to weaken their political enemies through personal attacks and intimidation. As long as she was the first daughter, and probably longer, she would need security. And security was an intrusion.

"I'd prefer that you not scare the hell out of me again for a while," Blair remarked after another kiss. I was terrified last night that you had been killed. I can't go through it again.

Cam brushed a kiss into silky blond hair. "I have no intention of scaring you again at any *time. I know it's hard to believe at the moment, but these situations are extremely rare. I hope you'll be able to believe that someday."*

"You're not resigning, are you?"

"I don't want to," Cam replied gently. She tightened her grip and held Blair closer. "It's what I do, Blair, and it feels right to me. It lets me be with you more than I would be able to under any other circumstances. I don't want to see you for a night every couple of months. Not for the next six years."

Blair tried hard to put her fear aside and listen. She couldn't deny the reality of the situation, because if Cam were not part of her security detail, it would be almost impossible for them to be together. Even with *her as the security chief, it would still be difficult for them to have a personal life, but that was not a new challenge for Blair. She'd been working outside the system, in that regard, all her life. She sighed.*

"I don't know if it will work, but I'm willing to try."

"If it doesn't work, I'll do whatever I have to do," Cam assured her. *"I love you."*

I'll do whatever I have to do. The words still echoed in Blair's mind, but she knew very well that Cam might not have a choice. She certainly couldn't resign, or even ask for a transfer, until the recent events in New York City were resolved. "Don't forget, I *know* the people lying in the intensive care unit back in Manhattan. And in case you hadn't noticed, I have pretty strong feelings about you, too."

Not for the first time, Cam reminded herself why personal relationships between Secret Service agents and protectees were forbidden. It wasn't exactly illegal, but it was an unwritten law throughout the Agency. And blatantly violating it could get you posted to a backwater embassy pretty fast. She heard the frustration in Blair's voice. *This is not going well.*

She wasn't worried about her career, but she was worried about fallout tarnishing Blair and her father. Her headache suddenly ratcheted up a notch, and she spoke sharply without thinking.

"This is Agency business, Blair. You're the president's daughter, for Christ's sake. It would be partisanship of the worst order for you to get involved. If it came out, it could damage him politically—even if catapulting your private life all over the front page didn't."

"I've been managing my private life and protecting my father's career for a long time without your help."

The silence that followed on the line sounded ominous even to Cam, three thousand miles away. She took a deep breath, blinked back the pain, and regrouped. "I'm sorry. I only meant—"

"I understand what you meant, Commander." Blair's tone was icy. "I know very well who I am to the public and how to behave in the political arena. I was under the mistaken impression that we were discussing something private. Something between *us*."

"Look, I—"

"There's no need for you to explain. Is there anything else?"

"I should speak with Mac." Cam rubbed her eyes wearily.

"I suggest you try him at the hotel. I'm sure you have the number."

"Yes."

"Good night then, Commander."

"Good night," Cam said softly, but she was already listening to a dial tone. She set the receiver carefully in its cradle and leaned back on the sofa. Lifting a remote from the end table, she shut off the room lights and closed her eyes, knowing she wouldn't sleep.

❖

Methodically, Blair stripped off her sweatpants, lifted her jeans from the back of a nearby chair, and stepped into them—all in under thirty seconds after dropping her cell phone onto the bed. It took even less time than that to finish dressing, and after pulling on a favorite hooded black sweatshirt with NYU stenciled on the left chest, she turned toward the door. As an afterthought, she put the phone in the front pocket. Even furious, she could not ignore the ingrained habits of half a lifetime and was too well trained to be foolish.

In the hall, Paula Stark, a young, dark-haired Secret Service agent—fresh-faced and with a hint of muscle under her dark suit— was leaning against the opposite wall, watching Blair's bedroom. She straightened quickly, momentarily surprised, when Blair stepped out of her room. The two women stared at one another, the silence deepening as the seconds passed.

"I'm going for a walk," Blair said at last.

"I'll notify Mac," Stark replied without inflection in her voice. She slipped her phone off her belt and flipped open the cover all in one practiced motion of her wrist. To her complete and utter shock, Blair Powell stopped her with a hand on her arm.

"Don't. Please. I just want to walk. I'm not going anywhere."

"You can't go alone," Stark responded emphatically, forgetting to appear impassive. She was still working on that. "Besides, the commander—"

"Isn't here, is she?" Blair retorted sharply, turning away before the agent could see the hurt in her eyes. *They might get to watch my life, but I'll be damned if they'll know what I feel.*

"Well, it's not like she won't know—Hey!"

Blair walked rapidly away down the hall, Stark close on her heels.

"Please—Ms. Powell, just let me call the cars."

"If you want to come along—fine. But just you." She started down the back stairs and would be outside, free, in a few seconds. "If you so much as lift your wrist to key that mike, I'll be gone."

Stark had no choice but to follow. She knew the president's daughter well enough by now to know that arguing would not work. She also knew that if provoked, Blair was perfectly capable of giving all of them the slip and disappearing. It had happened before, and that was a worse threat to her safety than going out with only one agent as protection. *Oh man, Mac is going to kill me. Thank* God *the commander is in DC.*

It was just after nine p.m., and the sky was clear, nearly cloudless except for wisps here and there that glowed silver with reflected light from the full moon. In a city famous for romance, on a night made for lovers, Blair was lonely.

Starting down the steep, twisting wooden stairs that led from the rear of Marcea Casells's house to Lombard Street at a pace too fast for the terrain, especially in the near dark, she steadfastly ignored the ache. She hadn't been aware of loneliness for a very long time, and on the rare occasions when she had, she'd known just what to do about it. A few hours lost in the arms of an attractive stranger, anonymous pleasures at no cost to anyone, had served her well until Cameron Roberts had come along less than a year ago and changed everything.

"Like I even asked her to."

"I'm sorry?" Stark was struggling to stay within touching distance of the president's daughter without actually touching her.

"Nothing."

They reached the street and wended their way down the sharply curving road in the general direction of the bay. When it became apparent that Stark wasn't going to do anything except dog her steps, Blair relaxed infinitesimally.

"What are you doing here, anyway? I though you were off for a while."

Stark blushed, grateful that her companion couldn't see it. The question caught her off guard—she hadn't realized that Blair

Powell, code name Egret, gave any thought to the schedule of her security team. Although Stark was the lead agent in Egret's personal security detail and spent hours with her every day under every imaginable circumstance, they had not had a personal conversation in months. Not since the night over six months before when they'd spent a number of frantic hours together in bed. *Well, I was pretty frantic. And come to think of it, we didn't do much talking even then.*

"Couldn't stay away?" Blair probed. She still couldn't quite figure out why these people were willing to risk their lives for a person to whom they worked so hard to appear invisible. Although she knew all the agents on her detail by name, she knew very little personally about most of them. They rarely looked directly at her because they were too busy looking everywhere else. If she stripped naked in front of them, they wouldn't blink. She grinned to herself—well, Stark would. But that was because the agent hadn't mastered the game face yet. *And besides, I wouldn't do that to her.*

"After everyone left for the airport last night, I felt useless," Stark confessed, stepping slightly to the right of Blair so that she could get between her and the traffic side of the sidewalk.

"You need to get a life, Stark," Blair commented, not unkindly.

"After what happened, I just...I don't know. I just wanted to be here."

Blair caught her breath, because she understood. All of them—the whole team—had been through hell together, and although they were strangers in many ways, they were also bonded by shared victory—and by shared loss. Despite understanding, she was amazed that Stark could admit it. "Don't you ever worry about saying things like that? It will ruin your macho image."

"Macho?" Stark laughed, then stopped at the corner of Hyde and Beach, unobtrusively blocking Blair's body from the intersection while glancing up and down the street. Thankfully, it was a weeknight and not many tourists were about. They crossed, heading steadily downhill toward the water. "As long as the commander trusts me, I'm not too worried about my image."

"It matters that much to you—what she thinks?"

"Of course," Stark replied, clearly surprised. "I mean—she's... well, she's what we all want to be."

"Be careful what you wish for." Blair's tone was sharp, but it wasn't anger. It was pain. *Can't you see what it costs her?*

Stark fell silent, and she and Blair walked on rapidly, eventually turning left onto Jefferson until they reached the beach. Blair threaded her way with Stark by her side down stone stairs to the sand and finally sat, knees drawn up, watching the moonlight play across the waves.

"How's Renee?" Blair's voice was low and pensive. She drew the fine white sand through her fingers, letting the grains fall in a steady stream by her side.

"She's okay," Stark replied hesitantly, still unsure how to talk to the woman she spent more time with than anyone else in her life. "She pretty much kicked me out of the hospital this morning, which is why I decided to fly out here in the afternoon. Catch up to you all."

"Why did she chase you off? Were you hovering?"

"Uh...well, maybe. Some."

Stark shifted in the stiff vinyl-cushioned chair, peering at her watch in the semi-darkness. Ten after five. In the morning. She'd slept all the previous afternoon after the commander had declared the entire first team off duty. As soon as she'd awakened, she'd come to the hospital, found Savard too sedated to talk, and had decided to sit for a while in case the FBI agent woke up. That had been at eight p.m.

She stretched and leaned closer to the bed, peering at the injured woman. In the dim light from the hall, Renee's usually deep-coffee toned skin seemed pale, almost lifeless. Heart racing, Stark quickly reached for the hand that lay on the covers, folding it into her own. It was warm. She closed her eyes, drew a shaky breath, and rubbed her cheek against the backs of the long, slender fingers.

"Hey," Renee said quietly, closing her hand weakly around Stark's.

Stark jumped. "Hey. You're awake."

"Kind of. Is there any water?"

"Yeah—right here. Wait a minute." Stark hurriedly poured *tepid water from a green plastic pitcher into a Styrofoam cup and fumbled the paper off a straw. Carefully, she tilted the cup and placed the straw between the other woman's lips. "Here you go."*

After a few swallows, Renee dropped her head back against the pillows. "Thanks."

"Should I call a nurse? Do you need something for the... pain?"

"No—not yet. Talk to me a little." Renee's voice was faint but her eyes seemed clear.

"Okay. Sure."

"What happened?"

Stark's heart thudded with anxiety again, because she'd already told her the story the day before. That was probably normal. Right?

Patiently, she recounted the tale from the beginning, leaving out the parts about the blood. And how fucking scared she'd been, kneeling by Renee's side with both hands pressed to her shoulder and the blood that just kept coming.

"Paula?"

"Huh?" Stark responded too loudly, jumping again.

"Have you had any sleep?"

"Yeah—lots."

"You seem...spooked."

"No. I'm fine."

"Good." Renee closed her eyes.

After a few minutes of watching Renee's chest steadily rise and fall, Stark figured she had fallen asleep. Gently, she disentangled her fingers and laid the slumbering woman's hand down on the covers. When she looked up, Renee was watching her.

"Are you leaving?" Renee's voice was just audible.

"Not if you don't want me to."

"I want you to."

"Oh." Stark looked away, swallowed.

"Paula."

"Huh?"

"Look at me."

Slowly, Stark brought her gaze to Renee's. The room had lightened enough to see the brilliant blue of them, and she couldn't help but smile.

Renee smiled back. "I'm going to get well...soon as I can."

"I know that," Stark said quickly.

"No—really. And you can't sit here worrying while I do."

"I'm not worr—"

"Go back to work if you don't want to take time off. Call me every day."

"Every day, huh?" Stark grinned. "Morning or night?"

"Either."

"Both?"

"If you like."

Stark's voice was husky when she replied. "Oh, I like."

"Hovering. Yeah, pretty much," Stark finally admitted with a faint laugh. "Yep."

Blair turned her head in time to catch the smile that even the darkness couldn't hide. *Aha! Our young Stark has a crush. I wonder—*

The phone on Stark's belt trilled, breaking the silence, and they both started in surprise.

"Don't answer it," Blair said quickly.

Stark shook her head, her hand already opening the phone. "I have to."

When she heard the familiar deep voice, she was very glad she had.

CHAPTER TWO

Is she with you?"

"Yes, ma'am." Stark leaped to her feet, her body rigid—nearly at attention—as she pressed the phone to her ear. "She is."

"Anyone else?"

"No, ma'am." Stark heard a muffled curse. She'd violated a cardinal rule—standard procedure dictated that a minimum of three agents accompany Egret whenever she was outside her residence. She'd known from the moment that they'd left the house that the president's daughter was seriously underprotected, and she also knew that it was her own fault for allowing it.

That's it. I'll be back doing site prep and background checks by morning. If I'm lucky.

Every public outing on Egret's calendar required weeks of preparation. It was mostly computer work and phone calls—memoranda to other security forces coordinating manpower needs and deployment, drafting shift schedules for all support personnel, charting itineraries for arrivals and departures, and mapping out every stop along every single potential travel route, all for every day of the journey. The procedure generated a mountain of paperwork. The assignment was considered a death sentence for any agent who coveted the excitement of field duty.

Stark waited for the ax to fall.

"Is she secure?"

"Yes."

"Read me the terrain."

"Ocean to the front; high ground to the left—uh, that would be Fort Mason, I think; the Embarcadero and piers to the right—pretty deserted this time of night; and the highway behind us. No one in the vicinity. Minimal anticipated contact with civilians."

"All right. Stay alert, Stark."

"Understood."

"Put her on, please."

Stark turned and extended the phone. Blair reached up from her seat on the sand and took it.

"Hello?"

"You're not answering your phone."

"I know."

Cam's voice over the line sounded more weary than angry. Blair turned slightly away from Stark, although she knew that the agent would do her best not to listen. *It's not as if she doesn't suspect. Not as if they all don't wonder. But suspecting and knowing are not the same thing.*

"Why not?" Cam asked. "You won't wear a radio or a pager. If you don't have the cell phone, you know we're completely unable to assist you. It's not safe for—"

"I brought it...just in case. I just don't have it turned on." It was fully dark, the water black now beneath a blacker sky broken only by shafts of moonlight and pinpoints of stars. *I knew if there was trouble, I could call for help.*

"Thank you."

"How did you know I was out here?"

Across the country, Cam shifted on the sofa, watching the lights of an airplane blink rhythmically as it banked over Washington, DC on its approach to Reagan National Airport. "I didn't know *where* you were. When you didn't answer your cell phone, I called the house line and got Davis. She checked upstairs and discovered that both you and Stark were missing. You weren't in the bedroom."

Blair laughed. "You didn't really think—"

"No."

"It's really not her fault."

There was no response, and Blair repeated, "Cam, it's not Stark's fault. I didn't give her any choice."

"No, you rarely do. However, that's no excuse."

Blair ran a hand through her hair and got to her feet. She moved ten feet away and glanced back over her shoulder. The Secret Service agent had moved to within three feet of her. One hand covering the phone, she whispered stridently, "Will you back off?"

"I can't do that, I'm sorry. There's just me here, and I need to be close."

"I'm fine. Look around—we're alone. So go away."

Stark didn't budge.

"God, she's almost as stubborn as you are," Blair said into the phone.

"She'd better be, if she's your only security."

"Why are you calling me?"

A second passed, then another.

"Cam?"

"I couldn't sleep."

It was Blair's turn for silence. Suddenly, there was a fist of emotion in her throat, blocking her breath, stealing her words. Cam always did this to her—took her by surprise just when she thought she was too angry to be touched. Somehow, Cam reached past the hurt and the anger and found the places that mattered most. She still wasn't certain that she entirely liked anyone having that kind of power, but she couldn't control what it did to her. It made her ache.

"The last time you couldn't sleep," Blair commented, her voice a mixture of challenge and regret, "you came to my bed."

"I would now, if I could." A moment's hesitation. "Would I be welcome?"

"You need to ask?"

"You left the house in the middle of the night with no word to the team. Your phone's off. You're three thousand fucking miles away and I can't see your face. *Yes*. I need to ask."

"You make me so angry," Blair muttered.

"I know," Cam said apologetically. "I don't mean to."

"I know."

"You piss me off pretty well, too."

"Yeah." Blair's voice was softer now, wistful. Lowering her voice, she added, "I just needed to get out. That's all."

"You didn't answer my question."

"Yes, the answer is yes. It will always be yes."

"I'm sorry I upset you." A regretful sigh came through the line. "Will you go home now, please?"

"Well, I had planned on a ferry ride to Alcatraz—"

"Blair," Cam threatened. "My sense of humor is running rather thin right now."

"All right then, Stark and I will head for home."

"No. I'll call Mac and have him send a car."

"Cam, no one noticed us, and we're only ten blocks from the house. Please. We'll be fine."

"Only if Davis walks down to meet you."

"Okay. If that's what it takes."

"Put Stark back on the phone. Wait..." After a beat, she added, "Call me later when you get settled?"

"Won't Stark do that?"

"It's not the same thing."

"I should hope not." Smiling, Blair held out the cell phone. "The commander—for you."

❖

Felicia Davis met them halfway to the house as they climbed back up Hyde Street to the top of Russian Hill. The tall, lithe, ebony-skinned woman nodded cordially and silently fell into step beside Stark, who shifted to her left so that the two Secret Service agents walked slightly behind and on either side of Blair Powell.

Completely oblivious to their presence, Blair replayed the conversation with Cam in her mind as she walked. She couldn't shake the feeling that something wasn't right. Even though they'd known each other less than a year, and, for a good part of that time, they had been either at odds or completely out of contact, she could sense the tension in Cam's voice. It was more than fatigue.

They'd only been lovers for the last two tumultuous months—following an even more harrowing four months during which Cam had been in the hospital and then on medical leave. She'd been struck—and nearly killed—by a bullet meant for Blair. A bullet which the Secret Service agent had intentionally blocked with her own body.

For the first time in her life, Blair had to face the hard truth that her life—by virtue of her father's position—was somehow valued more than that of another human being. It was a realization most protectees were never forced to consciously consider and one which she could not accept. Haunted by the image of what that reality had almost cost the woman she loved, Blair found it increasingly difficult to allow the agents to place themselves between her and danger. Whereas once she had eluded her protectors because she resented their intrusion into her life, now she tried to escape their presence so *they* wouldn't be in jeopardy. It was foolhardy, and she only hoped no one noticed.

Intellectually, she understood the need for intense security. If she were kidnapped, it would bring unbearable pressure on her father to give in to threats and manipulation. This was something that, as a man, and as a father, she knew he would want to do. However, as the president of the United States, it was something he would never be able to do. For that reason, *she* also bore the responsibility of seeing that he was never placed in that position. This conflict for her was a lifelong struggle, because she had been in the public eye since she was a teenager—first when her father was a governor and then during the eight years of his vice presidency when he was being very publicly groomed for the office of president. And now, she was having an affair with the chief of her personal security detail.

Life was a lot simpler a year ago.

"Do you need something, Ms. Powell?" Felicia Davis inclined her head slightly at the soft sound of Blair's voice.

"No. I'm fine."

The three women walked on in silence. When they reached the house, entering this time through the front door, Marcea Casells, Cameron Roberts's mother, was just bidding her other house guests good night. The dark-eyed, strikingly beautiful woman smiled as the trio came through the door.

"I see you've found each other."

"Yes," Blair replied, smiling in return.

Marcea, in a casual emerald green silk blouse and darker slacks, looked like a softer, only slightly older version of Cam. That alone would have drawn Blair's smile, but she also liked and respected the other woman. An artist herself, Blair was still slightly in awe of the critically acclaimed painter.

"Can I get you anything?" Marcea asked. "A drink or something to eat?"

"If there's port—that would be great," Blair replied.

"Perfect."

The two Secret Service agents declined. Davis crossed the living room and disappeared into the back of the house to check the rear entrance and grounds. Stark followed, assuming a station in the dining room, which adjoined the living room through an archway. She took up a post that provided a clear sightline to the front door, but a position that was far enough away to afford Blair and Marcea some privacy.

The house itself was a contemporary multilevel structure with many skylights, small decks beyond sliding glass doors that extended from the hillside rooms, and a general sense of uncluttered expansiveness. The sharp, cool lines were softened by the warm, muted colors of the rugs and furnishings. It was an *Architectural Digest* home made for actual living. Only one painting out of the many gracing the walls was Marcea's. Despite her international reputation, she had the same sense of intense privacy that her daughter displayed.

"Did you speak with Cameron?" Marcea poured the wine into two crystal glasses. She carried them to the sofa where Blair was seated, handed her one, and sank into one of the matching upholstered chairs that sat at right angles to the sofa. "She called looking for you."

"I spoke with her briefly a few minutes ago."

"I suppose she thought I wouldn't notice, but I did. She sounded...worried."

Blair hesitated. She wasn't accustomed to discussing personal matters with anyone—well, anyone other than Diane. Diane Bleeker was her business agent as well as her oldest friend, and although they had often shared a rivalry over the years for the same women, they understood each other. She thought that understanding, more than anything else, was probably the most important thing a friend could offer.

Nevertheless, despite her short association with Marcea, they had shared a critical experience and, in the sharing, had forged a deep bond. For nearly forty-eight hours after Cam had been shot, they'd waited together by her bedside. For those forty-eight hours, they hadn't known whether she would live or die. They had stood silent witness to her struggle, and they had shared grief and uncertainty. They also shared something else, although they had not spoken of it. They both loved her.

"She was worried." Blair drew a deep breath and smiled wanly. "That's my fault, I think. I decided to go for a walk, and I'm afraid I didn't follow 'Roberts's rules of order.'"

"I can imagine those rules must get very tiresome."

Blair shrugged. "They do. But I suppose, too, I should be used to them by now."

"I doubt very much I could ever get used to something like that," Marcea stated emphatically. "I also have a feeling that Cameron understands that." There was kindness in her tone and sympathy that sounded genuine.

To her absolute horror, Blair felt her eyes well with tears. Abruptly, she rose and crossed to the front window, desperately working to contain her emotions. "Cam understands," she said, her back to Marcea. "I know she does. But she has a job to do, and I'm her job. That comes first."

"Yes. I know how seriously she takes that responsibility. I'm sure that's why she was given the job." Marcea's voice was calm and gentle. "Loving you must make it quite a challenge for you both."

Startled, Blair turned sharply, meeting Marcea's eyes. "Has she said—"

"No," Marcea said with another smile. "But it's plain to see every time she looks at you. I'm not trying to excuse her, you know. She's like her father—completely devoted to her work, often to the exclusion of her own needs. But in her defense—"

"You don't need to defend her to me. I lov..."

Blair fell silent, shocked. She hadn't meant to say that; she'd never said that to anyone—about anyone—ever before. First, because there'd never *been* anyone about whom to say it. And even had there been, there was no one to whom she would've felt safe saying it. Not even to Diane—not because she didn't trust her friend with the knowledge, but because saying it would make it real. She'd have to acknowledge her own vulnerability. To say it would be to *feel* it, and that was terrifying.

The silence between them grew longer until Marcea spoke softly. "I didn't intend to defend her. I'm sorry—it's the mother in me. I only meant to say that despite her single-mindedness, she cares very deeply."

"I know she does." Blair tilted the glass and swallowed the rest of the wine. She carried it to the sideboard and placed it carefully on the silver serving tray. *I only wish I knew if it was me or the first daughter who came first in her affections.*

She turned and said tonelessly, "I need to call her. I promised I'd let her know when we got back."

"I hope I haven't offended you."

"No. You haven't."

Wordlessly, they nodded good night. As Blair passed Stark in the dining room, she informed her without turning in her direction, "I'm going to bed."

Stark did not reply, because no reply was required. She'd already radioed Mac to notify him that Egret was secured for the night, and she had called the commander in Washington, DC to tell her the same thing.

Now, she herself could go to bed. She glanced at her watch, wondering if it was too late to call the hospital in New York City.

❖

Blair showered quickly and got into bed, naked. She turned off the lights and punched in Cam's number by the faint glow of her cell phone screen. The line was picked up at the first ring.

"Roberts."

"It's me."

"All settled?" Cam asked gently.

"All secure."

"Good. How are you?"

"Tired, I think." Blair loved the sound of that deep voice. She sighed and closed her eyes, almost believing that Cam was nearby. "Jet lag, probably."

"It's been a busy few days."

Neither of them mentioned that in the last two weeks they'd weathered an assassination attempt, a car bombing, and several explosions—each involving Blair or a member of her security detail.

Blair shifted on her side so she could look out the window and watch the moon as it moved slowly in and out behind the few scattered clouds in the sky. The house was very still and quiet—unlike the ever-present city noises she was used to hearing, even from her penthouse on Gramercy Park. The view, too, was so different from New York, the sky somehow brighter and the stars more brilliant. It was beautiful, and she felt the stab of loneliness again.

"What does it look like...out your window?"

Cam was silent a moment as she focused on the night. "The sky is ribboned with clouds and very black. I can see the stars—a million of them it seems—and a lot of planes taking off and landing. There's a glow off to the left that reaches into the lower layers of the clouds—that's the White House. It's always flooded with light. I'm surprised anyone can sleep..." She laughed shortly. "Well, you know about all of that, don't you?"

"It's not easy to sleep there," Blair said thoughtfully. "For any number of reasons. The lights, the guards, the size of the damn rooms. It's like sleeping in a museum. As you know, it's not my favorite place."

Cam chuckled, lifting her bare feet to the coffee table in front of her sofa. She'd poured another scotch while waiting for word from Stark, and then wondering when—if—Blair would call. She reached for it, then turned the glass aimlessly in her hand. "I have noticed that."

"It's what, almost three there?"

"Just about."

"And what time do you bureaucratic types reconvene in the morning?"

"Seven." Cam tried to keep the weariness from her voice. "I think the bureaucrats feel guilty about not really doing anything, so they work extra long hours to make up for it."

"I believe you have a point," Blair agreed, laughing. "You should go to sleep, Cam. You've got to be even more tired than I am."

"At least I don't have to contend with jet lag."

"No, but you haven't had much sleep in the last week, and you're hurt."

There was silence, and Blair could envision Cam trying to find a distracting comeback. Which meant that she *was* hurting, because as much as Cam kept things to herself, she never lied. "How bad is it?"

"I've got a knot on the back of my head that throbs at inopportune moments. Of course, it could be listening to Doyle for twelve hours..."

"Cameron."

Cam heard the serious tone in Blair's voice and sighed. "I feel like a steamroller ran over me—coming and going. Twice."

"What else?" She'd seen the bruises the day before—*God, how can I miss her so much already*—and although they looked painful, it would take more than that to make Cam complain.

"Nothing too bad. A bit of dizziness, a little blurry visi—"

"Jesus." Blair sat up straight up in bed, the covers falling, leaving her breasts bare. "You shouldn't be working—you should be in bed. Can't you postpone this goddamned debriefing?"

"It's got to be done, and the sooner the better. Events tend to get skewed the longer we wait. People have selective memory loss, or fortuitous recollections, which tend to make themselves look good and everyone else look bad."

"You expect trouble, don't you?"

Again Cam hesitated, because she had spent more than a dozen years on the payroll of the US Treasury Department and she wasn't used to discussing her work with anyone. Even when she and Janet had been together, they hadn't talked shop. And Janet had been a cop. *If we'd talked a little more, maybe I would have known where she'd be that morning. Maybe I could have warned her off. Maybe she wouldn't be de—*

"Cam?"

"Sorry. I guess I *am* tired." She rubbed her eyes, pushed the memories aside. "We have one dead and two seriously wounded agents. You came very close to being a victim yourself. Any one of those events would be a serious issue. All of them together—there has to be an accounting."

"But you're okay in all of this, right? My God, Cam—you almost died. If it hadn't been for you, who knows what would have happened to Grant and Savard."

"I'll be fine. Don't worry."

"*Will* you tell me what happens?" Blair knew that she was asking Cam to cross a line. But they'd crossed so many already, and if they were ever going to have anything together...

She waited. *Please, don't shut me out now.*

"Full report."

"I miss you." It took all Blair's willpower to say it, but it was such an overwhelming feeling that she had nowhere else to put it. She had to give it voice or choke on it.

"I'd give anything I have to be lying next to you right now," Cam said very quietly. "Anything."

"You know what makes me so angry with you, Roberts?"

"No, what?"

"I can't stay angry at you very long."

Cam laughed softly, suddenly feeling better than she had in hours. "I have to have something going for me, because I know that most of the chips don't fall on my side."

"You're wrong about that, Commander." Blair reached for the sheet, suddenly chilled. *You have no idea how crazy I am about you.*

"Good." Blair's voice had been very quiet, too, but Cam heard her clearly. Closing her eyes and resting her head on the sofa back, Cam added, "Things will get better once these debriefings are done."

"Will they?" Blair sounded skeptical. "Washington politics never change. You know that, Cam. It's just more of the same in a different package."

"Things will get easier for *you*, at any rate. Now that he's been stopped—"

"You mean now that he's dead."

"Yes," Cam said softly. "Now that he's dead, your life will be a little bit easier."

"Do you have the final ID?"

Cam hesitated, but only for a second. "No, not yet. Everything is being handled out of Quantico, and you probably know how notoriously slow those wheels turn."

"But there isn't any doubt, right?"

"There isn't any doubt we got the right man," Cam said with as much conviction as she could convey. "The ID isn't positive until the forensics are completed, but Savard took care of him. That's all that counts. His name doesn't matter."

Blair shifted uneasily under the covers, acutely aware of what Cam *wasn't* saying. The FBI task force had indeed gotten someone. That *someone* was presumably the man who had been stalking her, threatening her life, and endangering her entire security team. She was too intelligent not to know that what Cam left out was that only time would tell if indeed the dead man was the perpetrator they'd been tracking.

"Are you going to make it for your mother's opening?" Blair asked, changing the subject intentionally. Neither of them could do anything to change the circumstances regarding Loverboy. There was no point in talking about it.

"I'm going to try," Cam replied. "I haven't made it to very many of them, and I know this one is particularly important. I'll do the best I can."

"Good. I know she wouldn't say it, but I can tell she likes it when you're there."

Cam sighed again and rubbed at the tension between her eyes. "I know."

"Go get some sleep."

"I will," Cam assured her, wondering if she possibly could rest now—having heard the touch of forgiveness in Blair's voice.

"Call me tomorrow?"

"I will. As soon as I get a break. About the morning...Mac will be—"

"Cameron, Mac can handle things. I'm fine."

"Right." After a moment, Cam added softly, "Good night, Blair."

"Good night," Blair whispered.

Then Blair shut off her cell phone and laid it on the bedside table. She drew the covers up to her shoulders and continued to stare out the window.

❖

Cam placed the receiver in the cradle, then stood and stretched. Her shoulders ached due to the bruising she'd sustained from being slammed to the ground by the concussive force of the explosion. She crossed the short distance to the window, drink in hand, and contemplated the skyline again.

Finally, she drained the scotch and set it on the nearby bar. She needed to sleep. But as she turned from the window, the phone rang.

Immediately, she grabbed it up.

"Roberts." She listened for a moment, then said, "No, that's fine. Send her up."

A minute later she opened her door to admit a tall, stately blond exquisitely attired in an expensive evening dress.

"Hello, Claire."

CHAPTER THREE

Cam opened her eyes in darkness, warm breath on the back of her neck. A woman pressed close—full breasts against her spine, an arm curving over the crest of her hip from behind, fingers moving softly over her skin. She started to turn onto her back, but the hand on her hip pressed forward, preventing her. A throaty voice spoke in her ear, familiar and commanding.

"No. Don't move. And keep your eyes closed."

Still on her side, Cam obeyed and closed her eyes. Every cell was acutely focused on the knowing touch tracing the hollow of her hip, the curve of her ribs, and the long plane of her abdomen. Light teasing strokes drew the breath from her lungs in sharp, nearly painful gasps as particularly sensitive spots were tormented, then abandoned.

"Ahh..."

"Shh."

Soon she was heavy and hard, and she tilted her hips to allow the questing hand to journey lower, between her thighs. Fingers parted her, sought her heat, and brushed feather-soft over nerve endings already twitching with arousal. Soft, sensuous lips explored her face, kissing her eyelids and jaw before finally claiming her mouth with deep, possessive thrusts.

She heard herself groan, shuddering as the fist of release pounded between her legs, and knew that surcease from the exquisite torture was not far away.

"Do you plan on making me come?" Cam whispered, her voice catching as her breath stuttered over peaks of excitement.

"Eventually."

The touch continued working her length, tugging at sensitive skin and tracing tender folds—drawing forth her desire on a flood of urgency.

"Now? Jes—"

"Be patient."

"It's not...up to me anymore," Cam managed, legs taut as the explosion gathered force. "You're...in command."

A husky laugh and the pressure of a thumb added to circling fingertips. "I've always been in command. Isn't that how you've always wanted it?"

"You know...that." Cam's hips lifted as her thighs parted, inviting entrance.

"Turn over on your stomach," the honeyed voice ordered.

"I'm so close. Can't I co—"

"Just do it."

Trembling, Cam turned onto her stomach, cradling the pillow in her arms, turning her face, offering her mouth. She moaned as a hand slipped between her legs and claimed her again, this time entering her while sliding simultaneously over her clitoris.

"Oh, God..."

She was too far along to contain the spiraling climax any longer—with another stroke or two, she would be gone.

"You're going to make me come," she warned, barely breathing now.

"I know. That's what you want, isn't it?"

"Yes. Yes, it's what I want. God, yes...Clai..."

Cam shot straight up in bed, shocked into wakefulness by the imminent orgasm. Gasping, she threw back the covers and swung her legs over the side of the bed, bracing herself with a hand on either side of her body, clutching the mattress as she struggled with her reeling senses.

"Jesus."

Legs shaking, stomach clenched in preparation for release, she rode the thin edge of orgasm, finally forcing down the swell of arousal. The red numerals of the bedside clock read 6:05 a.m. She'd been in bed an hour. She was quite alone.

Sweat drenched and breathing heavily, Cam stood on wooden legs and walked unsteadily to the bathroom. Viciously, she twisted the knobs on the shower, stepped in, and leaned her forehead against the cool tiles as water began to stream from the shower head.

"Fuck," she whispered.

She couldn't remember anything like that ever happening before, and to have it happen now, after the unsettling visit the night before, shook her. She trembled still with the unanswered demand pulsing in her depths, knowing that with the briefest touch, she could satisfy the physical need. Her body cried out for it, but her heart resisted. She wasn't fool enough to think that she could control her unconscious mind, but she still couldn't bring herself to orgasm with Claire's memory skittering along her nerve endings.

Turning her face into the still-cold water, she let it beat against her head and chest. Shivering, she placed her hands against the wall in front of her and lowered her head, soaking her hair and back. Finally, the churning pressure between her thighs began to abate, and she flung her head back, rubbing her face with both hands.

She stood in the shower a long time—until her body was quiet and her head was clear, save for the distant echo of the ever-present headache. Thankfully, that was barely a distraction, because she would need all her mental faculties when she met with Carlisle and the others in less than an hour.

For the time being, she couldn't afford to think about what had just happened—or what had taken place the night before.

"Let's wrap this thing up," Stewart Carlisle said with just a touch of weariness to the group convened around the conference table.

The fluorescent lights reflecting off the pale unadorned walls of one of many identical conference rooms in the Treasury Building made everyone look slightly sick. Cam hoped that fact would hide her own physical condition, because as the hours had passed she'd felt progressively light-headed and mildly disoriented. She tried to look alert as Carlisle continued.

"The statements of the individuals on scene all confirm the events as outlined in the reports of Agents Roberts and Doyle. There's nothing new or contradictory in them. Every contingency had been considered and prepared for. Protocols were followed without exception."

The accumulated field reports, generated by the FBI, Secret Service, and state police teams involved in Operation Loverboy three nights previously when an unidentified subject—UNSUB—had lured a woman thought to be Blair Powell to a deserted location with the intent of killing her, had been gathered into a file two inches thick. A copy sat in front of each of the representatives of the myriad security agencies present, along with an equally thick binder filled with preliminary forensic and laboratory results. They'd spent the better part of the past two days going through them, searching for strategic deficiencies, breakdowns in communication, or oversights by the agents in charge. Carlisle gestured to the documents as he spoke.

"I think we can all agree that the casualties were acceptable given the level of threat to the protectee. Acceptable and unavoidable."

The phrase was understood by all present to mean that no one was to be held responsible for the chain of events leading to the near fatal injuries sustained by several agents.

"My department, in conjunction with the New York Bureau field office, will follow up on the final ID and background checks," he added. "So—"

"There's the matter of the security breach in Central Park," Patrick Doyle interjected.

Warily, Carlisle regarded the blocky, thick-necked man who sat opposite him at the far end of the table. Hard blue eyes stared back from a broad, roughly handsome face. FBI Special Agent in Charge Patrick Doyle had headed up the task force formed to apprehend the man stalking the president's daughter after the first attempt on her life. Before Carlisle could respond, Cam spoke instead.

"That's a matter for the Secret Service to review, Doyle." She was stating the obvious, because everyone present knew that the Secret Service never discussed procedures and protocol with anyone outside the Agency. *Of course, Doyle knows that, too. So what's his game?*

"I should think that *two* nearly successful attempts on a high-level protectee's life would bring into question the adequacy of her security." Doyle was insistent, his gaze still on Stewart Carlisle's face. "After all, any time she's at a public function, it's *her* security team that coordinates all the other forces, right? Police, Transit Authority, tactical teams—the whole ball of wax. So, if someone gets through all that, who's to blame?"

"The Secret Service does not comment on procedure," Carlisle reiterated stiffly, but the gauntlet had been thrown. As the man directly overseeing the team providing the first daughter's protection, he couldn't ignore the implied criticism or the not so subtle accusation that her security had been lacking.

"I agree with Agent Doyle, Assistant Director," Robert Owens, the National Security Agency deputy director, added. "My department also needs an accounting of events."

"Fine. I'll send you a report," Carlisle snapped. *What the hell is this?*

"Perhaps something a little more formal is called for," Owens replied. "Such as an independent inquiry."

Cam's hands, resting on her lap, tightened into fists. "An inquiry by whom?"

"Justice should appoint a special prosecutor to review the facts." Owens answered with an alacrity that suggested he'd anticipated the question and prepared the response. "No chance of partisanship there, eh?"

"That kind of investigation will require exposure of information essential to the first daughter's security," Cam pointed out, her voice stone cold.

"Well, that remains to be seen, doesn't it?"

Cam waited for Carlisle to put an end to the discussion. As the seconds passed with no response from him, her fury grew. She couldn't break ranks to confront him on it, even though it was she, as commander of Egret's personal detail, whose competence was being called into question. Her head throbbed.

"I'll take it under advisement," Carlisle finally acceded.

"And I'll include the recommendation in my report to the security director," Owens rejoined, closing his laptop.

Carlisle's jaw tightened. "Are we through here, then, gentlemen?"

There was a general rumble of assent and the scraping of chairs as the group dispersed. Cam didn't look in Doyle's direction, because she was certain if she saw the smirk she knew would be there, she'd launch herself over the table at him. As soon as the last man filed out, she was on her feet.

"Jesus Christ, Stewart, are you going to let Doyle and Owens railroad you into an outside inquiry? What the hell kind of precedent does that set? We have our own internal review for this kind of thing."

"Nothing's been decided," he retorted, his temper frayed to breaking. "I didn't want to get into a skirmish with them today until I find out what prompted this."

She thought she knew—but she would refrain from saying anything until she had something concrete to back it up. Patrick Doyle had had a hard-on for her since the day they'd met. What she couldn't figure out was why. They worked for separate agencies, and she'd never met him before the day she'd learned he was heading the FBI task force to investigate Loverboy, so it couldn't be personal. *What does he stand to gain by discrediting me?*

"Why are you letting Doyle slide on the task force oversights? It was his operation that missed this guy for months."

"Roberts—you were an excellent investigator and you're an excellent security chief." Carlisle sighed. "But you're a lousy diplomat. There's no use in pointing fingers now—and if I cut Doyle and the FBI a break on that, I might be able to call in a favor in the future."

"Fine. How about you just tell them to stick their inquiry up their bureaucratic asses then?" She rubbed a hand over her face in an effort to shake her fatigue.

"Like I said—not very diplomatic." Carlisle began stuffing folders into his briefcase.

"Fuck diplomacy. We're talking about compromising our working strategies to accommodate these assholes." She tried to lower her voice, but she was too tired and too nauseous to control everything at once. "Look—call an internal Agency review of the whole thing. Let *our* people investigate me, if you think it's necessary."

"You could end up getting hurt that way. There's a lot of politics involved in a thing like that, and I might not be able to help."

"I'll answer for my actions."

"It's not that simple," Carlisle said with a shrug. "If Justice wants an independent review, I'll have to go along."

"You know that will put protectees at risk. I won't do it."

"You'll do whatever I need you to do, Agent," Carlisle said testily.

"Not if it means endangering Blair Powell."

"If you refuse to testify before a Justice board of inquiry, you'll be in contempt of a sanctioned federal investigative body. At the very least you'll lose your job—worst case scenario, you could be looking at jail time."

She studied the face of her boss, a man she thought she knew, and couldn't read what was behind his eyes. Then she decided she didn't really care.

"Fine. If you need to reach me, you know how to find me."

CHAPTER FOUR

Blair clicked off the phone with a sigh.

Still no answer. Not at her apartment. Not on her cell phone. Not on her two-way pager.

She glanced at the bedside clock. 9:42 p.m. It was after midnight in DC. Cam had said she would call during breaks in the meetings, but she hadn't. Even in Washington, bureaucrats didn't work this late on Friday night.

Blair had spent a good part of the day with Marcea in her studio, a jutting extension of the top floor that was all windows and light. While Marcea packed up the remaining canvases for the show the next night, Blair curled in a soft leather sling chair and sketched. It had been peaceful and companionable, even though they rarely spoke as the hours passed.

Late in the afternoon, Marcea stopped by Blair's side. She gestured to the sketchpad Blair had balanced on her knees and asked, "May I?"

Blushing faintly, Blair turned the pad in Marcea's direction, amazed at her own shyness with the woman who had never been anything but gracious and kind. But for Blair, art was her soul, and her work the one place where she had never needed to hide her feelings. She wondered what Marcea would see beneath the charcoal and paper.

"You have a very good memory," Marcea said with a soft smile, studying the images of herself and her daughter scattered across the page in various poses. In some views, their profiles overlapped, in others they blended and joined until finally transforming—one to the other. "You capture her perfectly."

"Do I," Blair said contemplatively.

Marcea's eyes were warm and caring as they rose to Blair's. "Yes, you do."

"Sometimes I...I'm not sure."

"Don't doubt it. I don't." Marcea's glance returned appreciatively to the images. "Might I possibly keep this?"

Blair nodded. "Yes, if you like. I'd be honored."

"Thank you," Marcea murmured, lifting long delicate fingers to Blair's cheek. "For what you see in her."

Transfixed by the touch, Blair grew still, feeling welcomed and, fleetingly, as if she had come home.

Remembering the interlude now, thinking of how much Cam resembled her mother, only made Blair miss Cam more. The last few weeks of confinement and constant threat of danger had worn on her, too. The long hours of waiting as others, including her lover, faced danger for her benefit had taken a toll. Her nerves were raw, and her heart was bruised.

Pacing fretfully around the confines of her room, she worked hard not to imagine where Cam might be. *Unwinding with a drink after two continuous days of meetings? In a bar? Lingering over a late dinner? Alone?*

In the two months they'd been lovers, Blair had barely had time to adjust to the fact that she had broken her own most fundamental rule—never become emotionally involved with anyone she slept with. Never let anyone touch her—not physically—most of the time, and definitely not emotionally, ever. She'd tried hard to keep Cam outside the formidable defenses she'd erected over the years, and she'd failed. She was in uncharted territory, and every step was new.

Cam, she knew, had broken more than one of her own rules, too—at least professionally. Most significant was the one about never becoming intimately involved with a protectee. Blair had a feeling that Cam had probably broken several personal rules as well, but they had not spoken of them. And there were other things they had not spoken of—fidelity, exclusivity, the shape of their future. These were concepts which to Blair had seemed foreign only a few months before. Now, the ideas had moved beyond philosophy to take on far greater significance. When she thought of the possibility of Cam with another woman, something between fury and despair welled within her.

"This is ridiculous," she muttered to herself. "I can't sit here any longer. I'm going stir crazy."

Blair stripped off her jeans and T-shirt and crossed to the adjoining bath. Quickly, mechanically, she showered and washed her hair. She left her hair loose, as she usually did when she was going out and didn't want to be recognized.

Over the years, she had learned that subtle alterations in her physical appearance and style of dress made it almost impossible for a member of the general public to recognize her as the president's daughter. Associating her with the image that appeared on television and in magazines, the average citizen expected to see a sophisticated, elegant woman in tasteful, expensive clothes, wearing just the right amount of makeup, and with her curling, shoulder-length blond hair gathered at the base of her neck with a gold clasp. With her hair down and free, in leather pants and a body-hugging sleeveless top, Blair bore almost no resemblance to the first daughter.

When she finished dressing, she slipped a slim leather wallet with nothing other than her ID and cash into her back pocket and opened the door to her room. This time, the hallway was empty, and she crossed quickly to the back stairs that led to the kitchen and the rear exit. To her surprise, the kitchen was empty, too. She knew that Felicia Davis was off that evening and that Ed Hernandez was somewhere in the front of the house, probably in the living room. She didn't see Stark and was surprised, but grateful. She wasn't anxious to elude her and draw yet more negative attention to the agent.

Carefully, she slid open the glass doors in the darkened kitchen and stepped out onto the cedar-planked deck. It was cantilevered over the slope of Russian Hill, which fell steeply away below. Moving quietly, she started down the first of many wooden staircases that cut back and forth across the lower portion of Marcea's property toward the street. Halfway down, she stopped at the sound of a voice just below her.

"Another walk?"

Blair leaned over the railing and looked down into the shadows. Paula Stark looked back. "I'm going out for a while."

"Then I guess I am, too."

"Why don't you continue your perimeter check and pretend you didn't see me?" Blair started down the stairs again.

Stark met her at the bottom. "We both know I can't. I don't even want to. It's my job to be with you tonight, especially if you're outside this building."

Blair regarded her steadily, surprised by the somber tone in her voice. She'd always known Stark was incredibly responsible and almost exuberantly dedicated to her job, but tonight, there was something else in her voice. Maturity perhaps. For a moment there, she'd sounded like Cam.

"Any room for negotiation?"

"Nope. I need to inform Mac that we're leaving home base. I'd like to be able to tell him where we're going."

"I don't know yet. I just want to get a drink and—"

"Please. You don't need to explain to me, Ms. Powell. It's only our destination I have any interest in. Would you object to taking the Suburban?"

"I'd rather walk." As they spoke, Blair moved off down the path that cut through the dense shrubbery toward the street and the sidewalk.

Stark fell in beside Blair and pulled the cell phone from her belt. She spoke softly as they walked, informing Mac that Egret was moving, destination undetermined. Mac, she knew, would instruct Hernandez to follow with the car, and eventually, wherever she and Blair stopped, the other agent would show up, too. In all likelihood, Mac would detail one other agent to join Hernandez in the car for backup.

It was somewhat unorthodox to have only one agent on foot, but typical of the way they were forced to deploy with the first daughter. She didn't welcome their presence and rarely made it easy for them. However, the commander had made it clear that despite Egret's objections, security *would* be provided. Stark had no intention of leaving her unguarded, no matter what she had to do.

"Let's take the cable car," Blair said impulsively, hurrying to catch the car as it trundled away from the stop on its way up the steep hill.

Hastening to follow, Stark grabbed onto the rail as Blair jumped up onto the step that ran on the outside of the car.

"Grab on," Blair called, extending her hand and laughing as Stark ran a few steps alongside and finally caught her hand.

"Thanks," Stark puffed as she pulled herself up. *Wouldn't that have been just terrific if I'd lost her because I was too slow. I've got to start running regularly. Pumping iron is just not enough.*

Their hands touched again as they both grasped the vertical pole for support. The cable car lurched down the other side of Russian Hill, and the two of them rocked back and forth, shoulder to shoulder, facing one another. It was the kind of thing that tourists always did, but Stark had never been a tourist in San Francisco before. It was the kind of thing that lovers did as well.

The experience was both exhilarating and slightly confusing. Blair Powell was a beautiful woman, and Stark remembered all too clearly what it felt like when the hand that lightly brushed hers now had done much more than that for the few hours they had spent together in a remote hotel room in the Rockies. Those hands had been accomplished and unexpectedly tender, and the memory echoed forcibly in her flesh. Their faces were only inches apart, and in the flickering glow of the street lights, she could see Blair's slightly parted lips and her sensuous smile, and for a moment, desire twisted within her.

Quickly, Stark averted her gaze.

"You okay?" Blair leaned back to let the wind course through her hair.

"Yeah, sure." *Damn, when will I learn not to telegraph my every thought and feeling. Cripes, some Secret Service agent.*

"Come on," Blair said a few moments later, leaping down before the car had even pulled to a stop at the circular turn around. "This is Market Street, the end of the line. Let's walk a while."

Painfully aware that Egret was once again underprotected, Stark did a quick three-sixty and her stomach lurched. There were more street people than she had anticipated—a motley gathering of homeless and transients, many of whom were aggressively panhandling or standing around in groups of two or more watching the tourists. Definitely a security nightmare. She could only hope that no one recognized Blair.

"This is a bad idea, Ms. Powell. Please, let's wait for Hernandez and the Suburban. It'll only be a minute or two."

"Come on, Stark—where's your sense of adventure?" Blair turned to her right and started walking southwest down Market toward the Tenderloin, away from the relative safety of the more populated downtown area.

"I don't think I have a sense of adventure," Stark mumbled, hastening to catch up. She lifted her wrist and radioed their location, grateful that Blair did not complain about that, at least. The Suburban, outfitted with everything they could possibly need, including automatic weapons, body armor and extensive medical equipment, would be in the vicinity in a minute or two. If they were going to walk, at least they'd have someone at their backs.

❖

They trekked the length of Market Street to the corner of Castro. At nearly eleven p.m. on a Friday night, the heart of the Castro District was alive with activity. The sidewalks were wall-to-wall people—tourists and locals alike. Whereas once the area had been the exclusive domain of gay men and somewhat clandestine, it was now much more upscale and civilized. Nevertheless, interspersed with the trendy restaurants and boutiques, the gay bars and sex clubs still flourished.

For the next hour, Blair browsed the bookstores and bars with Stark shadowing her at a respectable distance. They didn't speak. The first few bars were relatively bright, airy places that catered to an upscale clientele. They stayed awhile in each, while Blair sipped a glass of wine or seltzer and pensively watched the couples or soon-to-be lovers dancing. The scene seemed pretty uneventful, and Stark began to relax.

Big mistake.

Around midnight, Blair halted at the door of a nondescript establishment that bore a simple, hand-lettered board sign: "Skins." From the look of the men and occasional woman entering, it was a leather bar. It fulfilled every story about the seedier side of the Castro.

Blair glanced at Stark. "You want to wait outside?"

"I'll come in, thanks," Stark replied, as if she had any particular choice in the matter.

As soon as they entered, Blair said, "See you in a bit." And promptly disappeared.

One look around the dark, smoky club and Stark's stomach dropped. Visibility was zero, the music was loud, and sex was in the air. At the far end of the single square room, a small dance floor was crowded with bodies in various stages of undress writhing to a heavy metal beat. The unadorned bar along one wall was three-deep in people jostling to get their drinks.

Stark judged that unless she stayed physically attached to Egret, she wouldn't be of much use as security. And staying attached to her was neither advisable nor possible. Deciding she had no good alternatives, Stark moved deeper into the room to look for a vantage point along the wall opposite the bar from where she could watch the entrance and still have some view into the darker recesses to the rear.

It was the best she could manage. When she finally staked out a two-foot-square spot that would do, she radioed her location to Mac and the agents in the car. Mac's blistering response did not help her nerves.

❖

Blair insinuated her way through the bodies and eventually reached the bar. A few minutes later, beer in hand, she made her way to a rear corner where she could get her back against the wall and have a view of the dance floor. The crowd was almost all men, most of whom were shirtless in threadbare jeans or tight leather pants that displayed what they had come there to offer and left nothing to the imagination. Here and there she saw a woman, dressed in denim or leather, too, and usually wearing a tight tank top like her own that showed off toned muscles and untethered breasts.

It was a bar like dozens of other bars that she had been in, heavy with the scent of booze and sex and something dangerous. It was no different than it had ever been, and yet, it was completely different. Instead of feeling her pulse begin to beat in time with the music and the promise of sex, she felt remote, a stranger in her own land.

The first person to approach was a heavily muscled, dark-skinned woman with close-cut hair and a row of silver studs in her left ear. Her sleeveless black T-shirt fit so seamlessly that she might have been naked. Sweat glistened on the expanse of chest left bare by the deep vee in the neck, and her skin-tight leather pants outlined every sinew in powerful thighs.

"Dance, sugar?"

Blair smiled and shook her head. "No, thanks."

Clearly surprised, the other woman cocked her head and ran her eyes slowly up and down Blair's body, lingering on her breasts before meeting her eyes again. Hands in pockets, hips jutting forward, the stranger said pointedly, "That's not the message you're sending."

"I'm not hunting. But I appreciate the offer."

"You look hungry to me."

"Sorry, not tonight."

"You just come in to tease the animals, then?"

Again Blair shook her head, still smiling. "No." She shrugged. "I'm just here to pass the time."

"Suit yourself, baby, but you don't know what you're missing."

As the woman turned to walk away, Blair flashed on Cam's face. *Oh yes, I do.*

Over the next half-hour as she finished her beer, she refused several more invitations to dance and, in one case, a less subtle offer to share a few moments of bodily contact in the alley behind the bar. She had turned her back to the front of the room and was watching a particularly handsome male couple dancing when she felt a hand close over her shoulder from behind, the fingers spread over her collarbone and dip onto her upper chest.

She didn't stiffen or react in any way, but she shifted her weight until she was centered and slowly set her bottle down on the ledge near her elbow. Turning her head only slightly to keep her balance, not trying to see who was there, she said, "You better remove that hand. Right now."

A body pressed close against her, a crotch thrust against her ass, and fingers stroked down her bare arm. Lips brushed her ear.

Just as Blair prepared to grasp the intruding wrist and twist away, a voice murmured, "I'd give anything I have to be—"

Blair spun around, her arms coming up and around Cam's shoulders as she pushed her lover against the wall and kissed her, all in one swift motion.

It didn't matter to her a bit that she'd been vacillating between worry and anger all night—wondering where Cam was, wondering why she hadn't called, wondering how she herself was ever going to be able to control the terrible ache that consumed her when they were apart. What mattered was that at the sound of Cam's voice and the touch of her hand, every single thing in her life made sense. Every cell came alive, every breath felt sharper, every thought clearer. Urgently, hungrily, she molded her body to Cam's, her blood running hot and fast just from the feel of her skin.

Finally, breathing heavily, Blair leaned back, her thighs and pelvis still glued to Cam's. The hard press of the agent's inside-pants holster registered against her leg, and she was reminded of where they were and what she had just done. Breathlessly, she whispered, "Jesus, Cam—Stark is in here somewhere."

"No, she isn't. I sent her out when I came in. I assured her I'd be able to provide close protection."

"Not if I distract you, you won't," Blair retorted, one hand sliding up the inside of her lover's denim-clad thigh.

"That might do it." Cam thrust lightly back into her palm.

"Might?" A hint of challenge in her voice, Blair squeezed the triangle between Cam's legs and smiled at Cam's swift intake of breath.

"Except I may have to chase off some of the competition first," Cam murmured, covering Blair's hand with her own. "You're attracting attention."

"I didn't notice."

"*I* certainly did," Cam said. "And I've only been here five minutes."

"You have nothing to worry about."

"Hmm—I'll take that under advisement."

Even in the hazy light, Blair saw Cam's electric grin. She saw something else as well. Cam looked gaunt—dark circles under her eyes marred her handsome face, and the tightness in her jaw betrayed the strain that she couldn't hide. Blair moved her hand back up to Cam's waist, suddenly forgetting her own arousal.

"Cam, you look beat. Did you get any sleep at all?"

"I slept some on the plane."

"How do you feel?"

"Rough," Cam admitted reluctantly, because she knew she wouldn't be able to hide it for long. She *had* slept on the flight, and that had helped. The headache persisted, though. The neurologist who'd seen her in the emergency room, the one who'd wanted to admit her after the explosion three nights before, had warned her that it might. Still, the fleeting dizziness seemed a little better, and her stomach was more settled. "Nothing that a few days away from DC won't cure."

"Why didn't you call me—tell me you were coming?"

"Sorry. I drove right to the airport from Treasury. I always carry an emergency bag in my trunk, and I just grabbed that and caught the first plane out. By the time I had my weapons permit cleared, we were boarding, and I couldn't use the cell."

"That's not like you—to just up and go without checking in—at least with Mac." She brushed a lock of dark hair back from Cam's forehead. "Was it that bad?"

"About what I expected."

Blair nodded, hearing the evasion in her lover's voice, and knew there was more. But for the moment, all she really wanted to do was hold her. She kissed her again, less frantically this time but no less demandingly, then murmured, "Look, let's get out of here. We can..."

Suddenly, she remembered the car somewhere outside filled with Secret Service agents. In the past if she'd wanted to be alone with a woman she'd met in a bar, she'd use the back door and disappear for a few hours. But this was different; this wasn't just any woman—this was the superior of the agents waiting outside.

"Fuck, what *can* we do? I need to be alone with you. Just for a little while."

"Let's go to the beach."

"*What*?"

Cam took her hand. "Trust me on this."

Chapter Five

They caught a cab on the corner of Castro and Market, and while Blair directed the driver, Cam radioed instructions for the agents in the surveillance vehicle to follow them. When the cab pulled to the curb at the end of Polk across from the bay, they paid and climbed out.

"I'll just be a second," Cam said as she and Blair walked back toward the Suburban that sat idling behind their cab. When she leaned down to the open driver's side window of the Suburban, Hernandez looked up. "Two of you stay with the car—whoever's on swing shift is relieved."

"Yes, ma'am."

"Keep your eye on foot traffic on the beach."

"Roger."

As she turned away, the rear door opened and John Fielding climbed out. She nodded to him. "Fielding."

"Commander," he rejoined before heading off to find his way back to the hotel.

Guided by starlight, Cam and Blair crossed the sidewalk and climbed down to the beach, then walked a hundred yards over the sandy soil toward the bay. As they drew close to the water's edge, Cam pointed toward a prominent outcropping of stone.

"This looks good."

Taking Blair's hand, she led her around the far side of the rocks and settled them both on the hard-packed earth. The surf was only a few yards away, tossing ghostly fingers of froth up onto the moonlit sand. The salt spray rapidly misted their skin, and in the middle of the night, the air was chilly, even in August.

"You cold?" Cam had her back against the stone. Their location was isolated from view of the car, and no one could approach them without being seen by the agents stationed on the road above. It was at once private and secure.

"No, not with you here." Blair settled against Cam's right side, her arm circling Cam's waist, her head nestled on Cam's shoulder. "If I didn't know better, I'd think you had practice at this kind of thing."

"Oh? What kind of thing would that be?"

"Eluding the Secret Service."

"Ah. I *have* been giving it some thought," Cam murmured, pressing her lips to Blair's temple. "I didn't sleep *all* the way here—the rest of the time I thought about you."

"They've got to be wondering," Blair said quietly, tugging Cam's shirttail free from the waistband of her trousers and slipping her hand beneath, resting her palm on the warm skin.

"I'm sure they are—but you needn't worry about it." As she followed wisps of clouds streaking across the face of the moon, she thought how much better it was to be watching the sky with Blair beside her. DC seemed a world away. Slowly, she stroked the length of Blair's bare arm, fingertips lightly tracing the firm muscles. "Blair, you're the president's daughter. That works for us as much as it works against us. The Secret Service has a long legacy of silence when it comes to protecting the privacy of the president, and that extends to his family. My agents will not betray you."

"It's not me I care about." She traced a rib, smoothing her fingertips over the scar. *It's you. It's my father.*

"I know that. But *I* care about you." Cam tightened her hold, shifting on the sand until her chest and thighs were pressed to Blair's. "If and when you want to share your personal life with the world, it should be your choice. And it shouldn't be the fodder for anyone else's political agenda."

"*My* personal life has a lot to do with you," Blair whispered, just before her lips found Cam's and she lost her words in the warm welcome of Cam's mouth.

"Yeah," Cam agreed a lifetime later when she finally thought to breathe again. "But no one will care about me—"

"People in DC—at Treasury—could make it difficult for you."

People like Doyle, maybe. Cam shrugged and drew her finger along the edge of Blair's jaw. "I'm not worried about that."

"Then what are you worried about?" Blair leaned back enough to study Cam's face. In the slanting shadows cast by starlight off the water, the sharp angles and planes were even more strikingly handsome. Her voice suddenly thick, she asked softly, "What happened in DC the last two days?"

Cam sighed. "You don't give up, do you?"

"If I did," Blair said as she moved her hand to the inside of Cam's thigh, stroking upward along the thin material of her trousers, "we wouldn't be here right now."

"True." Cam lifted her hips into Blair's palm as the teasing touch turned firmer, more insistent. "It *was* mostly routine, but with something this critical—agents down and a high-profile target like..." She hesitated, realizing how clinical her words sounded. Blair's hand stopped moving, then drew away.

"Like me?"

"Yes," Cam admitted gently. "Like you. It has to be looked at carefully."

"So, is it over? Are you okay?"

Cam hesitated. "I don't know yet." She found Blair's hand and placed it back on her thigh. "But when I do know, I'll tell you."

"Good." Blair leaned close again, finding the heat high between Cam's legs. Her breath caught at the way her lover's body surged in answer to her touch. "I love the way you feel," she whispered. "I want to be all over you, inside you—I feel like I could swallow you whole."

As she spoke, Blair's fingers found what she was seeking through the folds of material, and she squeezed Cam's clitoris lightly. "I could start with this."

Cam's body grew weak, and if she hadn't been sitting, she probably would have fallen down. "Ah, hell. We can't...here."

"Mmm, I know. But God, I want to."

"Uh-huh, that makes two of us," Cam muttered, wondering if she could possibly stay awake long enough, because it wouldn't take much. Her blood was raging but her mind was on the verge of shutting down. "Blair, I'm..."

"What?"

"I'm beat. I don't think I can."

Blair sat up, instantly serious. "Let's go."

"I'm sorry, I—"

Blair laughed, cupping a hand behind Cam's head and leaning over to kiss her—no less passionately, but with a definite sense of finality. When she pulled back, she said, "Cam. You almost got blown up a few nights ago. You've been on your feet the better part of a week. You've got a concussion and God knows what else."

Now on her knees, Blair pushed back her hair with both hands and took a deep breath of the cool night air. "Come along, Commander. I can wait."

Cam caught her hand and held on, preventing her from rising. "I'm not sure *I* can. I've missed you."

"Oh," Blair replied softly. "I've missed you, too."

She bent forward, kissed Cam, long and hard, then pushed quickly away and got to her feet. From a safe distance, she placed her hands on her hips and said mock-threateningly, "I've never been known for my patience. Now, move it."

Laughing, her heart lighter than she could ever remember, Cam got to her feet and followed the retreating form of the first daughter into the shadows.

Within minutes, they were both seated in the rear seat of the Suburban. Stark rode in the front passenger seat while Hernandez drove. Cam leaned her head back against the seat and closed her eyes. The next thing she knew, Blair was gently shaking her shoulder.

"Commander, we're here."

Disoriented, Cam jerked awake and looked rapidly out her window, body tense and battle ready. As soon as she recognized the unique architecture and topography of her mother's street, she relaxed perceptibly. Clearing her throat, she said hoarsely, "Right."

Stark opened Blair's door and held it as Blair stepped out. Cam exited on the other side of the vehicle and walked around to meet her, by which time Hernandez had joined them as well. The four of them moved up the sidewalk to Marcea's front door in a formation so practiced it had become second nature.

A dim light glowed through the windows of the first floor living room fronting the street, and Cam smiled to herself at the welcoming beacon. She'd rarely had time to visit her mother's home, but it was the only place on the planet where she ever felt truly at ease.

Stark unlocked the door and preceded the small group into the still house. Apparently, Marcea and guests had retired. As soon as the door closed behind them, Stark and Hernandez moved quietly away to perform their routine house check. Cam and Blair climbed the stairs leading from the far side of the living room to the second floor. They stopped in the hallway at the end farthest from Marcea's bedroom.

"I guess I won't be sleeping with you tonight," Blair said with resignation as she ran her fingers lightly down Cam's chest. "That's going to be hard. I seem to be...stirred up a bit."

"You're not alone." Cam caught her hand and their fingers immediately entwined. "I don't believe there's any law against you tucking me in."

"That could be a dangerous suggestion, Commander," Blair replied, her voice husky.

"I'll risk it."

Cam led the way partway down the hall and opened the door to the second guest room. As Blair waited in the darkness just inside, Cam crossed to the bathroom, switched on the light, and pulled the door closed until only a thin shaft of illumination cut through the bedroom. It was enough for them to navigate between the dresser, an upholstered chair next to a reading lamp, and the bed.

Wearily, Cam shrugged out of her jacket and tossed it over the back of the chair. With a much-practiced motion, she released the clasp on the right side of her shoulder harness and slid it down her arms and off. By that time, Blair had crossed the space between them and stood close.

"Let me do the rest."

"Now *that's* a dangerous suggestion," Cam murmured. She stood still as Blair's deft fingers unbuttoned her shirt and drew the narrow black belt from her trousers. Obediently, she lifted her arms as her lover stripped the shirt from her and dropped it onto the chair with her jacket. When she reached out, intending to place her arms around Blair's waist, Blair stepped back out of reach.

"Hey," Cam protested, surprised.

"Cam, don't." Blair's voice was oddly still. "I'm not that strong."

"Blair..."

"I mean it. You need to get some rest. And if you touch me, I'm going to forget that." She stepped forward again. "Now, stand still."

Efficiently, she unzipped Cam's pants and worked them down over her hips along with the underlying briefs in one motion. Cam kicked out of her loafers and stepped free of the clothing.

"Now what?" Cam asked thickly, her heart thudding just from the unintentional flicker of Blair's fingers over her skin.

"Now, you get into bed," Blair replied, her voice just as hoarse.

Reluctantly, Cam complied and couldn't quite prevent her sigh of exhaustion as she stretched out under the sheet.

Blair leaned down, kissed her lover chastely, and ran her fingers through Cam's thick dark hair. "I'll see you tomorrow."

As she turned to go, Cam's lids were already fluttering closed. Just as Blair reached for the doorknob, she heard the deep voice float to her on the night air. "I love you."

I love you. Then she let herself out and crossed the hall to her own bed, knowing it would be a long time before she slept.

Chapter Six

A t 9:20 the next morning, Cam rolled over and opened her eyes.

Sunlight streaked through the window on the left side of the room and for a moment, she lay still, basking in its warmth, listening for sounds of life in the house. It was very quiet.

Much of her fatigue had been assuaged by six hours of solid sleep. The headache was a very distant echo and, for the time being, of no consequence. What was much more disruptive at the moment was the persistent pulse of desire that had not abated during the night. She briefly considered crossing the hall to Blair's room and perhaps finding her there alone.

Stellar idea, Roberts—sex in your mother's house with an agent or two practically outside the door. Either prospect should cool you down pretty fast.

It didn't. Instead, she recalled the way Blair had looked the night before—sleek and taut and dangerous in the half-light of the bar. Then on the beach in the moonlight—her face softer, but the hunger still burning in her eyes. Cam remembered, too, how ready she had been to be devoured. How ready she always was.

Time to douse the coals before I go up in flames.

Smiling to herself, she swung her legs over the side of the bed, stood, and stretched. Naked, she walked to the bathroom, turned on the shower, and waited for the water temperature to equilibrate. She showered and dressed with her usual efficiency, noting that she'd have to buy clothes before the gallery opening that evening. It was one thing to travel light, but there were social events scheduled. She wasn't certain how long Blair planned to stay in San Francisco, and if it was any longer than another twenty-four hours, she'd run out of things to wear.

As it was, she pulled on chinos and a black polo shirt, which for her was unusually casual for a workday. Since she wasn't wearing a jacket to hide her shoulder harness, she once again slid the slim body-contouring holster into her trousers and went downstairs to check in with her team.

The dining room and living room were empty, as was the kitchen. Fortunately, a carafe of coffee waited on the counter with a ceramic mug she recognized beside it. She'd made that cup for her father when she was ten.

A piece of paper extended from under it. She pulled it out and read her mother's distinctive hand. *Cameron, I'm in the studio. Come up when you're ready.*

Cam poured coffee and found a banana in a basket next to the refrigerator. Carrying her mug and fruit, she climbed the rear stairs to the third floor. She paused at the studio door, uncertain if her mother might be working and reluctant to disturb her if she was. She admired what Marcea created far too much to interfere with the process, and she knew from experience that when her mother was in the throes of the inspiration, she was lost to anything but the muse.

"Hello?"

"Cameron? Is that you?" Her mother's voice came from the far end of the studio, muffled somewhat by the mountain of canvases in the center of the room.

"Yep. Okay to come in?"

"Yes, do. I'm just finishing up." Marcea turned, smiling fondly. When Cam, who was an inch or two taller, drew near, Marcea stood on her toes to kiss Cam's cheek. "It's good to see you."

"You, too," Cam said, looking around for a safe place to rest her coffee mug.

"Here." Marcea removed a cork coaster from underneath a pile of loose sketch sheets, pencils, and drawing pens. She placed it on a nearby stand. "How are you?"

"Fine," Cam responded, wondering just how much her mother knew about the recent events. The threats on Blair's life and the bloody resolution had been downplayed in the press, but Blair could have told her. She doubted, though, that Blair would have mentioned her own injuries to Marcea. Not after what had happened earlier that year. She rested a hip on the edge of a long counter that held an assortment of art supplies and peeled the banana. "It's been hectic. I'm a bit tired is all."

"Well, I hope the opening tonight won't be too taxing." Marcea pulled over a tall stool and sat next to Cam. "The usual glitterati and media hounds will abound. Here and there a real art lover, too, I expect."

"For your show?" Cam scoffed. "It will be a zoo."

"You flatter me."

"And you're too modest." Cam sipped her coffee. "Where is everyone this morning?"

"Blair went running, and Paula and Felicia went with her."

Cam frowned momentarily, mentally reviewing the intelligence reports of the immediate area they'd hastily gathered before Blair's trip. Nothing to be worried about, but still..."Is someone in the car, too?"

"I don't know. I take it her decision to go out was rather sudden."

"It would be," Cam said with a resigned shake of her head. "I'd better call Mac for a status report. Have you seen him today?"

"He was here earlier, very briefly, and talked to Paula."

"All right. Thanks." Cam started to move away.

"Do you really have to leave immediately? She's quite safe with Paula and Felicia, isn't she?"

Startled, Cam halted. Her mother had never really shown much interest in her work before and had rarely talked to her about the details. But then of course, this wasn't about her work. This was about Blair.

"Yes, she should be fine."

"Well then, stay and finish your coffee, and I'll catch you up on all the latest gossip from the art scene."

For a second, Cam considered refusing. Then she reminded herself that until she officially relieved Mac as crew chief, he would be keeping a very close eye on what happened with Blair. A few more minutes wouldn't matter, and she rarely got the opportunity to speak with her mother.

"In that case, let's start with the good stuff. What's happening with you and Giancarlo?" She was astonished when her mother blushed.

"Ah...let's say we are exploring possibilities."

"Well, that's an intriguing answer." Cam laughed. "*Romantic* possibilities?"

"Yes."

Cam's surprise was surpassed only by her pleasure. Since her father had been killed over twenty years before, she had not known her mother to have a serious—or even casual—relationship with any man.

"I like him," Cam announced, finishing her banana and placing the peel on a crumpled piece of paper near her coffee mug. "I think it's terrific, and I hope this *exploration* brings you happiness."

Marcea studied her daughter's face, taken aback by the calm certainty in her tone and expression. She was used to more emotional detachment in her driven offspring, and the insightful directness of her response was new. "Thank you. And by the same token, might I ask about you and Blair?"

Cam stiffened, denial rising automatically to her lips. Instead, to her amazement, she said, "We are exploring possibilities, too."

"I have the feeling your exploration is a little further along than mine and Giancarlo's—and I'm not talking about the bedroom."

"It's complicated," Cam acquiesced, looking away.

"Cameron, my love, romance is always complicated." Marcea laughed and rested her palm on Cam's cheek. "She's very much in love with you, you know."

Cam swallowed, her voice suddenly deserting her. She reached for her mother's hand and held it lightly, staring at the strong tapering fingers that brought life to bare canvas with simple swatches of color. In a voice so low that Marcea had to lean forward to hear, Cam whispered, "God, I hope so."

She raised her gaze to her mother's, the depths of her gray eyes nearly black with emotion. "I shouldn't even *think* about her, but I can't help it. I can't stop feeling what I feel for her."

"Good. Because she doesn't want you to." Marcea kissed Cam on the forehead. "It will be all right. Just follow your heart."

"I'll try," Cam said softly.

She stayed a few more minutes while her mother brought her up to date on the latest news, until finally, her need to check in with

Mac became so urgent that she couldn't listen any longer. "I'm sorry. I need to get to work."

"Of course, you do." Marcea laughed. "I'm surprised you managed to sit still this long. Go ahead."

"I'll see you tonight," Cam said before she hurried toward the hall.

"Wonderful."

Marcea listened to Cam's footsteps fade away on the stairs and fervently hoped that, against the odds, her daughter and Blair would find their way to happiness.

❖

"Mac?"

"Good morning, Commander." Mac's voice sounded cheerful and welcoming through the line. The blond-haired, blue-eyed agent was ordinarily her communication coordinator, but when she was away from the security detail, he assumed the role of crew chief in her stead. He'd fulfilled that role admirably during the months when she'd been recovering from the gunshot wound. "Welcome aboard."

"Thanks." Cam stood in the sun on the rear deck of her mother's home, watching the white triangles of sails cut across the blue water of the bay far below. "Feels good to be here."

"After New York? Yeah."

"Where are you?"

"I'm still at the command post in the St. Francis. Since she's always moving, I figured *I* should be stationary. I've pretty much been coordinating from here." Mac gave no indication of the fact that he'd been taking calls almost twenty-four hours a day from the agents on shift who were guarding Blair Powell, apprising him of her whereabouts and providing status reports.

"Sounds right," Cam agreed. "Where is she now?"

"At Gold's Gym on Market and Noe."

"Who's inside?"

"Stark. It's quiet."

Cam wanted more details, but she had to admit she just wanted to know where Blair was, what she was doing. Her position as Blair's security chief gave her the power to know more about Blair's life than Blair might choose to share, and that was one of the dangers of crossing the line between protector and lover. Blair had never had a private life, not since she was twelve and her father had burst on the political scene as a very visible governor already slated to be a future power player in Washington, and she was entitled to as much privacy as they could give her while still keeping her safe. The fact that Cam was in love with her didn't change that.

"Okay," Cam said brusquely, annoyed that her mind was wandering. It never wandered when she worked, but just thinking about Blair..."Right. I'll take over—"

"Things are under control, Commander, if you want to take some down time. At least until the gallery opening tonight."

She was about to refuse when it occurred to her that she hadn't had an entire day off in weeks. "Thanks, Mac. We'll run through the assignments at 1700 hours, then. Call me if there's any change."

"Roger."

❖

As it turned out, Cam did not see Blair for the rest of the day. At six p.m., she waited in the living room of her mother's house to accompany the president's daughter to the opening of Marcea's latest show at the Rodman Gallery just off Union Square. She looked out the window to be certain that John Fielding had the Suburban idling at the curb in front of the house and that Felicia Davis rode in the shotgun seat beside him as planned. At the sound of footsteps descending the stairs from the second floor, she turned and the breath stopped in her chest. Blair stood ten feet away, regarding her silently, a curious expression on her face.

Cam's heart started triple-timing as she took in the sleek black dress with its nearly imperceptible straps encircling each sculpted shoulder and the subtle cut that outlined the lithe, toned form. A glint of diamonds sparkled in each ear and a delicate gold chain rested at the base of Blair's neck. Her artist's hands were without rings, graceful and strong. Cam cleared her suddenly very dry throat.

"Good evening, Ms. Powell."

Blair smiled, aware that they were truly alone for the first time in four days. "Commander."

"The car's just outside."

"Are you to be my escort this evening?" Blair walked slowly forward, her blue eyes dancing as they searched Cam's face.

The corner of Cam's mouth lifted in a grin. "Unless you have someone else than mind...in which case there could be a problem."

"No, no problem at all." Blair ran a single finger down the pearl studs on the pleated shirt that Cam wore beneath a fitted black tuxedo jacket. "How did you manage to get this into your handy-dandy all-purpose travel bag?"

"I didn't. I'm afraid my planning was not up to par this week—I had to have an emergency fitting this afternoon." Cam shrugged. "Off the rack, but the best I could do."

"Believe me," Blair murmured as she found Cam's hand and ran her thumb in small circles over the back of it. "Armani in any condition suits you."

"You look beautiful." Cam's tone was low and intimate.

"So do you."

"And you have an engagement." Cam straightened her shoulders and gestured to the door. "Shall we go?"

"Yes, of course." Blair's features transformed into the composed, coolly elegant lines that the world was accustomed to associating with the president's daughter. As they stepped outside, she asked, "Are you coming inside the gallery with me?"

"Yes."

"Good. I don't want you to waste that suit waiting in the car."

"Is that the only reason?"

"What else?"

Cam laughed as she led the way down the sidewalk to the waiting vehicle. The two of them settled into the back where the seats were rearranged to face one another. As Fielding pulled away, the first daughter and her security chief held each other's eyes, silently bridging the distance between them with the intensity of a caress.

❖

They were two blocks from the corner of Sutter and Mason when Cam's cell phone rang. She shifted on the seat and pulled it from her belt. "Roberts."

A crease developed between her brows as she frowned out the window, eyes scanning the street ahead. "How many? All right. Fine. Have Stark meet us curbside."

She terminated the call and gave Blair an apologetic smile. "That was Mac. There's a crowd of reporters and photographers waiting outside the gallery. More than we anticipated. I don't know if their presence has anything to do with what happened in New York or not, but the front entrance is the only reasonable way into the gallery. I'm sorry—it's probably going to be hectic."

"That's all right." Blair's voice was remote and her expression unreadable. Usually, her public comings and goings were documented as a matter of course by the local news media. Depending on the event, and the availability of other good news clips, reporters might then put the story out on the wire to be carried in the public interest section of the national newspapers. She was used to it.

As the Suburban slowed to a stop, Cam opened the door and, one leg extended to the curb, partially blocked the interior of the vehicle as she rapidly assessed the dozen or so people gathered on the sidewalk in front of the gallery. Stark appeared out of the crowd and stepped up opposite her so that they flanked the open door from which Blair would emerge.

"All clear," Stark advised quietly.

Cam nodded and turned to Blair, who had been waiting just at the edge of the seat. "Ready, Ms. Powell."

Blair exited just as Felicia Davis came around the front of the vehicle and moved behind the three of them as they started up the sidewalk.

They'd only gone a few feet when a wiry, shaggy-haired man in rumpled slacks and an open-collared shirt stepped in front of them and said, "Ms. Powell, do you know the identity of the man who tried to kill you in New York?"

He had a laminated card hanging around his neck on a lanyard, but the image and identifying logo were turned toward his chest. He could have been a reporter; he could have been a fan; he could have been an assassin.

"Step back, please," Cam said firmly, her left arm out palm first at chest level. She eased her right hand under her jacket to the gun she now carried in a shoulder holster snugged to her left side.

"Keep moving," she said quietly to Blair, Davis, and Stark.

He was barely three feet away from them, and Cam edged slightly to her left until she was in front of Blair, obscuring her from the man's view. "Please, step back."

"Is it true that you once had a sexual relationship with him?" he asked again, walking backwards up the walk toward the gallery, maintaining the distance between them as he spoke.

Cam raised her left wrist with the radio band attached, her right now closed on the grip of her automatic. "Mac—Stark, if he makes any move toward her, restrain him. Davis, prepare to extricate."

Cameras clicked, people shouted questions, the crowd followed—surging closer with each passing second. Blair looked neither right nor left. The door to the gallery was ten feet away. Mac stood there to one side, his right hand under his jacket, his gaze locked on Cam.

Behind them, the engine of the Suburban revved.

Stark took two quick steps forward, moving slightly ahead of Blair, and reached for the door. "Step away," she said to the man.

The stranger had no choice but to move aside as Stark gripped the doorknob and pulled. Still, he was half in front of the entrance and easily within touching distance of Blair.

"Ms. Powell—" he said one last time.

Cam shouldered his chest hard with her right elbow and side, pushing him off balance into Mac's waiting arms and out of the way as Blair walked between her and Stark into the gallery.

Once inside, Cam spoke again into her radio. "Do you have him? I want him ID'd—complete background check. Do not let him inside until you clear with me."

In the lull after the hurried entrance, Blair drew a deep breath and tried to settle herself by focusing on her surroundings. She loved galleries—the purity of the clean, uninterrupted space; the startling shock of pristine white walls splashed with vibrant color; the lighting—so intentionally directed only where it mattered, as if the people were insignificant in the shadows. Tonight the soothing hum of muted voices and soft click of heels on hardwood floors failed to calm her.

"I wish you wouldn't do that," Blair said in a low voice that only Cam could hear.

"What?" Cam asked absently as she nodded to Stark, who moved a few feet away to a spot where she had a better view of anyone approaching Blair through the crowd.

"Stand in front of me."

"It was nothing to be concerned about," Cam said dismissively, her complete attention fixed on the layout of the space and its inhabitants.

Not for you. Not this time. Why can't I make you understand what it does to me?

More frightened than annoyed, Blair shook her head slightly but before she could protest further, she recognized San Francisco's mayor approaching with a welcoming smile. She held out her hand and murmured a few polite words as they greeted one another. For the next few minutes, she was occupied fulfilling the social obligations that accompanied her position. It was a function she had performed countless times, and she did it without conscious thought.

As she moved around the room, Cam and Davis moved with her, one on either side, keeping a distance of five feet between themselves and her. Not close enough to appear intrusive but near enough to physically shield her if need be. Stark had disappeared into the crowd to institute roving surveillance, observing the attendees to ensure that no one suspicious approached the president's daughter.

Eventually, Blair had attended to all of the political requirements. She then made her way through the people gathered in pairs and small groups to where Marcea stood, wine glass in hand, talking to Giancarlo and several well-wishers.

"Blair, my dear." Marcea leaned to kiss her cheek. "Thank you so much for coming." Her eyes moved to her daughter's face, but she did not greet her other than with a smile.

"It's my pleasure." Blair returned the kiss with a brush of her lips against Marcea's skin. "It's truly wonderful. Very impressive—congratulations."

"Believe me, *I* am anything but impressed." Marcea laughed and took Blair's hand. "Probably the reason I don't have very many shows is that I can't tolerate all the pomp. I'm glad you've come, though."

"So am I. I hope that I'll actually be able to look at your work now. I think I've finally talked to everyone here."

"Please, escape while you can." Marcea squeezed her hand and turned with a smile to yet another patron, and Blair slipped away.

For the next few moments, she moved slowly around the large room. The space was partially subdivided by white half-walls upon which Marcea's paintings had been hung and lit with overhead track lights. She was familiar with Marcea Casells's work, of course, as any serious artist was, but she had never had the opportunity to see so many in one place. She was aware of Cam just outside her field of vision, keeping pace with her as she walked from one canvas to the next. Eventually, she lost herself in the color and form and captivating fluidity of Marcea's work and forgot everything except the experience.

She jumped, startled, when a voice close by murmured, "There's a particularly interesting work just ahead."

"Oh?" Turning her head, she met Cam's eyes.

"Yes. It doesn't appear to be my mother's, though."

Blair followed the direction of Cam's gaze and saw her own charcoal sketch of the day before mounted on the wall. The simple card beside it read, *Untitled,* by *Anonymous*.

"Interesting," she remarked noncommittally.

"It's more than that. It's beautiful," Cam declared, her voice husky with emotion. "When did you do it?"

"How did you know?"

"Several reasons," Cam said quietly. "First, I recognized your style."

Blair waited, watching Cam's eyes darken, feeling their heat on her skin. "And?"

Cam shrugged, at an unusual loss for words. "No one else could do that—no one knows me well enough."

"Sometimes," Blair replied quietly, "I'm not sure how well I really know you."

"What do you mean?"

"Like outside tonight—I thought we'd agreed you wouldn't be doing that again."

Cam looked genuinely confused. "I'm sorry?"

"Putting yourself between me and danger."

"He wasn't a threat—just a nuisance."

"And if he *had* been dangerous?"

Cam was silent a beat, because they both knew the answer. "I guess I don't always make it easy for you, do I?"

"No, you don't." Blair reached for her hand, then suddenly stopped, remembering where they were. "I suppose on occasion I'm guilty of that as well."

"Sometimes." A grin flickered across Cam's features and then quickly disappeared. "But I'm not complaining."

"Do you suppose there's any chance at all that we could disappear for a while?"

"Considering that we're surrounded by over a hundred people, including four of my agents? Not right at this moment," Cam replied with a regretful smile.

"I was afraid you'd say that."

"I should let you continue your tour of the paintings. I just wanted to...thank you." She gestured to the charcoal drawing. "I know my mother won't part with it—even if I beg."

"I know the artist. I'll see if there might be another in the series."

"I'd like that."

"You might have to sit for it."

"I could do that," Cam murmured as she stepped away. "Anytime you want."

CHAPTER SEVEN

When Blair eventually said good night to Marcea, the honoree kissed Blair on both cheeks, smiled fondly at Cam, and informed them that she planned to attend a late-night gathering at the Regency and would most likely not see them until the next day.

Blair and Cam, alone together in the rear of the Suburban, were silent on the short ride back to Russian Hill. As soon as Blair was safely inside, Cam posted Fielding to the Suburban for perimeter watch, relieved Davis for the night, and gave Stark the inside duty. Offering polite good nights to Blair, the three agents dispersed in various directions to carry out their assignments. Cam and Blair were left facing one another in the living room.

"Fancy that. Except for the agent out front and the agent in the house, we're...alone at last." Blair's eyes were hot on Cam's face as she spoke.

Cam nodded, standing two feet away, her hands at her sides, wondering if Blair could sense her trembling. It had been so long since they'd really touched, and the look in Blair's eyes set her skin on fire. In a voice that sounded amazingly calm even to her own ears, she asked, "What are your plans?"

"You mean for the rest of this evening...or for the next couple of days?"

"I think tonight is pretty well settled," Cam said with a regretful smile. She wished they could be together and knew she'd be disappointed. There was no way they'd find time alone. "I'd like to bring the team up to speed on your schedule now that we're all back in one place again."

"If I could, I'd stay here indefinitely." Blair settled on the arm of an overstuffed chair, her bare arm draped along its back.

"I really enjoy Marcea's company, and San Francisco agrees with me." She shrugged. "But I need to get back to New York. My work is there, and we're leaving for Paris soon. There are things I need to take care of before we go."

"Is it all right with you if I book a flight back for tomorrow evening?"

"Fine." Blair arched a brow. "Just make sure you get a seat next to mine."

"Understood," Cam said with a grin.

"How's your headache?"

"What headache?"

"Cameron." The threat in her voice was real.

"Practically gone."

"And the rest of it? The dizziness, the vision thing?"

"I'm fine. Really." Driven by the concern in Blair's voice, Cam stepped up to her, placing her fingertips lightly on Blair's waist, meaning only to reassure her. Too late, Cam realized that touching her was a mistake. Then she stopped thinking all together.

Blair tilted her head so she could study Cam's eyes, the one place she could always see the truth. Right now, those dark eyes were slightly wild, ebony shadows swirling through their depths. She knew what those shadows meant.

"Cam," she breathed as Cam's lips drew closer to her own.

At that moment, the sliding door to the kitchen opened with a thud, an unusually noisy entrance for the ordinarily stealthy Stark.

Cam sighed, her mouth a fraction from Blair's. "I believe that was an announcement."

"Yes," Blair said regretfully as Cam backed away. "I think I'll turn in, since it appears that sex on the sofa is out."

"Good night, Ms. Powell." Cam drew a shaky breath and smiled.

"Commander." Blair's tone made it sound like a caress before she turned hastily away.

As Blair disappeared up the stairs to the second floor, Stark entered from the rear of the house.

"All clear, Commander." She walked directly to the television in an alcove on the opposite side of the living room and turned it on.

"Thank you," Cam said. "I'll be upstairs if there's a problem."

"Yes, ma'am. I don't expect to need to disturb you."

Cam paused halfway up the stairs and looked down at the back of the young agent's head. "I appreciate that."

❖

When Cam reached the hallway on the second floor, she noticed a faint light filtering from beneath Blair's bedroom door. Silently, she stood before it, debating whether to enter. She knew it was unlikely that anyone would notice or, if they did, would care. And if one of the agents did see her together with Blair in an intimate situation, it was something that would never be mentioned. Even if they weren't loyal to *her,* one did not betray the confidences of a member of the first family and keep one's job.

Nevertheless, she turned away, more out of long habit than anything else. She *wanted* to be inside with Blair. She wanted to lie down beside her. She was weary from the past weeks of tension and struggle, tired in body and spirit, and she missed the comfort of Blair's arms. A comfort she found nowhere else.

Sighing deeply, she told herself that a few more days wouldn't matter. Once they were back in New York City, on home ground, Blair would have a greater degree of freedom, and they could relax their vigilance somewhat. Also, Blair was in the habit of secluding herself for hours or even days at a friend's apartment, and there she and Cam might steal a few hours of time alone. It was far from ideal, but for a public figure such as Blair, it was the norm to have to manufacture privacy.

Resolutely, Cam opened the door to her own bedroom and slid her right hand along the wall toward the light switch.

"You might want to leave that off."

Cam dropped her hand and quietly pushed the door closed behind her, remaining motionless while her eyes adjusted to the dim illumination offered by the street lamps and starlit sky outside the windows. "Do you trust me to do this by feel?"

"Well," Blair said musingly, stepping from the shadows into the slash of moonlight cutting across the center of the room, "it *has* been a while, but I imagine that given a little time and encouragement, you could manage."

As Blair spoke, Cam quickly shed her jacket and shrugged out of her shoulder holster, placing them on the chair just inside the door. She walked the ten feet to Blair and stopped with a sliver of the night still between them.

"Not tired?" Cam asked, her deep voice a register lower than usual.

"I was afraid I wouldn't be able to get to sleep...and I only know one sure remedy for that." She hesitated, then added mischievously, "I suppose I could go it alone—"

"Trying to make me jealous?" Cam interrupted softly.

"Me? Never." Blair laughed. "Besides...with you across the hall, there really is no other choice. At least...none that compares."

It was Cam's turn to laugh. Then, carefully, she placed her fingertips on Blair's bare shoulders and turned her so that she faced the window and the night. Moving so close that her pelvis just brushed Blair's rear, Cam slid her hands to the clasp that held Blair's hair confined at the base of her neck and released it. She combed her fingers through the thick curls, fanning the strands over Blair's neck, then caressed her palms over the slope of her lover's shoulders and down her arms. "You look very beautiful tonight."

Relaxing into the embrace, Blair leaned back into Cam's body, resting her head against Cam's chest. "Have I ever mentioned how much I love it when you undress me?" Her voice was throaty and just a bit ragged.

"I seem to remember something about that." Cam placed her lips on the firm curve of muscle where Blair's neck met her shoulder, exploring for an inch or so with her mouth before pressing her teeth to the tight flesh. Then she bit slowly until she heard Blair's breath catch and a small moan escape her. Finally, she lifted her mouth away. "May I take that as an invitation?"

"Please," Blair breathed.

Cam drew her fingers back up the outside of Blair's bare arms and insinuated her palms under the thin spaghetti straps, lowering them smoothly halfway down Blair's arms. She stopped then, causing the fabric of the dress to draw tightly across Blair's breasts just above her nipples. With one hand, Cam reached around Blair's body, spreading her fingers over Blair's chest, dipping into the cleft between her breasts. With the other, she slowly pulled the studs from her own shirt, letting the silver-encased pearls drop one by one to the hardwood floor.

Blair's body tightened each time the small clink broke the silence.

They leaned into one another, Blair's back pressed against the front of Cam's body, subtle curves fusing to long lean angles. Cam's white shirt was open, her chest naked against the flesh exposed by the nearly backless black dress.

"Four days is a long time," Cam murmured, her mouth brushing the curve of Blair's ear, her breath quickening as she felt her own nipples harden against Blair's soft skin. "It was hard to work tonight...trying to ignore how much I wanted to touch you."

"Why, Commander," Blair whispered huskily, "I didn't think anything could distract you from your work."

"*You* do." Cam tore her shirt from her trousers and threw it behind her on the floor, then pulled the zipper down the back of Blair's dress. With both hands, she lowered the sheer fabric over Blair's body, exposing her breasts to the moonlight, marveling at the way the pale skin glowed with the rush of blood and something altogether more elemental just below the surface. In the next instant, she closed her fingers around one taut nipple, splaying her hand under the full curve of hot yielding flesh. "You always do."

As much as she had wanted to go slowly, Cam found it more difficult with each passing second. Blair's flesh was soft and smooth, but the muscles beneath were tight, her body humming with tension. The quick rise and fall of her breasts under Cam's palms spoke of her lover's desire, and Cam's body soared in response, her thighs trembling as she rocked against Blair's buttocks. When Blair returned the pressure with a thrust of her hips, Cam moaned deep in her chest.

"You know I like it fast the first time," Blair gasped, relinquishing her passivity by insinuating one hand into the nearly nonexistent space between them and rapidly sliding up the inside of Cam's leg to grasp her firmly through her trousers. "I haven't stopped wanting you since the bar last night, and if I get any more swollen, there's going to be permanent damage."

Urgently, Cam grasped Blair's shoulders and pulled her around so they were face to face, their naked chests cleaving as they kissed. A kiss that spoke of need and longing and raw hunger. As the seconds passed, the first rush of desperation soothed into welcoming recognition, and when they finally parted, each breathing heavily, they were both smiling.

"Let's try something new. Let's see how we do with slow this time," Cam whispered.

"You're asking a lot." Blair gave a small shake of her head, her hands trailing over Cam's abdomen to the top of her trousers. Deftly, she unbuttoned the silk tuxedo pants and slid down the zipper. "But I'll try if you do."

And then she slipped her hand inside.

Cam flushed hot, and her head reeled with sudden dizziness at the unexpected force of Blair's fingers gliding over her exposed and ready nerve endings. Her hands trembled on Blair's skin and her voice shuddered. "I can't if you do that."

"If you insist..." Blair laughed lightly and took her hand away, then laughed again at Cam's unintentional whimper. "Let's at least do this on the bed then. I don't have the strength to stand."

They drew apart only enough to strip free the rest of their clothing. Then, as if fearful of being separated, they hastily embraced, their limbs entwining as they rolled together on top of the sheets.

Twisting her torso, Cam drew Blair beneath her, one leg between Blair's thighs as she claimed her lover's mouth. When the heat of Blair's breath in her throat wasn't enough to assuage her need, Cam reared up on both arms and pushed downward on the bed, settling her chest between Blair's spread thighs. Instantly, her mouth closed over a nipple, and she bit lightly, feeling Blair's fingers push into her hair. She found the other breast and cradled it in her hand, working the nipple between her fingers. She didn't stop until Blair was arched bow-tight beneath her, her breath a series of short gasps.

"Please," Blair whispered, framing Cam's face with trembling hands. Her eyes were cloudy as she tried to focus on her lover. "I need you so much."

Only then did Cam ease lower still, kissing her way down the center of Blair's abdomen, moving both palms to the inside of Blair's thighs. Blair was wet against her skin. Pulse pounding, so heady with lust she could barely hear, Cam rested her cheek against the soft down at the base of Blair's abdomen and rasped, "Slow enough?"

"Any slower...and I'll...go off without you."

Cam laughed shakily. "Oh, I don't think so."

Unhurriedly, Cam drew her fingers through the thick heat between Blair's thighs, thumbing firmly against her clitoris as she passed, then dipping inside her for a fleeting moment. Withdrawing despite Blair's cry of protest, she grew still with her fingers spread over the hot, swollen flesh, feeling the blood pound wildly against her palm. Blair pushed against her hand.

"Don't. I want you to come in my mouth."

"Then kiss me," Blair begged, "and I will."

Very slowly, Cam lowered her head and drew Blair carefully between her lips. When Blair's thighs tensed suddenly, signaling she was close, Cam took her more deeply into her mouth, matching the rhythmic movements of her lips to the tempo of her fingers stroking within. The thrust of her tongue and fingers danced counterpoint to the blood pulsing and muscles spasming around her hand.

Blair's hand was fisted in Cam's hair, clenching fitfully as small cries ripped from her throat. When she climaxed, Blair choked out Cam's name, partway between surrender and benediction.

Eyes closed, not breathing, Cam fought back tears at the soaring wonder of being united with the only woman in her life that mattered. She had no idea how long she lay without moving before Blair broke the silence.

"Are you asleep?"

Cam shook her head slightly, her lips moving faintly on Blair's still-pulsing flesh. "No. I don't think so. Maybe...or I could just be dead, and this is heaven."

"Oh yeah. Feels...like heaven." Blair laughed unsteadily, flexing her cramped fingers and easing her stiff legs back and forth on the sheets. The titanic contractions at the peak of her orgasm had been nearly painful, and probably would have been if the pleasure hadn't been so acute. "Come up here...if you can. I want to touch you."

"I'm fine," Cam mumbled, her eyes still closed and her heart beating erratically in her chest.

"Come up here anyway."

With heavy limbs, Cam managed to eventually move the three feet before collapsing on the pillows next to Blair. "What do you think?"

"Slow is okay, I guess." Drowsily, Blair shifted into Cam's arms and rested her head on her lover's shoulder, one hand on the taut abdomen.

"Mmm," Cam agreed. "Not bad for starters."

Blair pressed her lips to Cam's neck and licked the salty sweat that filmed her skin. A pulse beat hard beneath her lips, and she inched her fingers lower, finding her way between Cam's thighs. Cam groaned as Blair fingered the hard prominence of her clitoris.

"Fine, are you?" Blair chuckled faintly. "You are *so* out of touch sometimes, Commander."

"Well...there's fine—" Cam's pelvis arched as the pressure abruptly escalated beneath Blair's knowing touch. "And then there's...fine."

"I don't think slow is a possibility here," Blair observed as Cam's stomach muscles contracted hard and her whole body shuddered. "Is it?"

"I...I'm losing it," Cam confessed desperately, already jerking with the first wave of spasms. "Oh God..."

"It's all right," Blair murmured, her lips pressed to the curve of her lover's ear. "I have you."

❖

Quietly, Blair opened the door to the elevated rear deck and stepped out into the night. She had pulled on a loose pair of workout shorts and a sleeveless T-shirt and carried a can of soda in her hand. She stopped just outside the door when she realized that she was not alone.

Paula Stark spoke quickly into her cell phone. "Listen— you take it easy, understand? I'll call you soon. Yeah...all right. I remember. 'Night."

"Sorry." Blair crossed the fifteen-foot deck to join the agent at the railing.

"No problem. I'm in between checkpoints, and I was just—"

"Paula, for God's sake. Do you think I care if you make a telephone call?"

"Well, strictly speaking, I'm—"

"Please." Blair snorted. "Strictly speaking, you should stand in the dark and do nothing for twelve hours?"

"Well," Stark rejoined seriously, "*strictly* speaking, it wouldn't be for twelve hours. I'm working the swing shift, so, actually, I've only been on duty for—"

"I get the picture, Secret Service Agent Stark."

Stark shut her mouth and peered at the president's daughter in the moonlight. Blair was smiling, and as it never failed to do, Stark's heart gave a slight stutter. This time, however, she recognized it for what it was. She liked the president's daughter. More than liked her.

She respected Blair Powell's official position, and she valued the work that Blair did in that capacity, representing the nation well whenever she stood in for her deceased mother as the president's closest female emissary in situations where that kind of position mattered. She appreciated her, too, as an individual who was talented in her own right and passionate about important causes, particularly the fight against the cancer that had claimed her mother's life.

And more than all of that, Stark admitted, she had a history with her. A very brief history, to be sure, but it was a part of her past that, on balance, she was not sorry to have experienced. So when she looked at the woman next to her, all of those things affected her, even if they weren't supposed to. Even if, as a Secret Service agent, she wasn't supposed to feel anything at all for the person she guarded, other than responsibility.

Stark sighed. So maybe she would never be the best Secret Service agent because of that, but she knew she probably wasn't going to be able to change. Maybe no one would ever notice these failings. At least the commander trusted her as Egret's primary protector, and that was really all that mattered.

Blair watched the moonlight flutter across Stark's features and watched, too, the kaleidoscope of emotions—not all of which she understood but some of which she clearly recognized. Fondly, she smiled again. "So, checking in with Mac, were you?"

"Um..."

"Never mind, Stark." Blair took pity on her and dropped the teasing. "I know it wasn't Mac, because I know your tone of voice when you talk to him. How is Renee, anyhow?"

"She's good, I guess," Stark said glumly, picking at a splinter of wood on the edge of the railing.

"You guess? What's wrong?"

"They're letting her out of the hospital in a day or so."

"That's wonderful," Blair exclaimed, leaning her elbows on the railing so that she and Stark both faced the bay. "That's a lot sooner than expected, isn't it?"

"Yeah, and that's the problem. She's already talking about when she'll be going back to work."

"Why am I not surprised?"

"Huh?"

"Never mind," Blair said with a slight shake of her head. "I can't imagine that she'll be able to go back to work right away, even if she wants to. Don't worry too much—she's going to need physical therapy, right?"

"Yeah, she is. Still, I'm sure she'll figure out a way to get a desk job even if she can't get back to field duty right away."

"You know, Stark," Blair said pointedly, "most of you on my team probably shouldn't even be working right now, so you might try to put yourself in Savard's position."

Genuinely perplexed, Stark turned her head to meet Blair's eyes. "What are you talking about? None of us were hurt except Ellen."

"Jesus. Is it a requirement that all Secret Service agents be blockheads?"

Stark stiffened at Blair's criticism, ready to defend her colleagues, but before she could get a word out, Blair continued.

"We're not just talking about physical injury, although God knows, Cam should probably be on sick leave."

"Is the commander ill?" Stark asked immediately with genuine concern.

"Nothing she would admit to, but the point is, she *was* hurt. And all of you lost a colleague and had two others badly injured. It could have been any one of you. That kind of thing hurts, too."

"It comes with the job, Ms. Powell." Stark suddenly sounded somber and years older.

"Yes." Blair was likewise subdued, with noticeable sympathy in her voice this time. "I guess it does."

Very briefly, in an unusual movement for her, Blair squeezed Stark's forearm in a friendly gesture, then brought her hand back to the railing. "At any rate, I don't imagine that Renee is going to be any different than the rest of you, but hopefully, she'll be sensible enough not to push for anything too physical until she's ready."

"The one good thing is that she's going to be staying with her sister in New York City while she recovers," Stark explained, the enthusiasm back in her voice. "So if she *does* get an assignment, it will most likely be in the local field office, at least temporarily."

"Ah—so she'll be nearby then."

"Yeah. She will."

Blair couldn't miss the excitement in the young agent's voice, and she couldn't help but feel just a twinge of jealousy. Renee Savard and Paula Stark were free to explore whatever was happening between them and to do it with all the joy and anticipation of any two people who might be falling in love. It was something she had never had the opportunity to do.

Now, she *was* in love—hopelessly, achingly, desperately in love—and she still found the joy tinged with sadness, and sometimes anger. It was three in the morning, and she had just left her lover's arms because she could not awaken with her, even in one of the safest places she had ever known. *If we can't share that simple pleasure here, then where, and when, will it ever be possible?*

Chapter Eight

A t seven-thirty the next morning, feeling refreshed and unusually light-hearted, Cam walked into the kitchen and headed directly for the coffeepot. The pot was warm and the coffee smelled fresh. Someone from the night shift had probably just made it. Gratefully, she helped herself and headed toward the rear deck. She'd already called Mac at the hotel to review the daily updates from DC as well as the myriad of intelligence agencies that monitored foreign and domestic events, and now she planned to take advantage of the rare morning sunshine and exceptionally clear sky. Even in summer, fog was the norm on a San Francisco morning.

At the sound of the door sliding open, the woman standing at the rail turned in her direction.

"Good morning," Cam said, pleasantly surprised. She hadn't heard anyone moving about upstairs, and she'd thought she was the only one awake. Leaning a shoulder against the open door frame, she sipped her coffee and took a moment to appreciate the sunlight on her lover's face. In a faded Yankees jersey that looked older than she was and a pair of baggy sweats, Blair was easily the most beautiful woman she'd even seen. Cam's heart, and most other places, began to pound.

"Good morning." Blair leaned back against the railing with an arm outstretched on either side of her body, her hands curled over the top rail. She smiled faintly, watching Cam's expression go from pleasure to desire.

"I thought you were still asleep," Cam remarked, still nailed to the door. She didn't quite trust herself to go near Blair just yet— not on the deck in broad daylight. She'd thought her hunger had been temporarily sated the night before. Apparently, she'd thought wrong.

"No. I've been up for a while." Blair saw no reason to mention that she'd lain awake for most of what remained of the night after leaving Stark. Knowing that Cam was just across the hall had not helped. It had only made her more restless.

"Are you all right?" Cam frowned, sensing something left unsaid.

"Yes." Blair smiled, a real smile as she shook off the vestiges of melancholy. It was a beautiful day and Cam was standing there, looking impossibly sexy in worn jeans and a white shirt—frayed at the collar and cuffs. "Perfect."

"Mind company?"

"Not yours."

Cam crossed the deck, then looked down to quickly survey the densely shrubbed rear property as it sloped toward the street, a barely visible ribbon of grey as it fell steeply away below them.

"Felicia is down there somewhere," Blair noted as she watched Cam do a perimeter scan. "It's her shift."

Scrutinizing the area below, Cam merely nodded until she saw the faint shadow of her agent move across her view. Satisfied, she turned to Blair. "How are you really?"

"Better than I was yesterday morning at this time," Blair answered, a husky tone in her voice. "I'm content...for the moment."

"And *I'm* sorry," Cam replied with a laugh. "I fell asleep—"

"Don't apologize. First of all, you needed it. Second, it makes me feel like a stud."

"Huh...I'm wondering just how to take that. Does that mean that I'm *not?*"

Blair met her eyes, noting with relief that the shadows beneath them were rapidly fading and that the pain, which Cam thought she couldn't see, was gone as well. "Oh no, Commander. Your stud credentials are well intact."

"That's good to know," Cam said, grinning. She leaned on the rail and worked on her coffee, drifting in the postcard-perfect view. "Have you heard anything from my wayward mother this morning?"

"I certainly wouldn't expect to—not this early. Not if I've read the situation with Giancarlo correctly."

"I believe you have." A fond smile spread slowly on Cam's face. "If she's not back by this afternoon, I'll call her before we depart for the airport."

"I'll be sorry to leave here," Blair said quietly.

Cam moved her left hand along the rail until it covered Blair's right. Their shoulders were nearly touching, but only someone on the deck with them could have seen the movement. Automatically, their fingers entwined, thumbs brushing over the tops of each other's hand.

"Yes, so will I. It takes being here with you to make me realize how truly beautiful this place is. Being with you makes the entire world look different."

For a moment, Blair was speechless. It was one of those times when Cam took her completely by surprise, and it was just the way she had always imagined that being in love would feel. She had just never imagined she would ever feel it herself. "We don't have to leave that feeling here, do we?"

Cam met her gaze again, marveling at the myriad shades of blue that moved in the depths of her lover's eyes. "No. We don't. In fact, let's make sure we don't."

"Cam, I—"

The cell phone on Cam's belt interrupted. Grimacing, she said, "Sorry," as she pulled it off and flipped it open. She turned slightly away and answered, "Roberts."

Something about the way Cam's shoulders stiffened nearly imperceptibly caught Blair's attention. Ordinarily, these frequent calls from an agent checking in or an intelligence update being relayed to Cam were so much a part of the daily routine that she barely noticed. Now she found herself listening without really intending to do so.

"Where are you calling from?...You're sure?...When?...Are you all rig—...No. Not for a day or so...Yes...Yes...I'll find you... Okay...Yes. Good."

"Problem?" Blair asked as Cam terminated the call. She was certain that Cam had been timing the conversation.

"No," Cam said automatically, her eyes cloudy, her voice distant as she moved back to the rail. She met Blair's eyes and saw the disbelief in them. She let out a long sigh and raked a hand through her hair. "I'm not sure. Maybe."

"Is it fallout from what happened in New York?"

Distracted, still thinking about the phone call, she replied offhandedly. "No. It was something personal." The words were out before she realized how they must sound.

Blair tried to keep her face expressionless as the words registered. *Personal. Personal as in personal call—as in something that is none of my business. As in...what? A lover? Why not—we never talked about being exclusive.*

"Oh," Blair replied flatly. "Sorry."

She started to turn away, gathering her coffee mug and the book she'd carried out onto the deck earlier, when Cam's hand on her arm stopped her.

"Blair...it's not what you're thinking."

"You have no idea what I'm thinking." Blair's voice was low-pitched and controlled. Too controlled. She kept her gaze averted because she didn't want Cam to see the hurt in them. *Stupid. Jesus, Blair. Grow up!*

"All right then," Cam allowed softly, her fingers still curled around Blair's forearm, "in *case* you might have gotten the idea that it was a...romantic issue. It wasn't."

Blair's head came up, and she was about to make a vehement denial when she saw Cam's face. The angry retort died on her tongue. Secret Service Agent Cameron Roberts, twice commended for bravery by the president of the United States, stood looking at her with worry and uncertainty in her eyes. Incredibly, Cam seemed vulnerable and defenseless. Blair wanted to hold her and never let go. "You don't have to explain. It's none of my busi—"

"Yes. It is." Cam stepped closer, forgetting where they were or who might come out through the kitchen behind them. Urgently, she said, "There's no one else. No one..."

Blair placed her fingers lightly on Cam's lips. "Stop. It's okay." Then she kissed her security chief, swiftly but with intent, and just as quickly pulled away. "I'm going for a run. Come with me."

"All right." Cam followed her into the house, hoping that Blair really *did* believe her, because the wounded look in those blue eyes had made her own heart bleed.

❖

After the run, Blair showered, dressed, and spent a few hours shopping on Union Square. Davis and Foster accompanied her while Cam met with Mac to review the flight arrangements and double-check the pilot dossiers for the evening's departure. She and Cam hadn't mentioned the morning's phone call again, and Blair didn't plan to. Cam had said it wasn't a lover, and even if it had been, they hadn't talked of monogamy or even a commitment. She wasn't sure she really wanted to bring those issues up. The very fact that she was *thinking* about exclusivity made her uneasy. She'd fallen so hard, so fast, and she needed to get used to that before she could contemplate the future.

Later in the afternoon, she read her book again out on the deck, napping on and off in a lounge chair. Marcea returned in time for a late lunch, for which, to Blair's delight, Cam joined them. It was different, having Cam by her side, sharing the moment, than it was when Cam stood a little away from her at some social function, all her attention focused on the crowd.

The three of them talked of art, of old friends of Marcea's whom Cam knew from childhood, and of Blair's plans for a new project. It was the sort of easy, casual conversation that friends and lovers might share. She had to remind herself again to take things slowly, because for those few hours, it felt as if she and Cam were just an ordinary couple, and she liked it. Despite her misgivings, their relationship was still exhilarating. By the time they were ready to leave for the airport, Blair was finally able to put the disquieting effects of Cam's mysterious call out of her mind.

The chartered Gulfstream II turbojet seated sixteen when fully occupied and was large enough to allow the team to spread out a bit for the transcontinental flight. As was customary, after the plane had been checked, the Secret Service agents boarded last and filled the forward seats in the cabin, affording Blair, already seated in a small separate area at the rear, some privacy.

Blair looked up from her book as the last passenger boarded and moved slowly down the aisle, stopping occasionally to murmur something to one of the agents along the way. She enjoyed watching the dark-haired, handsome woman approach—enjoyed the way her suit fit her so well it looked ordinary, though Blair knew it was custom cut and tailored, enjoyed the intense focus on her face as her gray eyes scanned every inch of the interior, and especially enjoyed the flicker of a smile that softened the concentration on Cam's face when their eyes met.

The security chief settled beside her just as the aircraft began to taxi down the runway of the small airport outside the city limits of San Francisco. The seats were roomy in the luxury craft, but the length of their thighs touched and their shoulders pressed lightly together nevertheless.

"Good book?" Cam asked as she buckled in.

"Mmm." Blair nodded, closing it on one finger to mark her place. "Funny, sexy, and well put together."

"Sounds like a winning combination."

Blair brushed her fingers lightly over the top of the agent's hand where it rested on her trousered thigh. "Yes, I think so."

"Be good," Cam whispered, suppressing a grin. "I'm working."

"Oh, really?" Blair raised an eyebrow, then laughed. "All right—I'll give you a reprieve. But only for the rest of the flight. Then I intend to tease you as much as I like."

"I'll look forward to it."

Blair eased the seat back and rested her hand on Cam's forearm, below the sightline of the agents in the front of the plane if they happened to turn around.

"Any pressing plans for the rest of the week?" Cam inquired. "We haven't had an itinerary review since we've been here, and I want to get everyone back to routine. It's better after what happened."

"Nothing special. Since we're going to be traveling again soon, I want to paint. I hope to have a full show this fall, and as of right now, I don't have enough canvases completed to do that." Blair sighed. "There's always the chance that something will come through from the West Wing that I'll need to do—I haven't heard anything for a few days, and that's never a good sign."

"I'll get a full briefing in the morning," Cam reminded her. "We can go over the week's itinerary after that."

"Fine."

"And...I need to go out of town for a day or so," Cam said quietly.

Blair stiffened, withdrawing her hand from Cam's arm. "Oh?"

"If everything is quiet, I thought I'd leave tomorrow night. Mac will have the detail."

"I'm sure he can handle it." Blair opened her book again.

Cam didn't reply. She didn't have any explanation that she could share, and she knew that half-truths would only make things worse. They were both quiet for the rest of the flight—Blair reading and Cam sleeping on and off. Despite their silence, they remained leaning close together—their bodies touching, their connection not completely broken.

CHAPTER NINE

The jet taxied to a stop on the runway at Teterboro airport in New Jersey, just across the Hudson River from Manhattan, and the team prepared to disembark. Cam walked to the front of the plane and stood at the top of the stairway that had been rolled across the tarmac to the open door. She pressed a finger to the receiver in her ear and listened to the report from the agent who was transmitting from the first of two black Suburbans that approached the terminal along an access road on the far side of the airport. Satisfied, she turned to the agents behind her.

"Two minutes. Let's proceed inside."

Stark passed by on her way down the stairs to take the point position on the ground, and then Blair was beside her.

"Ready?" Cam knew this was always an anxious moment.

"Yes."

As soon as Blair stepped onto the tarmac with Cam and Stark flanking her, a horde of reporters who had apparently been hiding around the corner of the building appeared out of the darkness with video cameras and microphones at the ready. Harsh halogen lights flashed on, striking Blair in the face and blinding her. For a moment she was disoriented...and afraid.

The light touch of Cam's hand on her arm immediately settled her despite the explosive barrage of questions.

One reporter, only feet away, called loudly, "Ms. Powell, can you comment on the photograph in the *New York Post?"*

"Who was the person with you?" another man demanded.

Then the voices, male and female, blurred into one continuous, chaotic cacophony.

"Where was it taken?"

"Can you confirm that you were with a lover?"

"Who...?"

"...name..."

"...comment..."

"...father know..."

"Ms. Powell...Ms. Powell...Ms. Powell..."

Voices accosted her from every direction. Only one voice penetrated the pandemonium.

"Don't worry—we're going to move quickly now. Just let me lead," Cam instructed calmly.

As the onslaught continued, Cam and Stark, an arm under each of Blair's elbows, quickly herded her toward the small, single-story terminal. The other agents clambered down the stairs, shouldered through the trailing crowd of reporters, and converged on her as well. Mac double-timed to get in front of their group while Hernandez, along with Felicia Davis, closed in behind. The entire team formed a human wedge with Blair in the center, and the reporters scurried to get out of the way of the phalanx of fast-moving bodies.

Nevertheless, the clamor of shouted questions followed the group through the doors, down the brightly lit hallway, and into the private VIP portion of the terminal.

"What are they talking about?" Blair whispered harshly to Cam as soon as the double doors closed behind them. She hated to be manhandled, even when it was for her own good, and in that moment, Cam was the nearest target for her anger. "Why didn't you know about them? Jesus."

"Whatever it is, it must have hit the wires after we were in the air," Cam muttered, lifting her wrist to bark questions and instructions into her microphone. She was beyond furious. Up-to-the-minute intelligence was critical if she was to anticipate precisely this kind of occurrence and ward off problems. "Whoever is monitoring the news services in DC either didn't pick it up or didn't think we needed to know about it."

Had she known that a bevy of reporters would be waiting at the gate, Cam would have arranged for the transport vehicles to drive directly onto the runway so that Blair would not have to walk to the terminal. *It's my job to protect her.* "Ms. Powell, I'm sorry about this. I didn't have an advance team on the ground—I should have."

"No," Blair shook her head, already calmer now that the unexpected assault had stopped. "It's not your fault. Let's just collect our luggage and get out of here before they find their way in."

"Don't worry," Cam said harshly, her temper close to boiling. It was not only her responsibility to project Blair physically, but also to see that she was not ambushed by intrusive media hounds. She would have been angry if *any* of her protectees had been left open to such an affront, but the fact that it was her lover who had been subjected to the onslaught made it even worse. "They won't bother you again."

At that moment, Mac approached from the main part of the terminal, a folded newspaper under his arm and a grim look on his face.

"What have you got?" Cam asked sharply. To her surprise, Mac blushed.

"Uh..." He lifted the folded newspaper in his hand and glanced from Cam to Blair and then quickly away. "You might want to look at this in the car."

"Let me see it," Blair said brusquely, extending her hand. "It's not going to get any better if I wait."

Wordlessly, he handed it to her. The Secret Service agents standing around averted their eyes but did not move from the protective circle they had formed, shielding her from the few airport personnel carrying bags in from the plane.

Cam watched Blair's face as she opened the newspaper and quickly scanned the front page. She couldn't detect the slightest change in Blair's expression. When Blair silently folded the newspaper again and put it and the book she had been carrying under her arm, Cam said abruptly, "Okay, then. Let's get out of here."

Two of the men walked to the pile of luggage and collected everyone's bags, loading them quickly and efficiently onto a wheeled handcart. Within minutes, the team loaded into the pair of Suburbans which then headed rapidly out of the airport toward the Lincoln Tunnel and Manhattan.

Stark and Davis were in the front seats of the lead vehicle while Blair and Cam occupied the rear. The majority of the other agents, most of whom were now off duty, had remained at the airport, making separate arrangements for cabs, friends, or family to pick them up there.

"Are you all right?" Cam leaned forward and extended one hand to lightly touch Blair's knee.

Blair had been mutely staring out the window since they had gotten into the vehicle. Turning to face Cam, Blair smiled sadly in the irregular illumination of passing headlights and flickering neon signs. "I've been waiting for this. I was just sitting here, trying to think how long I've been waiting."

"What is it?" Cam remained as she was, her fingertips moving gently on the fabric of Blair's slacks.

When Blair wordlessly passed the newspaper to her across the space between their seats, Cam unfolded it and leaned toward the window to catch enough light to read. Prominently displayed below the fold was a picture with the caption, "President's Daughter and Secret Lover?" In a hazy night shot, a woman who looked very much like Blair could be seen kissing someone, although the other individual's features were difficult to determine because of the camera angle and the obvious distance from which it had been taken.

"Son of a bitch," Cam whispered. It was a photograph of the two of them on the beach in San Francisco, the first night that Cam had arrived from DC. She raised her eyes to Blair. "I'm so sorry."

"About what? The kiss or the photograph?"

"Definitely not the kiss."

Blair nodded once, sharply. "Good."

Cam struggled in the poor light to read the short paragraph underneath the picture. It didn't say much—just the usual titillating inferences about Blair's alleged liaisons with movie stars, underworld kingpins, or elected officials that were common in similar publications. Precisely because Blair was so private, and because the White House tried diligently to keep her out of the public eye unless it was a sanctioned official function, the press loved to conjecture about her love life. Except this time it wasn't gossip and innuendo.

"What do you think?" Blair sounded wary.

"I think it's interesting," Cam said after a minute more of staring at the photograph, "that they don't name names and they don't specifically state that you are with a woman. Whoever took this photograph must know those facts."

"I noticed that, too," Blair said darkly. "It's almost as if someone is teasing me—or taunting me. But what in the world for?"

"I have no idea." Cam clenched the paper so tightly in her fist that it crumpled. She had to force herself not to fling it on the floor. She was angry for Blair at the invasion of her privacy and incensed with herself for being so careless as to let someone close enough to get the photo. "But what I want to know is where the hell he was and why my people didn't see him."

"Well, I have a feeling this is only the beginning. This is probably going to be embarrassing for my father." Blair laughed bitterly. "The big question really is—what is this going to do to you professionally if someone recognizes you?"

"I don't think that's the most important thing right now," Cam disagreed with a swift shake of her head. "There's something off about this entire situation, because if this were just some reporter looking to make a story, my name would already be in this article. The fact that you're kissing a *woman* would be the headline— *above* the fold. As these things go, this is pretty tame, which makes no sense at all."

"Blackmail?"

"If it is, they've got more balls than brains. You don't blackmail the daughter of the president of the United States. Not like this and—God damn it—not on my watch."

Suddenly very tired, Blair leaned her forehead against the glass window, watching the night slide by. The stretch of highway outside the speeding vehicle was barren and seemed to echo the emptiness in her heart. Of course, she had been foolish to think that she would be allowed to love anyone in peace, let alone the woman seated across from her. She closed her eyes, knowing that she would sleep alone this night and wanting more than anything else for that not to be true.

CHAPTER TEN

Cam watched Blair as wordless moments passed. It was the quiet that worried her. Anger she would have expected, even embraced, considering the circumstances. Accusations of her own complicity in allowing the photo to be taken, however unfounded, would have been more welcome than the curtain of silence that fell heavily between them.

She tried to imagine how it must feel to have one's most private experiences on display, not just once, but repeatedly. She couldn't, even though it was *her* picture in the newspaper as well. And she knew, too, that even had her face been clear and her name printed in bold letters beneath the image, it wouldn't have been the same thing for her as it was for Blair. *She* wasn't recognized the world over, nor was her family likely to be held up to scrutiny by self-appointed guardians of right and wrong whose true motivation was nothing loftier than their own political gain. She was guilty of nothing, but even if she were, her transgression would soon be forgotten.

Such was not the case for Blair Powell or her father. The president was not immune to the effect of public opinion—just the opposite. Right or wrong had nothing to do with the fact that powerful groups constantly jockeyed for position and influence in the Washington political arena. Something as inflammatory as Andrew Powell's daughter's love affair—especially her *lesbian* love affair—would give his opponents one more piece of ammunition with which to threaten him.

"Blair," Cam began gently, "is there anything I can do?"

Turning away from the window, and the night, and her own troubled thoughts, Blair straightened. When she spoke, her voice was stronger, carrying a hint of its old steel. "Yes. You can tell me right now if you're up for what's coming."

"What?" Cam exclaimed, too shocked by the question to even absorb it completely. As the reality of what Blair was asking finally hit her, she responded heatedly, "You can't really think that this would matter to me?"

"It's one thing to talk in the abstract about the possibility of exposure. It's quite another thing to be the center of a media circus where everything about you is fair game for discussion. Believe me, I know."

"Jesus Christ." Cam shook her head in disbelief, struggling to bite back an even angrier retort. Blair's voice had been calm, steady, and her face expressionless. She looked the way she'd looked the first day Cam had met her—cool, controlled, untouchable. Cam remembered very well the angry, wounded woman Blair had been, and how in recent weeks that rage had burned less brightly and the wounds had seemed less raw. Until this.

Christ, she's scared.

That realization defused Cam's ire in a way nothing else could, because fear was not something she associated with the president's daughter. Perhaps for the first time, she understood the price of Blair's strength—the isolation and the impenetrable defenses and the expectation of loss.

Quickly, Cam shifted across the narrow space between them until she was sitting on the seat next to Blair. She found her hand in the semi-darkness and whispered vehemently, "I intend to identify the person behind this. Once I do, I intend to kick his—*or* her—ass from one side of this continent to the other."

"By then it will be too late. The damage—"

"I *love* you," Cam insisted, her quiet voice loud with conviction. "Nothing and no one will ever change that."

Blair tightened her grip on Cam's hand and leaned into the reassuring solidity of her lover's body. "You can't imagine what kind of pressure there's going to be for us to stop seeing one another."

The words hit Cam in the center of her chest like a sledgehammer. Even being shot hadn't hurt as much. "No. Don't even think it, because it gives the possibility power. Please."

"When you were shot," Blair said as if reading her thoughts, "I felt parts of me dying with you." Her voice was hushed; she might have been speaking in a dream. "I had only just begun to let you in, and I was nearly lost already. Now, I don't think I could survi—"

"Listen to me, Blair. I love you. I am not going anywhere. I swear."

Blair searched dark, direct eyes and saw only truth. "It scares me how much I need you."

"Don't think you're alone." Cam lifted Blair's hand, brushed her lips swiftly across the back of her knuckles. "I need you, too. More than you'll ever know."

"I'll try to remember that." Blair drew the first full breath she'd taken since the airport. "So—what do we do now, Commander?"

Cam laughed, but there was an edge to the laughter. "I'm a Secret Service agent. Do you think I can't track down the little bastard that gave that photo to the wire service?"

"Just be careful, Cam," Blair warned. "A person doesn't need a gun to be dangerous. In the right hands, a camera can be lethal."

"Any coward who chooses this underhanded way of going after you is no threat to me. Don't worry."

"Why don't I feel reassured?"

"I'll be careful. But this is what I do."

"I suppose I have to accept the logic of that," Blair conceded. Again she sighed. "I'm surprised I haven't heard from the White House by now. The chief of staff must be having kittens all over the West Wing."

"I thought Lucinda Washburn was a personal friend of your family's," Cam said, referring to the woman who most people considered the most powerful woman in Washington. As the first female chief of staff, she held the president's ear and served as his primary adviser. When Andrew Powell ran for the presidency, he had made it very clear that no decision would be made without her input. That had proved to be true over the first months of his tenure when economic crises at home and the reemergence of violent foreign unrest had placed his administration in the spotlight. "Surely she'll be on your side."

"Trust me," Blair said without any hint of animosity. "Lucy's number one goal from the day my father was sworn in has been to get him reelected. She's known him since they were in college, and I think she's been working to get him where he is today since then. She'd sacrifice almost anything or anyone to keep him in the White House for a second term."

"And you think that includes forcing you to...what?" Cam asked in frustration. "Give up our relationship?"

"I think Lucy considers relationships expendable if they stand in the way of a higher goal."

"What about your father? Does he feel the same way?"

"I don't know." Blair glanced out the window as they emerged from the Lincoln Tunnel into Manhattan, realizing that they were only moments from her building. "Since I've never had a relationship that mattered, it's never come up—and I don't know him well enough to guess." She couldn't quite hide the concern in her tone. "But I don't think it will be very long before we find out."

❖

A few minutes later, the security cars pulled up in front of Blair's apartment building, and the occupants of both vehicles fell into the familiar, choreographed routine of disembarking. Once through the doors and into the small but ornate lobby of the elegant building, Blair hesitated. The elevator was twenty feet away. Stark walked directly to it and keyed the single locked car which went only to Blair's top floor apartment.

Turning her back to the elevator and the agents waiting nearby to escort her upstairs, Blair faced Cam and spoke in a voice too low for the others to hear. "Is there any way you can stay?"

Cam could only imagine what it cost Blair to ask that. Her eyes swept over her agents, several of whom would remain in the command center one floor below Blair's apartment for the remainder of the night shift.

"I want to. You know that, don't you?" Cam asked, her voice a strained whisper.

"I'm sorry." Blair's eyes swiftly became unreadable. "I shouldn't have asked."

"Blair..."

Abruptly, Blair turned and walked directly across the lobby and into the open elevator. Stark followed her in and the doors closed soundlessly behind them.

Facing Davis and the others, Cam bit off her words. "I'll be on my pager."

"Roger," Felicia Davis replied, her expression carefully neutral.

The security chief turned without another word, pushed through the double doors, and was quickly lost to the dark.

❖

Cam hesitated briefly on the sidewalk. It was two o'clock in the morning. She glanced up and diagonally across the block-wide oasis of trees that comprised Gramercy Park to the building where she lived when in New York City on assignment. The prospect of pacing for several sleepless hours in her well-appointed but essentially impersonal apartment held little appeal. The further prospect of tossing in her solitary bed, trying to forget the disappointment Blair hadn't been able to hide, held even less.

Decision made, she walked quickly to the southeast corner of the square and flagged a cab. She gave the cabbie an intersection in the East Village.

Traffic was light in the small hours of the morning in Manhattan, though any hour evidenced more activity here than in any other American city. When she paid the driver and stepped out, people still strolled on the sidewalks, and here and there music wafted from the open doors of taverns and all-night restaurants. It was a short walk to her destination, and less than half an hour after leaving Blair's building, she was seated on a corner stool in a small neighborhood bar.

The bartender—a hard-bodied, hard-eyed brunette—came over almost immediately. The muscles in her well-developed shoulders and upper arms strained the fabric of the tight white T-shirt she wore tucked into faded blue jeans. "What can I get ya?"

"Glenlivet. Double—straight up."

"Sure thing."

A minute later, Cam was sipping the aged single malt scotch and trying to make sense of the last few hours. *Hours? Hell, the last few days.*

She turned the glass aimlessly on the bar top, struggling with a puzzle with too many pieces still missing. It had started with the debriefing in Washington and Stewart Carlisle's odd capitulation to Doyle's bullying threats of an investigation and had culminated with the night's oblique threat to Blair. And then, of course, there was Claire.

"Claire." Cam sighed wearily.

From beside her, a voice softly questioned, "Girlfriend?"

Cam jumped, startled, and that in itself spoke volumes about her muddled state of mind. Or perhaps just her persistent state of fatigue. She turned her eyes to the redhead who had slipped onto the next barstool without her even noticing.

The woman looked to be in her early twenties, but might have been a decade older. Her green eyes were wide and liquid with invitation, and her high, full breasts—shown off to their full advantage in a scoop-necked tank top that exposed plenty of cleavage and did little to conceal the sharp prominences of her nipples—were ripe with promise.

"Has to be a woman to make you look that down," the redhead remarked again.

"No." Cam shook her head. "Just thinking out loud."

"If there's something—or someone—you'd like to forget for a few hours, I can suggest a couple of interesting ways to help you out."

"No, thanks." Cam smiled slightly. "What I need right now is to think, not forget."

"It never pays to think alone," the woman persisted, pressing closer, her fingers flirting lightly on the top of Cam's right hand.

"I'm not alone," Cam said softly.

The redhead studied her silently for a moment, then nodded. "In that case, I'll let you get back to whatever is keeping you up tonight."

With that she moved away, and Cam returned to studying her drink. The touch of the stranger's hand had evoked thoughts of Claire again. Until a few days ago, she had thought that chapter of her life closed.

Claire. Is she a part of this?

After she hung up the phone, Cam hurriedly crossed to the bedroom, stripped off the robe, and grabbed for the first thing that was handy. She was just buttoning the fly of her jeans when the doorbell rang. Quickly, she pulled on the T-shirt and opened the door.

"Hello, Claire."

"I'm sorry," the woman in the hallway said. "I know I shouldn't have come—"

"No. It's all right." Cam extended her hand, and Claire took it. It was the first time they had touched in more than six months. Claire grew very still, and Cam said gently, "Come inside."

Claire was dressed as she often was—tasteful evening dress and matching heels, her blond hair in a French twist, her makeup flawless, her jewelry expensive. She hesitated just inside the door, then dropped her purse onto the mail table in the small foyer. "You look tired. It's late, isn't it? God, I should go."

"Come into the living room. Can I get you a drink?"

"Wine, if you have it."

Several minutes later, Cam joined Claire on the sofa in front of the windows where less than thirty minutes before she had been gazing into the night and speaking to her lover. She forced the image of Blair from her mind and handed the glass of chardonnay to the woman who had made love to her countless times. The lines of stress around Claire's eyes were obvious.

"What is it?"

"I've been hearing things from my...colleagues...for the last several weeks. Someone has been asking questions."

Cam frowned. "Someone has been trying to get information out of the...escorts?"

Claire smiled, her blue eyes troubled. "First you must understand—with this particular agency, confidentiality is absolutely the most critical service we provide. Every one of us is thoroughly screened. There are background checks to rival those of the federal government. Known associates are identified; resumes, transcripts—everything ever documented—are reviewed. No one gives out information about a client. It just doesn't happen."

"But now you think someone's been talking?"

"I don't know." Claire's eyes were dark with concern. "All I know is that someone, or several someones, has certainly been asking questions."

"And why are you telling me?"

"Because they've been asking questions about the president."

"That's not news." Cam shrugged. "There have been rumors going around Washington since before he was elected that he uses a...service...for his...social needs."

"I know," Claire said. "But this is the first time any of us has been approached. For one thing, no one outside our organization has access to an escort's true identity, so it's almost impossible for us to be individually linked to any particular establishment or client. Our names are carefully omitted from any transactions— even on paper."

Cam didn't think it prudent to point out that if someone, having enough time and resources, really wanted to find out who ran the escort service, and who utilized it, and exactly what tastes and proclivities the clients demonstrated, he could. She'd never thought that possibility very likely. Maybe she'd been wrong.

"Has anyone talked to you specifically?"

"Not yet. But I gather more than one of us has been questioned about the president."

Cam was quiet, considering the information. "Which means that someone may have identified your organization and accessed your files."

"True. And if that's the case, he might have access to much more than just the escort identities. He may have the client lists."

"Ah, I see." Cam rubbed her forehead with one hand, trying desperately to assuage the pounding headache that was making it difficult for her to think. "Are you here to warn me?"

"Partly, and..."

"What?"

"I know who you are."

"Meaning?" Cam asked quietly.

"Your picture has been on television."

"Yes," Cam acknowledged with a sigh. "I suppose you've known for a long time."

Claire rested her hand on Cam's thigh with a familiarity borne of countless other nights spent alone together in the long hours just before dawn. "It's my business not to know who you are. My only responsibility is to know what you need."

The touch of Claire's hand evoked a visceral memory that was as automatic as the awakening of hunger stirred by a familiar smell. For months after Janet's death, Cam had wanted nothing more than the few hours of dreamless sleep that the satisfaction of Claire's caress had given her. Now, her senses responded to the remembered heat of Claire's body in the dark and the practiced stroke of her fingers. Cam's nerve endings held the memories, too, and her breath quickened. Deliberately, she ignored the sweet stab of unbidden desire.

"Has anyone asked about me specifically?"

"Not that I know of, but there may be things I haven't heard about yet."

"I'm not sure what I can do with this information—or what I can do about it," Cam said.

"I don't know that there is anything to do, especially if we're as compromised as it seems. But I don't want to see anyone hurt—especially not the president." She lifted her eyes to Cam's, resting her fingers lightly now against her cheek. Her lips were very close to Cam's when she whispered, "Or you."

Cam jerked, as if feeling the warmth of Claire's fingers again. That was a memory she had no desire to ponder. She rubbed her eyes, then quickly downed the rest of her scotch. Tomorrow, she would meet with Claire. Then, perhaps, she would find some answers.

❖

Blair turned over in bed and looked at the clock. The glowing red numerals read 1:10 a.m. With an exasperated sigh, she threw back the light sheet and swung her legs to the floor. Naked, she walked through the moonlit loft and stopped in front of the floor-to-ceiling windows overlooking the park below. From her vantage point, she could see Cam's building and sought out her windows. Her lover's apartment was dark. Blair knew she shouldn't wake her; she had recognized the subtle signs of pain that Cam would never mention—the faint deepening of the lines around her eyes and the slight, nearly imperceptible tightening of her shoulders as she shifted position in a chair. What Cam needed now was to sleep and to heal.

After several moments, caught between reason and desire, Blair returned to her bed and sat on the edge. She watched flickers of otherworldly light dance across the hardwood floor. A very long time ago, she had taught herself not to need the solace of a woman's body in the dark. She never spent the night with anyone she made love to; she never sought the sound of another's voice to console her pain or assuage her fears. She slept alone, and she bore her uncertainty and disappointment and loneliness in silence.

Without meaning for it to happen, she had lost her heart to Cam, and she hadn't expected the need, so much deeper than flesh, that followed. Sometimes the hunger was like a hand on her throat, and she didn't know whether to run or strike out. Then she would hear Cam's deep voice or catch a glimpse of her grin, and the pain, which was so much a part of her that only its absence was notable, vanished.

Almost against her will, Blair reached for the phone. A minute later, after listening to the unanswered ring, she laid the receiver carefully into its cradle. Then she stretched out on the bed, rolled onto her side, and closed her eyes. It was a long time before her breathing eased into the steady, quiet cadence of sleep.

CHAPTER ELEVEN

Cam shook her head groggily as the alarm droned beside her. She wasn't certain how long it had been buzzing as she slowly emerged from a dreamless sleep to the insistent sound. Stifling another groan, she reached out with one arm and blindly swatted in the direction of the clock. With a lethal jab, she finally succeeded in silencing the din. Another minute passed before she forced herself upright and headed for the bathroom. With the shower set to cold, she stepped in and turned her face to the pinpricks of frigid water.

It was early, and she wondered if Blair was still asleep. In that one unguarded moment, a swift stab of loneliness pierced her chest. Then, just as quickly as it arrived, she forced it from her consciousness.

At precisely 0730, Cam, looking crisp and fresh in a dark jacket, matching trousers and open-collared shirt, walked into the conference room on the eighth floor of Blair's apartment building, the level directly below Blair's loft that was entirely occupied by the Secret Service team. The major portion of the floor was a high-ceilinged open space, subdivided by shoulder-high walls into workstations and monitoring consoles. In the far corner past a warren of cramped desks was the glass-enclosed area which served as the meeting room for Cam and her agents.

At the moment, most of the team was present, since the night shift had stayed to give report before going off duty and the day shift had just arrived to take over the watch. Usually, there were one or more swing agents available as well to cover unexpected events or to supply double coverage on short notice whenever needed. Almost everyone had coffee of some form in hand—carryout cups from nearby delis a subtle indictment of the office brew that was often hours old.

Cam strode to the head of the table and nodded to the men and women facing her. This was the first time the team had convened at Command Central since the night the operation to apprehend Loverboy had nearly ended in disaster. Ellen Grant's absence was conspicuous.

"I presume all of you have seen the newspaper article from last night. Obviously, we can anticipate increased media attention whenever Egret leaves the building. There's a camera crew on the northeast corner of the square right now and a TV van at the intersection."

This statement was met with several groans and a few unflattering comments as to the nature of the fourth estate.

"That means we can also expect close approach from the press—individually and in groups. Be alert for press credentials and maintain a very low threshold for containing or diverting anyone who is without the appropriate identification or who encroaches on her personal perimeter. If at all possible, move Egret quickly from the vehicle to any public venue. We'll go to high security status as of this morning. We have no reason at this point to think they know about the gym or any of her private appointments. Nevertheless, don't make any assumptions."

Everyone nodded. Then Cam looked to Mac. "I'll be meeting with Egret per usual at 1100 hours. Hopefully, I'll be able to update the weekly schedule with her and pass along that information to you for a more concrete itinerary." Surveying the group again, she added, "Mac will have your schedule assignments at that time. Any questions?"

"What are we going to do about finding the slimeball who shot that photo?" The righteous indignation in Paula Stark's voice was obvious.

"For now, nothing," Cam responded bluntly. Briefly, she wondered how many of her agents knew that she was the person depicted in the photograph kissing the president's daughter. She almost smiled at the expressions of outrage on their faces. The fact that they were all ferociously dedicated to Blair pleased her. She raised a hand to stem this line of questions. "I need to brief first with DC, but I can tell you this—we're not going to take this lying down."

That statement prompted an assortment of *goods, for sures,* and *damn rights.*

"In addition to routine matters, we need to gear up for the transatlantic trip. I want status reports on my desk by this afternoon as to the identity of our liaison in Paris, the itinerary down to the minute, the report from the security chief at the hotel regarding manpower, deployment, and background checks on hotel employees, an update on all terrorist cells known to be operating in France with particular emphasis on Paris and its environs, and dossiers on the French security members assigned to every venue at which Egret will be present." She rubbed her eyes and focused on the far side of the room, as if checking her mental list. "Guest lists for all functions, alternate motorcade routes, evacuation routes, and safe house locations."

"We're on that, Commander," Mac assured her, glancing at his laptop and his own agenda items. "I'll collate the material we have and get it to you this afternoon."

"Very well." Cam shrugged her shoulders to ease some of the stiffness in her neck and back. Finally, she smiled slightly. "I guess it's just business as usual then."

Everyone smiled back, and some of the tension left the room. Any crisis, it seemed, lost some of its punch when the hand on the helm was steady.

"Mac, I'd like to see you, please. The rest of you, carry on."

Once the room had cleared, Cam sat down across from her second in command and rubbed absently at her temples, the headache having ignited again in the night. Then she leaned forward and met his steady gaze. "I want to know where that photograph came from. I want to know who took it, and I want to know who gave it to the press. Make some inquiries to the wire services, contact the managing editor of the *Post,* and dig around at the Intel Ops center in DC. Be discreet if you can, but pull rank if you have to."

Mac, a scrupulous detail man, had conspicuously *stopped* taking notes. What Cam was asking of him was outside the Agency chain of command. Strictly speaking, the assistant director in DC should coordinate the investigation and intelligence acquisition with the FBI. But in reality, in matters directly impacting operating procedure, the Secret Service did not share intelligence with the FBI, nor ask them for any.

"I'll get on it. What do we know about the specifics—time frame, location?"

For a moment, Cam was silent. Mac had not been present for the late night trip to the beach in San Francisco and did not know the circumstances under which the image had been captured. She didn't have to tell him the details now. She could keep her part in it under wraps—at least for a while. As a Secret Service agent, she was indoctrinated in the policy of silence. One did not discuss a protectee; one did not discuss Agency business with other departments; one did not discuss procedure.

Solitary since childhood, circumspect with her own emotional pain—unable and unwilling to add to her mother's agony with her own seemingly inconsequential anguish and guilt after the death of her father—she had learned to keep her own counsel. The habits of a lifetime compounded by the requirements of her profession made it difficult for her to disclose anything to anyone, no matter how much she trusted him—or loved her. The silence in the room grew, a silence during which Mac sat quietly, simply waiting.

"The photograph was taken at approximately 0130, three nights ago, on the waterfront in San Francisco." Cam's tone was even, matter-of-fact.

One blond eyebrow raised, his only sign of surprise—whether at the information or the fact that she knew it, Cam couldn't tell. "I never got a report that we'd lost her at any time in San Francisco."

"We didn't."

"Then how did she manage to get away from us long enough for anyone to get that shot?"

His confusion was evident, and Cam made a decision that in all probability would alter the course of her career forever.

"She didn't leave our sight. She was always covered. The person in the photograph with her is me."

"Well then, where the fuck were the rest of our people? How in the *hell* did they let anyone get that close to her? Jesus, talk about a security breach."

"I missed something." Cam shrugged, a rueful grin on her face. His reaction was not *precisely* what she had expected. "The Suburban was on the street—the agents were inside. She and I were not directly in their sightline, although they should have had an excellent perimeter view. I thought we were secure."

"Any theories?"

His expression and tone had not changed after her revelation. If he had an issue with her relationship with Blair, either personally or professionally, it certainly wasn't apparent. She had sensed his unspoken support, but sometimes the appearance of collegiality was just that—a show. Career agents kept their thoughts and opinions to themselves because they never knew who might someday become their superior or want their job. Despite her fundamental trust in him, she had irrevocably exposed herself, and it wasn't an altogether comfortable sensation.

"One thought I had—after the fact, unfortunately," she added with a grimace, "is that he was on one of the nearby piers with a night scope. After the initial feeding frenzy in New York over Loverboy, and the press statement Blair gave upon her arrival in San Francisco, they'd pretty much left her alone. I hadn't considered we'd be photographed. He could have gotten fairly close to us but probably wouldn't have raised any particular suspicion from the team. They were most likely focusing on foot traffic on the beach."

"Commander, may I speak freely?"

"Go ahead, Mac."

He held her eyes as he said firmly, "I consider it my responsibility—the responsibility of the entire team—to protect Egret not just physically, but from this kind of invasion as well. I know it's not completely possible to deny the press access to her, but the public has no right to know this. It's no one's business but hers, and I don't want it to happen again."

"I don't know that we can stop it." Frustrated, Cam strafed her hair with a hand. "I'm not even sure I know *how* to stop it. But someone released this photograph, and I want to know who and why. I want to know..." She hesitated; the next words came hard. Harder than almost anything she had ever said. "I need to know if it came from one of us."

His blue eyes grew dark with pain, but he answered crisply. "Yes, ma'am. If I may, I'd like to look into this personally."

"That might not be viewed favorably by DC," she warned.

"So noted."

She pushed back in her chair and rubbed both hands briskly over her face. When she spoke, her voice was calm and steady. "I may go down for this, Mac. If I do, I want you in the clear. I'll need you to take my place. Blair needs you."

"I would *not* want to be in Egret's path if anyone tried that, Commander."

Cam smiled. "No, I don't suppose it would be pretty. Just the same, if it comes to that, I want you to disavow any prior knowledge. We never had this conversation."

"Yes, ma'am."

"Thank you, Mac."

CHAPTER TWELVE

As Cam stood in the small carpeted foyer between the elevator and the broad, carved oak door to Blair's apartment, she thought of the first time she had come here and how much had changed. She hadn't wanted the assignment; she hadn't wanted a woman in her life; she hadn't wanted to feel anything for anyone at all. Now all she cared about was on the other side of that door. She raised her hand to knock, but the door opened before her fist met wood.

"Good morning," Blair said, her tone unusually subdued.

She wore loose white cotton drawstring pants and a matching ribbed tank top. Her shoulders and arms were bronzed from the sun, sharply etched with muscle from her workouts in the kickboxing ring. Her hair was down, and there was a dab of brilliant blue pigment on her shirt, just above her left breast. There were circles under her normally vibrant blue eyes, though, and Cam caught sight of something moving in their depths, something dark and wounded.

"Have you been working all night?" Cam swallowed against the sudden thickness in her throat stirred by too many feelings to consider all at once—love, desire, wonder, worry.

"Yes. What else? The antidote to every problem."

Cam stayed on the threshold, waiting to be invited in. "Did you sleep at all?"

"Some. Did you?"

"Some."

Blair pulled the door open wide and gestured with a sweep of her hand. "Come in. This shouldn't take too long, because I don't have much in the way of plans for the rest of the week. Especially not now."

"Fine." Cam followed her inside and trailed behind to the breakfast bar, puzzling over Blair's odd detachment. It was rare for them to be anywhere alone that Blair did not touch her, however fleetingly, and here in the apartment, she had grown used to Blair greeting her with a kiss. The absence of that small gesture echoed hollowly in her chest.

Silently, Blair set out two mugs and poured coffee. She passed one to Cam and leaned her elbows on the counter, one hip edged up on a stool. When she finally looked at Cam, her expression was remote.

"Have you heard anything from Washington?"

"Carlisle called bright and early—rather, his secretary did." Cam settled on the neighboring stool. "I've been summoned for another briefing. I don't know if the fact that he didn't contact me himself is a good sign or not. What about you?"

"Lucinda phoned just after nine this morning. She was in a rush, because my father was on his way to a meeting with the Senate minority leader about the budget, and she was getting ready to brief him in the car at the same time as she was talking to me. I believe her precise words were, 'Tell me it's someone you can bring home to dinner.'"

"Huh," Cam snorted, wondering if she fit the bill. What would the president think of her with his daughter? "Anything else?"

"Nope. She said she'd get back to me later. That could mean midnight."

"What are you going to tell her?"

"At the moment, I'm going to tell her it's nobody's business. Not even hers."

For the first time, Blair looked and sounded like herself. When she was angry, Cam was certain she was fine.

"I suppose for now, that makes sense," Cam said, nodding. She pushed the mug away and reached for Blair's hand, then stiffened when Blair eased back from the counter, just out of touching distance.

Silence fell again, and finally Cam asked quietly, "What's wrong?"

"Nothing."

"Something's happened."

"Are we done here? I'm in the middle of something."

"Damn it! *No,* we're not done." Cam's sharp retort erupted from a combination of frustration, worry, and fatigue threatening to get the best of her. "Not until you tell me what's happened between now and when we said good night eight hours ago."

"Not a thing."

Blair looked away, but before she did, Cam saw a glint of tears. In a heartbeat, her anger died. She slid off her seat and moved to Blair's side, lightly touching her bare arm with her fingertips. "Is it because I didn't come up with you last night?"

"No," Blair said abruptly, still not looking at her, but not moving her arm away either.

"I couldn't think what to do," Cam said as if she hadn't heard. "Sometimes, I can't seem to figure out who I am—whether I'm your lover or your security chief."

"What?" Blair asked in surprise, meeting Cam's eyes now.

"When push comes to shove, I guess I'm more used to being your security chief. I'm sorry."

"Oh, Cameron, that's not the problem." It almost hurt to hear Cam apologize for something Blair knew she couldn't help. "Can't you just finish this goddamned briefing and go do whatever the security chief part of you needs to do?"

"No." Cam shook her head, smiling softly. "The security chief is finished. It's just your lover here now."

"Then maybe you should tell me which one of you I ought to ask about this." Blair drew a manila envelope from beneath the counter and handed it to Cam.

Perplexed, Cam studied the envelope. Standard office issue. Blair's name and address in block print. No return address. No stamp, either.

"How did this arrive?" Her tone was formal, her expression intent. It was definitely the security chief asking.

"Courier."

For one heart-stopping moment, Cam expected what her rational mind knew to be impossible—that she was about to read yet another threatening message from Loverboy. Fixing her eyes on Blair's, she asked quietly, "What is it?"

"Open it."

Carefully, Cam folded back the small metal clasps that held the flap closed and withdrew an eight-by-ten photograph. She stared at it, anger boiling in her chest. "Christ."

"The date stamp on the print is last night," Blair remarked with no inflection in her voice.

"Yes."

"I don't know what to do. I don't even know what this mea—"

"Blair, I swear I don't know who she is."

Blair didn't respond.

Furious, Cam couldn't stop staring at herself in the photograph, leaning toward a woman who appeared to be whispering in her ear. The woman's hand was resting on hers. The pose was intimate, as if the shot had been taken during an intensely private moment, an image stolen from a lovers' tryst. The woman was the redhead from the previous evening, and although only their faces were in focus, the grainy background was clearly the bar where she had gone for a drink. Still glaring at the photo, Cam said, "Last night after I left here, I went downtown—"

"You don't need to explai—"

"Yes, I goddamned well *do* need to. And *we* need to get something straight," Cam replied heatedly, lifting her eyes from the image of the redhead and fixing her gaze on Blair. "I haven't been with anyone but you since right before I was shot. I haven't *wanted* to be—"

"Cam—"

"I'm not done." Cam's dark eyes were smoldering. "I don't want anyone except you, and I have no intention of being with anyone else. Not now—not ever."

"Stop, please." Blair's tone was somewhere between embarrassed and confused. "I feel ridiculous putting you in a position where you need to say that."

"Why?"

"Because," Blair answered, her voice hushed, "I've never before wanted anyone to say what you just said."

"Do you now?"

"Oh, yes."

"If it makes you feel any better, I've never said it to anyone before." Cam gently moved closer and slipped both arms around

Blair's waist. They faced one another, their thighs touching, their eyes locked—leaning back in the circle of one another's arms. "I don't know what the hell is going on. I don't know why someone is trying to drive a wedge between us...if that's even what this is about. I can't imagine that our relationship is a threat to anyone."

At that, Blair laughed out loud. "Uh—visited the Bible Belt recently?"

"This isn't their style. The photograph in the newspaper, maybe, but even that's a stretch. You're the president's daughter, for God's sake. Even the right-wingers aren't crazy enough to sling mud at you."

"Maybe. I'm not sure my position affords much protection any longer."

"I'm sorry you have to deal with this." Cam kissed her forehead, the feel of Blair's body in her arms easing the tightness in her chest that the photo had evoked.

"So—who is the bitch?" Blair asked abruptly, but there was a light dancing in her eyes that hadn't been there before.

Cam laughed. "I have no idea. I couldn't sleep last night. That seems to be a common theme when I'm not with you."

"Hmm, I know what you need when you can't sleep," Blair remarked lightly, but her eyes were troubled again. Resting her cheek against Cam's shoulder, she kissed her neck above the collar of a pristine white shirt.

"What I need is you." Cam brushed a kiss into Blair's hair. "So I was just sitting at the bar, trying to get my thoughts in order, when she appeared out of nowhere. I wasn't really paying any attention, and, I have to admit, I really don't know who else was in the bar. Going there was a last-minute decision, but obviously, someone must have followed me, was inside watching, and took the picture."

"What did she say?"

"Uh..."

"Cameron?"

"Just a pick-up line—nothing too serious."

"I'm going to hunt her down—"

The flow of words was stopped by Cam's mouth on hers. A long moment later, their lips parted, but they remained pressed close together, both of them a little breathless. Blair found her voice and spoke again, her cheek nestled against Cam's chest, one hand under her jacket, stroking her back.

"Do you think she was trying to set you up for something?"

"I don't know. She could have been an innocent bystander, and someone just took advantage of the moment. What *is* clear, though, is that I was tailed from here to the bar." She rested her chin on the top of Blair's head and sighed. "Some Secret Service agent I've been this week. First I let someone photograph you in a compromising position, and now I've managed to get myself a tail that I didn't even see. Maybe it *is* time for me to retire."

"Bullshit." Blair tilted her head while tapping a finger against Cam's chest. "You haven't had enough rest in a week to account for one full night's sleep. On top of that, you've had a concussion. Oh, and not to mention more stress than any one person should have to handle in a year, let alone a few weeks. If you've missed a few things, it's understandable. I still trust you with my life."

"The problem is, you *do,* and if I'm not up to the job—"

"Oh, for God's sake, Cameron, give yourself a break. When I require you to walk on water, I'll let you know."

For a moment, Cam simply stared at her. Then she laughed. "Yes, ma'am."

"And whatever someone is trying to do with us, it's had quite the opposite effect. All he has managed to do is piss me off." Blair was adamant. "And not at you."

"Thank God for that. I don't think I could take it."

"On the other hand," Blair said as she cupped Cam's cheek in the curve of her palm, "if I see her anywhere near you, her life isn't worth a dime."

For an instant, Cam was worried, and then she recognized the lilt of humor in Blair's voice. That laughter had been lacking for too long, and hearing it made her heart lift. "Let's hope for her sake she was just in the wrong place at the wrong time. For now, though, let's forget about her."

"Yes." Blair insinuated the fingers of one hand through the thick, dark hair at the base of Cam's neck and pulled her head down. Just before she melded her mouth to Cam's again, she whispered throatily, "Let's do that."

CHAPTER THIRTEEN

As the kiss turned hungry, Blair's thighs began to tremble, and she edged her hips up onto the stool behind her, pulling Cam with her until her lover was pressed between the vee of her legs. Lifting both hands to Cam's shoulders, Blair pressed her breasts against Cam's chest, the thin cotton of her tank top doing little to blunt the effect of her nipples hardening from the heat of her lover's body alone. Moaning faintly far back in her throat, she kneaded both hands down Cam's back and then underneath her jacket, finally pulling the shirt free of her trousers until her palms found skin.

As their tongues met in a rush of possession, Cam eased her hands between their bodies and rubbed her thumbs over Blair's nipples, drawing a small cry from her. Thrusting her pelvis hard into the space between Blair's thighs, Cam lifted both breasts in her hands while tugging sharply on Blair's nipples. She grunted softly as Blair rocked hard against her, her clitoris swelling instantly from the pressure.

"Oh, this is *such* a bad idea," Blair gasped, even as she worked at Cam's belt buckle.

"Why?" Cam's tone was short and tight with challenge, her fingers still tormenting.

"Because," Blair replied before she bit her lover's neck, "I know how you hate to be distracted when you're working."

By way of reply, Cam bunched the shirt in one fist and jerked it upward until Blair's breasts were exposed. The white fabric strained across the top of Blair's chest, calling the blood to the surface and painting her breasts with the hot blush of arousal. Swiftly, Cam lowered her head and pulled one nipple into her mouth. Blair's neck arched as she closed her eyes and whimpered.

Moving from one breast to the other and then back again, Cam alternately sucked and bit until Blair's hands flew to Cam's face and pushed her head away.

"You've got to stop. My God, I'll go crazy if you keep doing that."

"I thought you already *were* crazy...about me." Cam's voice was thick, her eyes heavy-lidded with need. She kept one hand on Blair's breast as she yanked the drawstring loose on the soft cotton pants with the other. "Didn't you..." she worked her hand under the fabric, "say that?"

"You know what I mean," Blair replied urgently, her lips swollen with kisses and lust. "You make me want to...oh..." Shocked by the sudden touch of Cam's fingers on her tensely distended clitoris, she nearly came. She gripped Cam's arms hard enough to leave bruises and struggled to contain the swift surge of pleasure. "Jesus Christ."

"I love the way you feel," Cam grated, pushing her hand deeper between Blair's thighs with the force of her whole body behind it, remotely registering Blair's fingers digging into her flesh. She slipped her free arm behind Blair's shoulders, then pulled her roughly against her, simultaneously stroking rapidly inside. Blair clung to her now, both arms wrapped tightly around Cam's shoulders—her face, damp with perspiration and the sweet sheen of sex, pressed to Cam's neck.

Cam breathed in Blair's ear, "I love to fuck you."

"Do it, just do it." Before the words had completely left her throat, Blair bucked on Cam's hand, then grew rigid, crying out helplessly as wave upon wave of pleasure ripped through her.

When Blair finally quieted, sagging back on the stool, her back propped against the breakfast counter for support, Cam spread her arms on either side of her and leaned close. She pressed her hips into the still tender places that made Blair gasp. With her lips brushing the outer edge of Blair's ear again, she growled, "I love you. Don't ever forget that."

Then, her legs still shaking from exertion and arousal, Cam stepped away, rapidly tucking in her shirt with trembling hands.

"What are you doing?" Blair's voice was rough with the lingering lassitude of satisfaction.

"I need to get out of here. I'm on duty, remember?"

"Are you out of your mind?" Blair laughed, her tone stronger this time. "Tell me you're not ready to come."

Cam grinned a little shakily. "What do *you* think?"

"Think? I *know*. Get over here and let me take care of you."

"I shouldn't. Really—I have things I have to do."

"Uh-huh." Indolently, Blair pulled her tank top the rest of the way off and ran one hand up her bare abdomen and over her breasts. "If you leave here in the state you're in now, everyone downstairs is going to know. You're shaking. You look like you're about to explode out of your skin."

As she talked, Blair absently brushed her fingers over one nipple, bringing it back to taut arousal. Cam couldn't take her eyes off those sensuous fingers. When Blair squeezed her own breast, her breath catching audibly as her hips lifted in invitation, Cam's head reeled again.

"Fuck it." Pushing into the space between Blair's spread thighs, Cam rapidly unbuckled her belt and opened her trousers. Then, grasping the counter again on either side of Blair's body, she leaned down and kissed her. Arms outstretched, locked in place, she waited for the touch that she knew would devastate her.

Smiling against Cam's mouth, Blair pushed past the zipper and under the last barrier of material. Then she slid her fingers along Cam's rigid clitoris and circled back up again, reveling in the swift jerk of her lover's hips into her palm. Cam's breath rasped in her ear, a choking desperate sound that might have been pain, but Blair knew it wasn't.

She could have teased her—she loved to tease her—but this time she knew neither of them could bear it. She worked the pulsing flesh under her hand as she stroked back and forth through the hot swollen tissue, bringing Cam rapidly to the edge and then mercilessly driving her over. Cam shouted as she climaxed, shuddering in Blair's arms, and the weight of her body collapsing into orgasm was almost enough to make Blair come again with her. As if it were the first time, Blair held her, trembling herself—breathless with wonder.

Ten minutes later, Cam stood at the door, brushing a strand of damp hair from Blair's cheek.

"I'll be back tomorrow. Noon at the latest. If there's any delay, I'll call you from DC."

"Okay." Blair regarded her lover seriously, her gaze probing Cam's face. "The photograph of you in the bar last night—does it have anything to do with the call in San Francisco?"

"I don't know," Cam said after a moment's hesitation. "There are too many things that don't make sense right now. I hope I'll be able to find some answers in DC."

"Are you going to tell me?"

"Blair, if there were an...investigation into...alleged irregularities, you could be called to testify. Anything you know about me—or information I've shared with you—would be fair game. I can't put you in that position."

"I'm your lover, Cam," Blair insisted quietly, realizing she had never before thought of herself that way in relation to another person. It was so much more than physical, and the thought of being excluded from Cam's life bothered her more than she had ever imagined. "I want to know what's happening to you."

Cam brushed her thumb across Blair's cheek and let her fingers trail from neck to shoulder. With her palm lightly stroking Blair's bare upper arm, she murmured, "I don't want to keep secrets from you, but there's more than just you and me involved."

"You can't forget who I am, can you?" Blair's tone reflected more sorrow than accusation.

"You're a lot more to me than the first daughter," Cam replied, her tone gentle. "When you're not angry with me, you remember that, right?"

"I'm not *angry* with you now." But even as she said it, she knew that wasn't entirely true. She knew it wasn't Cam's fault—or even hers. They both had history, and being in love didn't change that. "I just can't take feeling like there's something standing between us, even though I know what you said makes sense. I *hate* that I'll miss you the minute you walk out the door, that I'll worry about what's happening to you, that I'll wonder about who you're with."

"Do you really mind feeling that way?" Cam's eyes had gone from gray to black, and they bore into Blair's, searching inside the places that no one else ever saw.

"No," Blair whispered, resting her palm under Cam's jacket over the strong heartbeat beneath. "God, no."

"I promise I'll tell you as much as I can."

"All right. I don't like it, but I'll accept that for now."

"Thank you."

Blair rubbed her hand lightly back and forth over Cam's chest. "You'll be careful, right?"

"Swear." Cam kissed her, gently this time, without the urgency of the earlier passion but with the certainty of belonging. "Don't disappear on Mac if you go out, okay? Take someone with you, no matter where you're going."

Sighing, Blair nodded. "Only for you, Commander."

Lightly, Cam stroked her cheek. "I love you." Then she opened the door and crossed the foyer to the elevator.

Blair watched until the elevator doors closed. Immediately, the longing, the other side of love, began.

❖

Downstairs in Command Central, Cam found Mac in his cubbyhole in one corner of the main room, reviewing the pre-Paris intelligence reports. "Where's Stark?"

"In the gym, I think. She's got the swing shift today, but I didn't have any intel that Egret would be flying. Do you need her now?"

"Not for Egret. She's settled in the nest." Cam pointed to the ceiling and Blair's apartment above. "But I want to talk to both of you. Let's go find her."

Five minutes later, they discovered Stark flat on her back on a weight bench, a barbell poised over her chest, counting reps out loud. She was alone in the twenty-by-thirty-foot room outfitted with weights and aerobic equipment.

"You should probably have a spotter," Mac remarked good-naturedly as he lifted the bar from her hands and settled it into the cleats.

Stark sat up, reaching for a towel as she did so. Quickly, she wiped the sweat from her face and off her bare arms. In a sleeveless T-shirt and gym shorts, her body looked sturdy and muscular.

"Sorry," she said glancing from Mac to Cam. "I didn't think there was anything on for me. I'll just grab a fast shower and—"

"Relax, Stark," Cam said as she slipped off her suit jacket. The air-conditioning in the workout room left a little something to be desired, and it was humid the way all gyms seemed to be. "This is not about Egret's detail."

Clearly puzzled, Stark remained silent as Cam settled onto a bench facing her and Mac sat down by her side. Reflexively, she moved over an inch to give him some room and herself space to maneuver. An agent never let their personal perimeter be encroached upon.

"I have to go to DC this afternoon," Cam said. "Mac, you'll have the watch."

"Okay. Do you need me to make flight arrangements?"

"No. I'll just catch a shuttle. I expect to be back tomorrow, but...something may come up." She paused, then said briskly, "Something *has* come up."

She handed Mac the manila envelope. "Take a look at that. Handle it carefully—there probably aren't any prints, but we could get lucky."

Stark checked the envelope over Mac's shoulder. "No postmark."

"It came by courier this morning. Hand delivered."

Mac drew in a quick breath, no doubt having the same uncomfortable feelings of déjà vu Cam had experienced at first seeing the envelope. "It went through to her?"

"Yes."

"Who was downstairs?" Stark's tone had a sharp edge.

"Taylor. He scanned it, then had it sent up to Egret. No reason not to."

Carefully, Mac pulled the photograph out by the corner and placed it atop the envelope in his lap. The two agents studied it for a minute without comment. Finally, Mac looked up at his chief. "Any message with it?"

"No."

"When was it taken?" Stark's tone was guarded. The training manual didn't cover this sort of situation, and she wasn't used to questioning her commander about anything, let alone something that was obviously personal.

"Last night about 0300."

"Jesus," Mac exclaimed. "How—"

"Someone must have tailed me downtown from here, because I never went home."

Neither of them dared ask how it was possible that she had been followed. Secret Service agents didn't worry about their own security. They were just anonymous faces on the fringes of the spotlight, nearly identical and interchangeable. And replaceable.

"What really worries me is that someone probably tailed us *from* Teterboro *to* here. Which means that we have a problem in terms of Egret's security."

"Do you think that she's a target of some kind?" Mac was already assessing the angles.

"Jesus, not again," Stark breathed, unaware that she had even spoken aloud.

"Probably not physically, but that remains to be seen." Cam's expression was grim. "We must assume that she is. Maybe this is the same photographer who took the shot in San Francisco."

Stark stared for a second, her thoughts practically written across her broad, smooth face. "On the beach—"

"Yes," Cam said quietly.

"Oh, man, I'm sorry, Commander," she said miserably. "I had the beach in view the whole time, but he must have gotten by me."

"He got by us both, Stark. Forget it." Cam tried to shrug away the fury that rose every time she thought of someone watching her and Blair together during an innocent, intimate moment—when they'd both felt safe. *Christ, this is how she lives all the time. No wonder she's angry. How in hell does she stand it?*

"Commander?" Mac asked uncertainly.

Cam flinched imperceptibly, her gaze refocusing on her agents. "I'd like to know who's taking such an interest."

"You want me to run this through forensics?"

"Like I said—we could get lucky. Maybe he licked the envelope and we'll get a DNA sample."

"Or maybe *she* did," Stark interjected.

RADCLY*f*FE

"I suppose that's possible," Cam allowed, keeping her tone carefully neutral.

Mac glanced again at the image, seeming to search for words. "Do you...uh...know her?"

"No, I don't," Cam answered crisply. "Try calling Walker in the New York City lab to run the tests. He's good."

"Excuse me, Commander," Stark said, "but maybe that's not such a good idea. Respectfully, ma'am."

Cam eyed her. "Go ahead."

"Well, this photograph is...telling."

"Interesting choice of words," Cam remarked dryly, hating the disclosure of something so private, even to those she trusted. The younger agent colored, and Cam regretted her brief loss of control. "Go ahead, Stark."

"I think we should handle this internally as far as possible."

"Are you up on your forensics?" Mac interjected. "'Cause I sure can't walk this through a lab."

"No, me either." Stark answered tentatively as if she were feeling her way along a narrow ledge that threatened to crumble under her feet. "But I know someone we can trust who *can* do it. Renee Savard."

"She's FBI," Mac exclaimed. "Since when do we trust *them?*"

"She's a friend," Stark insisted, holding his gaze steadily. "She won't betray us. And she's been assigned to a desk at the New York City field office."

"Isn't she still in the hospital?" Cam asked, surprised.

"Until today. I'm going there in a few minutes to pick her up." For the first time, she appeared unsure. "To give her a ride home... you know."

"Understood." Cam suppressed a grin. "But she's got to be on medical leave for a while."

Stark laughed derisively. "Sure—for about a day. She'll go in the first chance she gets."

"Mac?" Cam turned to her second in command.

He thought about the conversations he'd had in the past with the FBI agent. She had always dealt with them squarely, and she had been willing to give her life for Egret. Still, he had an inherent distrust of the FBI. "Yeah, I say we keep it in house. And Savard is

• 136 •

almost one of us."

"Agreed." Cam stood. "Stark, mind if I tag along with you to the hospital on my way to the airport?"

"I'll be ready in five," the agent responded, jumping up and heading for the shower.

"Keep me informed of any developments on this end, Mac."

"Don't worry, Commander," he assured steadily. "We'll be fine here."

"Of course," she said with confidence. But leaving Blair was getting harder every day, and it had less and less to do with her assignment as the first daughter's security chief.

CHAPTER FOURTEEN

Is she okay?"

"Sure," Stark responded automatically, watching the door swing closed on her departing commander.

Renee Savard, seated on the side of her narrow hospital bed, raised an eyebrow. Her coffee-colored skin had regained its luster, and her blue eyes were sharp and clear once again. If the bruise on her forehead or the healing gunshot wound in her shoulder were causing any pain, she didn't show it. Even in a faded, shapeless hospital gown, she was striking.

"The commander took quite a beating in the blast," Stark acknowledged uneasily. "Why?"

"She looks tired, that's all. I guess I'm just not used to seeing her that way." Renee's blue eyes probed the face of the agent fidgeting by the side of the bed, clearly uncomfortable discussing her chief. She noticed, too, the circles smudging the smooth clear skin under Paula's eyes, and she realized that *all* of them had taken a beating the last few weeks. Softly, she asked, "How about you? *You* okay?"

"Yeah. This whole thing is making me a little crazy, though. I feel like I did when Loverboy first showed up. Like there's something bad happening and all I can see is smoke and mirrors."

"It'll be fine," the FBI agent calmly assured her, "because we'll make sure it is."

Stark grinned, feeling some of the weight lift from her shoulders. "Damn right."

"It took guts for her to come here today and show me that photo."

"She doesn't back down from anything."

"Still, I *am* FBI," Savard pointed out. "For all she knows, I could send that straight to an assistant director, and she'd have a jacket by sundown."

"Yeah—like we all don't have one already," Stark retorted angrily. "You know Doyle investigated the whole security team when the task force was first formed."

"I know that sucked," Savard said gently, "but that's just SOP."

"Yeah, well, being a suspect doesn't exactly make me want to play ball with the Bureau again."

"What about me?" For the first time, there was concern in Renee's eyes. "Do you trust me?"

"Of course!" Stark's expression softened. "Sorry...I know what happened with the task force wasn't on you."

Savard finally smiled again. "Just so we're clear on what's between us."

"Crystal," Stark said firmly. "Do you really think you'll be able to help us out? I don't want you to end up in the middle of this. You could lose your job."

"Shouldn't be a problem. I know a guy in the lab who will run things through for me with no questions asked. He's such a total lab rat he probably doesn't even know who Roberts is. I don't think he'll make the connection from that photo in the bar."

"Is he good?"

"If there's something to be found, he'll find it."

"Good, because we need something." Stark sighed. "Right now, we don't know dick."

"It will buy her a little time," Savard said cautiously, "but she won't be able to keep a lid on this forever. Sooner or later, you know something is going to come out."

Stark was silent, torn between her desire to share her concerns and her loyalty to her commander's privacy.

"I saw the photo in the newspaper last night," Savard continued casually. "The one of Blair Powell and her mystery lover."

"Yeah, the whole team seems to be real popular with the candid camera crew these days."

"That's Roberts with her, isn't it?"

Once again, Stark hesitated.

"Paula, anyone with eyes can see what's happening between those two. You know damn well I don't care. Why should I? It's their business."

"Yeah." Stark couldn't hide a hint of bitterness. "It *should* be, but everything else aside, considering it's the first daughter and the commander of her security team, you know it's complicated."

"Complicated. Yes, I agree with you there. But it's still nobody's business. It's for them to work out the complications."

"I hope they can," Stark said fervently. She'd been on Egret's team since day one, and for a few months before Ellen Grant had been assigned, she'd been the only woman. She'd followed the first daughter through bars and guarded her at parties, watching her tear through one-night stands and dangerous liaisons—until the commander had come along. Now it was all different. Better.

Savard smiled, watching the concern darken Stark's eyes. "You're sweet, have I ever mentioned that?"

"Maybe." Stark grinned.

"They'll be okay."

"Sure, I know that." Stark straightened her shoulders, determined not to let her worry show. "I'm glad you didn't mind me suggesting that you help out. I just didn't know that the commander was going to brief you herself."

Savard reached out and took Stark's hand, running her thumb back and forth over the top of it as their fingers intertwined. "You did right. I'm glad you thought of me."

"I think about you all the time." Stark blushed, but her voice was firm and her eyes held Savard's without blinking.

"Good. Then let's get me dressed so you can take me home." Savard reached for her clothes on the bed. Carefully, she worked each leg into her pants and stood up by the side of the bed, frowning as she contemplated closing buttons and zippers one-handed. Her left arm was held tightly across her chest in a sling. "Uh...I think I'm going to need some help here. Sorry."

"No problem," Stark said nonchalantly, stepping forward to slide up the zipper on the FBI agent's pants, being careful not to touch the taut smooth skin of her abdomen as Renee held the hospital gown up with her good hand. Then she worked the button closed on the waistband and looked around for Renee's shirt.

Renee hooked a finger inside Stark's belt and tugged playfully. "This is where I should say something clever about how I wish you were *un*dressing me."

Stark colored and lifted the dark blue polo shirt from the bottom of the bed. Holding it in front of her, she said, "Here. I guess we'll have to take the sling off to get this on." She frowned. "Is that okay? I don't want to hurt you."

"I can't raise my arm. I think we're going to have to use something with buttons. Is there anything in the bag like that?"

Stark rapidly looked through the contents of the gym bag that Renee's sister had brought earlier that day. "No. Everything pulls on over your head."

"Well, I don't intend to leave here in this hospital gown—and I'm not staying one minute longer than I have to." Savard was silent for a few seconds, and then she smiled, her eyes twinkling. "You're about my size. Give me your shirt."

"My shirt!"

"Well, it buttons, which is the primary thing. You can wear my polo shirt."

"It'll be too small," Stark protested desperately.

"You've got a jacket. It will be fine. Come on, hand it over."

"There's another problem." Stark's face reddened again.

"Paula, I work mostly with men. I went through the FBI Academy with a class that was ninety percent male. A little sweat, especially yours, is not going to bother me."

"That's not it," Stark said stiffly. "I'm not...uh...wearing anything under it."

"Even better. A shirt and a bonus." Renee laughed out loud at Stark's expression. "Take off the jacket and give me the damn shirt. I want to get out of here—and don't even think about asking me to close my eyes."

Stark shed her jacket and pulled her pale-blue button-down-collar shirt from the waistband of her black trousers. Her gun was clipped on the right side of her pants, and she steadied the holster with one hand while she slowly worked the buttons free on the front of her shirt with the other.

"You want me to do that?" Savard feigned innocence.

"You only have one hand yourself, remember?" Stark was smiling now, too. She liked the way Savard's eyes widened slightly as the material over her breasts parted with each button that she loosened.

"You'd be amazed what I can do with one hand, given the right motivation." Renee's voice was lower, a bit husky. She reached out, and Paula stepped back a foot.

"I've got it."

"Thought you trusted me," Renee teased, her eyes on the muscled chest and small, firm breasts now nearly completely exposed.

"You, yes. Don't trust myself."

"I do," Renee whispered. She moved closer and placed a kiss on Paula's mouth. She held it, savoring the soft full lower lip exploring hers and the barest brush of breasts against her own. It was going to be very easy to get lost in Paula Stark's arms. Sighing with a mixture of pleasure and regret, she broke the kiss. "Time to go."

"I have to work tonight," Stark barely managed, her throat thick. She held out her shirt, unmindful of her nudity now. Her skin felt so hot, all she wanted was the cool touch of Renee's fingers. "I'm sorry."

Savard shook her head and took the shirt. "Until when?"

"Midnight."

"I'll nap." Savard tossed her the polo shirt. "You can return my shirt when you get off work."

Stark grinned. "Roger that."

❖

Not long after Cam left her apartment, Blair set aside her palette and brushes and washed her hands in the work sink tucked into the corner of the loft that formed her studio. Then she lifted the nearby phone and punched in a familiar number. A moment later, a woman answered.

"Hello?"

The whiskey tones were huskier than usual, and Blair smiled fondly. "Don't tell me you just woke up? It *is* the middle of the day, you know?"

"Listen, love, some of us *have* to work at night."

"Oh, please, Diane." Blair tossed back her head and laughed. "I know the kind of work you do after midnight."

"How do you know that I wasn't busy selling one of your paintings?" Diane Bleeker, her business agent and oldest friend, inquired indignantly. "And how do you know that I was *sleeping* just now?"

"If you were slaving away on my behalf, I appreciate it. If you weren't, I'd love to hear all the details."

"Where are you?" Diane was beginning to sound awake.

"Back in Manhattan."

"Is everything all right?"

The concern in her friend's voice was genuine. As many times over their fifteen-year friendship as they'd disagreed over the direction of each other's relationships—or been at odds over the same woman—their deep-rooted affection for one another endured.

"I'm fine," Blair hastened to assure her. "I wouldn't mind seeing you, though—if your *associate* from last evening isn't still there."

"Well," Diane said as if thinking it over, "let's say by the time you get here, my calendar will be clear."

"Don't let me rush you."

"Oh my dear, never that. Some things should definitely be savored."

"Is an hour good enough?"

"Perfect. Now, let me get back to what I was about to do. I'll see you soon."

After hanging up, Blair stripped off her soiled clothes and headed toward the shower. On her way, she picked up the bedside phone and dialed another number. It was answered immediately.

"Yes, Ms. Powell?"

"I'm going out in an hour, Mac."

If the advance notice, which was a distinctly unusual phenomenon for the notoriously unpredictable first daughter, surprised him, his voice didn't reveal it. "Very well. I'll call for the car."

"That would be fine. Thank you, Mac."

Fifty minutes later, dressed in jeans, a white short-sleeved ribbed cotton top, and running shoes, she keyed the penthouse elevator and rode down to the lobby. When the doors opened, Felicia Davis and a small, bespectacled agent, Vince Taylor, a relative newcomer to the team, were waiting for her. She assumed that one of the others was in the car, which idled at the curb. It didn't really matter to her, because it wouldn't be Cam.

As she walked between the agents, her mind replayed the earlier conversation with her lover. She had told Cam that she had no intention of discussing their relationship with Lucinda Washburn, but she knew it was only a matter of time before she would be forced to. The only reason her personal life had not become a matter of public record much sooner was simply because she'd never had a serious relationship. It was much easier to remain anonymous when one's love interests were anonymous as well.

As she stepped from beneath the awning that shaded the entrance to her building, a flock of reporters rushed down the sidewalk toward her, microphones extended and cameras at the ready. Clearly, her days of anonymity were numbered.

Fortunately, her security team was prepared for exactly this contingency and quickly escorted her to the Suburban, whose doors stood open to facilitate her entry. Once she was inside, the driver pulled quickly from the curb, and she was able to avoid making any kind of comment whatsoever in response to the shouted questions. Since New York City traffic prohibited easy pursuit, by the time they reached Diane Bleeker's Upper East Side condo, the media had been outdistanced and were nowhere in sight. Felicia Davis accompanied Blair to Diane's door and took up a post just outside after Diane answered her friend's knock.

"That's one I don't think I've seen before," Diane remarked after a quick glimpse at the tall ebony-skinned woman who somehow managed to look Paris runway elegant in the standard dark two-piece suit. "She's absolutely gorgeous."

"Forget it. She's straight."

"And your point would be?" Diane tossed a grin over her shoulder as she led the way through the apartment to a sitting area facing the balcony. Through the open French doors, the green expanse of Central Park was visible far below.

"Don't you think you have your hands full with your many other...ah...interests?" Blair teased.

"Well, darlin', variety is the spice of life and all that."

"Riiight."

"You want something to drink? Beer or wine?"

Blair shook her head and settled into one corner of the broad beige sectional. She kicked off her shoes, propped her feet on a footstool, and dropped her head against the back of the sofa. "No, I'm fine. Thanks."

"Yes, I can see that." Diane walked to a nearby serving cart and poured herself a glass of white wine, then returned and sat near Blair. Resting one hand on Blair's blue-jeaned leg, she said, "So. Tell me."

Blair raised an eyebrow. "What makes you think there's anything to tell?"

"Come on, save me the trouble of teasing it out of you." Suddenly, she held up a hand. "No—wait...let me guess. Roberts has done something to annoy you again."

"Why do you say that?" Blair asked in honest curiosity.

"Because you always get those double frown lines between your brows when she's driving you crazy."

"You guessed wrong this time." Blair shook her head and smiled. "She hasn't done anything. In fact, she's...fabulous."

"Oh my God." Diane's voice registered true shock. "You can't be serious."

"What are you talking about?"

"Are you really, truly, in love?"

Briefly, Blair wavered. She had said the words to Cam, but only rarely. She'd told Marcea. Still, saying it out loud, she was sure, would destroy the last barricade that stood between her heart and everything that had always threatened to hurt her. Maybe it had started with the loss of her mother, or maybe it had been the betrayal of her first love in prep school, or maybe it had been the long procession of women who had claimed to want her when it was only the spotlight that accompanied her father's name they wished to experience. She had managed to protect herself from the disappointment of a love lost by never allowing it to happen. Into the expectant silence, she loosed the fear and breathed the truth.

"Yes, absolutely. Utterly. Madly."

Diane stared at her, her face blank and unreadable for what felt like an endless moment. Finally, she sipped her drink and said quietly, "I envy you. And I'm happy for you."

Almost shyly, Blair nudged Diane's leg with her toes. "Thanks."

"So, if it's not Roberts, what's the problem?"

"I guess you haven't seen a newspaper recently."

Diane laughed, a deep-throated purr that at one time had been enough to make Blair want to throw her down on the bed and ravish her. But they had been teenagers then, and they had not been lovers for many years.

"There's a picture of me on the front page of the *Post* in a compromising position. You can't tell that it's Cam, but eventually someone is going to put it together. I am, to put it bluntly, about to be outed."

"You've had a pretty good run, you know," Diane pointed out quietly.

"I know. I'm just not sure how to handle it. The White House needs to be prepared, because my father is going to catch the fallout."

"I've always thought that a preemptive strike was the best way to deal with things like this."

"You think I should make a statement?"

"You intend to keep on with her?"

"God," Blair gasped, as if from a sudden pain. "I hope so."

"Well, that's the answer then, isn't it?" Diane shrugged. "If you aren't willing to give her up, then you're going to have to deal with the publicity that goes with the relationship. Better to have it on your own terms than ending up on the defensive."

"I'd say exactly the same thing, if it were just up to me." Blair ran her hands through her hair, then sighed. "It would be so much easier if I didn't have to worry about the spin doctors in DC wanting to control what I say and when I say it and who I say it to."

"Screw them. You're an adult—do what you want to do."

"I *have* been. But I can't this time." Blair regarded her friend seriously. "I can't pretend that my father is not the president of the

United States. He's got sort of an important job, remember. I think I'm going to need to run this by some people in the West Wing before I shoot him in the foot."

"I suppose you're right. You want me to come with you?"

"Thanks, I really appreciate it. But I'd better do this one alone."

"Will Commander Heartthrob go along with it?"

Blair thought about it, shrugged slightly. "She isn't worried about herself, but then she never is. I think she'd be happiest taking all the risks and bearing all the consequences, but this is about us. The two of us."

"So, she'll be pissed if you put yourself on the spot publicly."

Blair grinned. "I imagine."

"What do you plan to do?"

"I'm going to catch a plane to Washington." She leaned over, kissed Diane on the cheek, and stood.

"Any chance you could lend me one of your spookies?" Diane asked as she rose and threaded her arm through Blair's.

"Anyone in particular?" Blair asked playfully as the two friends walked toward the door.

When Diane opened the door, Felicia Davis stepped away from the wall and glanced in at Blair.

"She would do nicely," Diane said *sotto voce*.

Felicia raised one elegant eyebrow. "Ready, Ms. Powell?"

"As I'll ever be," Blair replied seriously.

CHAPTER FIFTEEN

At 1830 hours that evening, Cam sat in a deserted anteroom in front of a plain, varnished door with a discreet plaque bearing Stewart Carlisle's name. She settled in to wait, but just a few minutes passed before his administrative assistant appeared around the corner and said, "He's ready for you."

When Cam opened the door and stepped into the unadorned office, her immediate superior was making a notation on the bottom of a report. The room held little in the way of personal touches other than a small framed photo on the wall of a very young Stewart Carlisle with John Fitzgerald Kennedy and his brother Robert.

"Grab a chair," he said without looking up.

She chose one of a pair of institutional fabric-covered office chairs in front of his desk and crossed her right ankle over her knee, her hands resting loosely on the thin wooden armrests. When he finally closed the folder, pushed the pile of papers away, and looked up to meet Cam's gaze, his face revealed nothing.

"What happened with that newspaper photograph?" he began without preamble. "That's just the kind of thing the White House likes to chew my ass over."

"I was going to ask you the same thing," she said calmly. "We should have had intelligence that the photo was going out over the wires. We were unprepared for the article in the *Post,* and we walked into a hornet's nest of reporters at Teterboro when we arrived last night. We were lucky it didn't turn into a media free-for-all. So, where was the breakdown in the system?"

A muscle bunched in his jaw, but his voice, too, was even in reply. "Since you were there when the picture was taken, I assumed you'd be able to tell me."

For a second, before she realized that he simply meant San Francisco, Cam thought he was referring to her presence on the beach with Blair. Oddly, it didn't bother her. There was not one moment in her relationship with Blair that she would deny to anyone. On the other hand, in her professional life—a world rife with double dealing, political blackmail, and constant struggle for bureaucratic superiority—she had learned never to divulge information that could be used as a weapon against her or anyone for whom she cared.

"The photo was taken with a long-range telephoto lens, probably across the water from an adjacent pier. We had close physical surveillance in place, but no substantial perimeter. I had no reason to believe it was required in that particular location."

"The camera could just as well have been a long-range rifle equipped with a night scope," he pointed out, as if discussing an inconsequential notation in the margin of a not particularly interesting article. "She could be dead instead of just caught in an embarrassing moment."

The image struck like a shard of glass tearing through her chest, and it hurt even to draw a breath. Outwardly, her expression didn't change. "I've thought of that. Unless we keep her at highest priority twenty-four hours a day, we can't prevent it if someone decides to do something of that nature. Ordinarily, that kind of perimeter is not required for her, and I made the judgment call that our surveillance was sufficient."

"It's going to be one more piece of ammunition against you."

"Meaning what?"

"I received a call from Justice this morning; a request for a formal inquest into the outcome of the operation in New York has been lodged by the NSA chief and the deputy director of the Bureau."

"That's precedent setting, isn't it?" She was careful to keep her expression blank. The implication that she had not performed her duty appropriately stung. That she would have to defend herself to outsiders only added insult to the injury.

He shrugged. "It was a joint operation, so the Bureau is within their rights to ask for it. Bottom line, though, it's the casualties that resulted that make it difficult for us to object without looking like we have something to hide. There's not much I can do about it."

"All right. I understand."

"I'm not sure that you do. They were strongly *suggesting* that you be relieved of duty until the inquiry is completed."

Gray eyes hardened, but she didn't move a muscle. "What did *you* say?"

For the first time that day, and for one of the very few times she could ever remember, he looked uncomfortable. "I told them no, but I don't know how long that will last. Once the *request* is formalized..." He held out his hands, palms up, to indicate his powerlessness.

"Since when do you let other agencies tell the Secret Service how to run its business?"

"Since the president was forced to accept an FBI director who is just a little bit further right of Joe McCarthy," he snapped. "Damn it, Roberts, you know that ever since William Morrow was appointed, the FBI has been working nonstop to expand its investigative reach and to confiscate as much power as possible from the other security divisions."

"And you think that the Bureau is behind this move to investigate me?"

"That's my best guess."

"Why? Why do they care who's in charge of Blair Powell's security? What difference could it make to them?"

For a moment, he didn't speak, and she knew he was making a decision as to whether he could ultimately trust her or not. Bureaucratic politics superseded even friendship. Finally, he leaned back in his chair and grimaced.

"Think about it. In another six months, Andrew Powell will need to consolidate a reelection platform. He'll need money and backers and a very high popularity rating, or he may not win a bid for reelection. His left-of-center views haven't always played well, even with his own party. Remember, in the days of J. Edgar Hoover, the FBI had dossiers on every important political figure in the country, as well as leaders of industry, civil rights organizers, Hollywood stars—everyone with any conceivable connection to the men who held the reins of power. It didn't matter if they were upright citizens or criminals."

He leaned forward, held her eyes. "Hoover and his cronies used information as a weapon. They used it to buy mob informants—or to shut them up; they used it to undermine King and his followers; they bought and sold presidents at will. Some suggested that if they couldn't buy the appropriate people, they killed them. Or at least looked the other way while someone else did."

"But that was thirty, forty years ago," Cam protested.

"And you think that stopped when Hoover left? Look at the direction the Supreme Court has taken in the last twenty years— they don't even *pretend* to be nonpartisan. Andrew Powell is a very liberal president, and there are a lot of people in Washington— Democrats and Republicans alike—who aren't happy that he was elected. Right now, my best guess is that some powerful people want him out, and they're gathering as much ammunition from every quarter as they possibly can. Having an edge on the president's daughter—having some degree of control over the information flow to and from that quarter—might be parlayed into political leverage at some point."

"That seems like a stretch to me," Cam argued.

"Not if the person heading her security force reports directly to the FBI and not to me."

Cam stiffened. "If I'm out, Mac Phillips would replace me, and I guarantee he's no mole."

"It wouldn't necessarily be Phillips who replaces you." Carlisle stared at her silently as the words hung heavily in the air.

Her heart began to pound and her throat felt dry. "Is someone squeezing you on this? Stewart, if you're in trouble, I'll help if I can. But not at the expense of Blair Powell's safety."

Methodically, he straightened the file folders on his desk again, and when he looked up, his face was expressionless. "For the time being, consider yourself notified of a formal inquest. You'll remain on duty until such time as the panel convenes and makes a determination as to whether suspension is recommended."

"She's due to go to Paris in five days. It's a high security agenda, and I intend to lead the team. You'll have to throw me in jail to suspend me before that."

When he didn't respond, she got to her feet and leaned down over his desk, her palms flat on its surface. Her voice was low and strong. "Do whatever it is you have to do to me, but don't put the president's daughter at risk because of interagency politics."

"That will be all, Agent Roberts."

She continued to look at him for long moment, then straightened. "Yes, sir."

When Cam reached the lobby, she signed the log and retrieved her cell phone. Once outside, she punched in a number and waited until a familiar, but generic, female voice answered. Then she provided her account number and requested an appointment, again using only a similar anonymous code.

"I'm sorry, that employee is not currently available. May I substitute someone with similar qualifications?"

"No, thank you. Please check your priority list and cross-reference this account number."

"Just one moment."

A minute later, the pleasant tones returned. "I'm so sorry to have inconvenienced you. For what time shall I record the appointment?"

"Just relay the request and note this as an open-ended appointment for this evening."

"Certainly. If you would call the following number and relay the appointment address."

Cam memorized the number, thanked her, and rang off. Briefly, she considered calling Blair but realized that there was nothing she could tell her that she wanted to say over the phone. And she wasn't certain how much she *really* wanted to share with her in person. She wasn't sure she could make Blair understand what she might need to do.

❖

Blair nodded hello and murmured a brief "Good to see you" to those she passed as she walked hurriedly through the corridors of the West Wing toward a large office that was as close to the center of power as one could get without actually being in the Oval Office. She stopped by the desk of a pale, sandy-haired, intense-looking young man. "Is she in for me?"

In a flat Midwestern baritone, he replied, "Let me check. She was on with the secretary of state."

In another minute, Blair was getting a quick hug and a peck on the cheek from a woman she had known since childhood. Lucinda Washburn still managed to instill in her a certain amount of awe and temerity as no one else could.

"I figured I'd save you the quarter for the phone call." Blair sat down on the leather sofa that bordered one wall in the office of the White House chief of staff.

Lucinda, a statuesque auburn-haired woman in her early fifties, was wearing a navy dress accented by a few pieces of gold jewelry. She leaned back against the front of the wide desk, which was covered with thick binders, stacks of memos, and a computer, and regarded Blair with an amused smile.

"Must be serious if it got you to the White House voluntarily."

"I guess that's for you to tell me."

Lucinda's eyes were sharp as they probed Blair's. "Well, I think that depends."

"On what?"

Washburn fixed Blair with a look then that was known to make the Joint Chiefs sit up straight in their chairs. Blair didn't flinch. She knew Lucinda's stare and had learned not to let its effect show in her face.

"Let's cut to the chase, Blair. It depends on who was in the picture with you and whether there are likely to be any *more* candid photo-ops of an embarrassing nature. Aaron Stern has already fielded questions about the newspaper photo at this morning's press briefing. The press *and* the public want to know why they haven't heard about this romance of yours before now. Everyone wants details."

Blair did her best not to bristle, but it took every ounce of her formidable will not to snap back that *everyone* could go screw himself. Instead, she said, "I don't see why we need to give any explanation whatsoever. This will be yesterday's news by this time tomorrow."

"You may very well be right. On the other hand, there's nothing that the newshounds like better than something juicy involving the first family to use as filler while waiting for the next meteorological catastrophe or military atrocity."

"Fine. Tell them it was a date and let it go at that."

"Oh, come now. An assignation in the middle of the night on a beach in a city half the Midwest thinks is the reincarnation of Sodom and Gomorrah?" Lucinda snorted. "Don't pretend to be naïve, because I know better. Here in the White House, our motto is to be prepared. I don't like to be blindsided by anything, and particularly not by something that reflects directly on the president's family."

Blair was silent, because she knew that already. That was part of the reason she was here. A moment passed. "What do you want?"

"If you're going to embark on a public relationship, then we need to be able to say something about it when asked, and you know damn well we *will* be asked. So, give me the details now."

"You can say that I'm seriously involved with another woman." Blair assumed that this news was probably not a surprise, because Lucinda was too astute not to have known before this. But there was a world of difference between assumption and knowledge.

Lucinda's expression didn't change. "Who?"

"I won't give you that."

"Well, this will take some handling," Lucinda responded in a controlled tone. "If you refuse to name her, it will only make people think you have something *else* to hide. You'll be hounded to death over it. *Is* there something I need to know about her—some scandal, some dark hidden past?"

"No."

"It will come out, Blair. Don't put me behind the eight ball on this." There was a warning note in her voice.

"There's nothing. She's above reproach."

"Then why the secrecy with me?"

Blair didn't answer, and she could almost see Lucinda mentally shuffling cards, deciding which play to make.

"I don't suppose you'd be willing to put this affair on ice until after the president has the party endorsement for reelection?" Lucinda's tone was almost casual now.

"That's more than a year away."

"Do you mean to tell me that you think one year is too long for you to wait? Or is it her? Because if the woman has any substance—"

"You're stepping over the line, Luce."

Lucinda Washburn's dark eyes flashed with sudden ire, but she held her breath for a long second, then exhaled slowly. "Blair, your father has only eight years—maximum—to hold the most powerful position in the world. He can accomplish amazing things for this country and for the future of the world during those eight years. Tell me you don't care about that. Tell me you're willing to risk that."

That had always been the issue, of course. Everyone in her father's inner circle, Lucinda included, had sacrificed a personal life to put him where he was. Some never had time for relationships, and those who did rarely kept them long. For his daughter, the question wasn't as simple as how to balance her father's political ambitions with her own need for an independent honest life. It was the rightness of placing the personal above the greater good. Looking at it the way Lucinda had put it, her desire for personal happiness seemed selfish.

"I've been quiet about my life for over a decade." Blair met the chief of staff's hard stare without blinking. "I've avoided any kind of public statement or disclosure about my sexual identity. I didn't mean for that photograph to be in the newspaper. But I can't change who I am, even for my father's benefit."

"I'm not asking you to change. I *am* asking you not to advertise."

"I've tried the 'don't ask, don't tell' approach since I was fifteen years old. It's a lot like living in a prison."

For one brief instant, Blair saw sympathy in Lucinda's face. Then it was gone. "You're your father's daughter, Blair. You'll make the right decision."

They didn't embrace in parting. As Blair passed the closed door to the Oval Office and the pair of Secret Service agents flanking it, she saw Cam's face in her mind. *I wonder if I have the strength to do the right thing.*

CHAPTER SIXTEEN

It was just before midnight when Cam opened the door to her apartment and ushered Claire inside. The blond wasn't dressed for work. In street clothes—plain white blouse, dark slacks, and low heels—with only the barest hint of makeup, she seemed younger, more vulnerable than Cam had ever seen her. She was still achingly beautiful.

"Are you all right?" Cam asked immediately as they stood facing one another just inside the door, the two feet between them shimmering with the echo of a dozen other meetings just like this.

In the past they might have touched—silent until need and loss and pain had been muted by the fusion of their flesh. No words had been necessary then; what was to happen between them had been understood. Now, the rules had changed, and Cam was acutely aware of being alone with a woman who knew how to shred her control with a whisper.

"Yes, I'm fine," Claire assured her, although her voice rung hollowly.

"Come sit down."

Claire laid her purse on the table just inside the door and walked across the living room to the sofa. Cam joined her and, without being asked, handed her a glass of wine.

"Did you notice anyone following you?"

Claire shook her head, smiling wanly. "No, I don't think so, but I'm not certain I'd notice if there were. Subterfuge is not something I ordinarily need to employ. The safeguards built into our business are enough."

"It probably doesn't matter at this point."

"Are you in trouble?"

"No."

If Claire doubted that answer, she did not challenge it. "I called the other day because there've been more questions. I'm apparently on the list now, too."

"Who approached you—a client?"

"Yes."

"A man?"

"Not the first time, no."

Cam didn't let her surprise show. She'd thought it might have been Doyle. Now she didn't know what to think.

"Someone you know?"

"A new client. Apparently referred by an impeccable source, but I don't know who. I wouldn't."

"And she asked about me?"

"Not directly. Just vague questions about how many people from the Hill used the service. Wondering what kind of company she was in—nothing very specific, and if I hadn't known about the others being questioned, I might not have noticed." She drew a breath, as if steeling herself to continue. "Then a man asked about you."

"What exactly did he ask you?" Cam inquired quietly as she mentally assessed the level of threat.

"He didn't actually use your name. He showed me a photograph and asked me if I knew you."

"Was he a client, too?"

"He posed as one," Claire said with just a hint of distaste. "Ordinarily, I wouldn't have seen him, but he had connections and asked specifically for me. I could tell immediately that something was wrong, because he was uncomfortable."

Cam raised an eyebrow in question.

"The class of people with whom I deal is *not* uncomfortable about our transactions."

"Of course not." They were all civilized and businesslike and emotionally remote. Just like she had been. *When did that change? When we exchanged names?*

"At any rate, he wasn't interested in anything physical. He was clearly trying to get me to talk about the business. When I didn't, he resorted to strong-arm tactics."

"Did he touch you?" Cam stiffened and lightly clasped her fingers over Claire's forearm.

"No, not like that," Claire quickly replied, covering Cam's hand with hers. "He blustered and threatened and suggested that I could go to jail."

"For what?"

"That's what I asked him," Claire said with a dismissive shrug. "He must know this is not some backroom operation with a shady client list. In every sense of the word, this is a high-powered enterprise with even higher-powered clientele. Anyone who tried to expose our clients would probably end up in jail himself."

"That's when he showed you the picture?"

"Yes." She nodded. "I think at that point he realized he wasn't going to get anything from me and just decided to see how I would react."

"Claire," Cam said gently, removing her hand from under Claire's and placing both her hands on her own thighs. "You need to protect yourself, even if that means revealing your association with me."

Claire turned on the sofa until her knees were touching Cam's. She rested her fingers on Cam's blue-jean clad leg. The touch was intimate but not seductive. "I wouldn't do that."

"No matter what happens in the future, if for some reason you are called to testify to anything, don't perjure yourself to protect me. It's impossible to prove what you and I have done in private, and it's unlikely that the financial transactions could be traced. And even if they could, it's debatable whether any laws were broken."

"I'm sure you're right. Nevertheless, I *do* know things that I would not want to be compelled to reveal."

"What are you going to do?"

Claire smiled sadly. "I'm going to retire."

They were both silent, because they both knew what that meant. In all likelihood, they would never see one another again.

"Are you leaving DC?"

"I don't know yet. Probably."

"This whole thing may blow over. I have a feeling it's just a fishing expedition—probably a small group of people trying to dig up any kind of inflammatory information on anyone they possibly

can. There may be no point or direction to this investigation at all."
Cam rubbed her eyes and grimaced. "Still, I think you're making
the right choice, since they've clearly identified you as part of the
organization."

"I have a feeling I'd be out of a job soon anyway. With this kind
of security lapse, the service will need to restructure and probably
replace all the escorts. At this point, everyone is suspect."

"If you ever need anything," Cam said, "you know how to
find me."

"Thank you." Claire smiled and touched Cam's hand in a
fleeting caress. "Part of the reason I was in this business is that it's
very lucrative. You needn't worry about anything like that."

"I just meant—"

Claire placed her fingers gently against Cam's mouth. "I know
what you meant."

They were both very still, Claire's fingers motionless against
Cam's face. A heartbeat later, she stroked the edge of Cam's jaw,
then brushed the hair just above her collar. Claire's eyes searched
Cam's, and in a low voice, her body trembling faintly, she asked,
"Is there someone?"

Cam caught Claire's hand, drew her fingers to her own lips
again, and kissed them softly before letting them go. "Yes."

"I thought there must be," Claire whispered. "The pain in
your eyes is gone."

"I—"

The sound of the doorbell interrupted, and Cam murmured,
"I'm sorry. Excuse me."

Surprised that the doorman had not phoned to announce a
visitor, she quickly crossed to the door and glanced through the
peephole. Too stunned even to curse, she opened the door to Blair
Powell.

"What are you doing in DC?" Cam asked incredulously.

"Sorry to show up unannounced," Blair replied lightly. Hands
in the back pockets of her jeans, she grinned, her face alight with
the pleasure she couldn't hide. When Cam didn't answer, the smile
faded. As awareness of the consternation on Cam's face dawned,
she asked, "What's wrong?"

Cam pulled the door nearly closed, stepped into the hall, and glanced up and down. "Where's the team?"

"My primary detail is at a hotel. The White House detail thinks I'm asleep."

"*God damn* it, Blair, I thought we were past this by now."

"Listen, Cameron," Blair said sharply, confused by Cam's anger. She had expected her to be annoyed, but there was something else in Cam's voice—something that might have been fear—and that was enough to frighten *her*. "I wanted to see you. No, I *needed* to see you."

Cam closed her eyes and sighed. When she spoke, her voice was soft, the edge gone. "I'm sorry. I just can't seem to impress upon you that you can't be running around the city by yourself."

"I wasn't running around. I took a cab." She brushed her hand over Cam's chest and playfully bumped Cam's leg with her hip. "So, can I come in?"

"I'm sorry. No."

"What? Why not?" Blair asked, bewildered. "Don't tell me you're going to get all huffy about the fact that the team doesn't know where I am. If it will make you happier, I'll use my cell phone to call the White House detail commander. I've done it before."

"It's not that." Cam hesitated, searching for the right words, and then realized that there weren't any. "There's someone here."

"Someone…" Blair stared at her, searching Cam's eyes and finding nothing but sorrow. "Are you *finished*, or is she staying the night for round two in the morning?"

"Of course not. Damn it, Blair—"

"My mistake. I *should* have called."

Before Cam could protest, Blair turned on her heel, rapidly crossed the hallway, and pushed through the fire door to the stairwell. The last thing Cam heard was the hollow echo of her footsteps on the stairs.

❖

In a faint circle of light on the corner in front of Cam's apartment building, Blair leaned against a lamp post and, ten minutes later, watched a woman come through the front door. She didn't need to be told who the blond was—she just knew. As if by design, the woman turned in her direction and their eyes met. Blair pushed away from the pole and started up the sidewalk as the other woman walked toward her. They met on the edge of the flickering shadows cast by the streetlight.

"I'd introduce myself," the woman said in a smooth, rich alto, "but that might not be a very good idea."

"No," Blair agreed. "Cameron would only remind us that what we don't know, we can't testify to."

"Precisely."

"Your idea to leave or hers?" Blair asked conversationally.

"Hers. Did you doubt it?"

Blair shrugged. "Now and then."

"You don't have to."

"I might believe that in a decade or so."

The blond smiled wistfully. "I should go—she's terribly worried about you."

"I seem to have that effect on her."

"Apparently, much more than that. You're very fortunate."

"I could say the same thing about you," Blair said without rancor. "You've held her, haven't you?"

"Not the way you think. You have her heart." The blond extended her hand. "Good night then. I don't believe I'll be seeing you again."

Blair took it. "Good night."

And then Claire was gone.

CHAPTER SEVENTEEN

When the elevator doors opened onto Cam's floor, Blair found herself face to face with a very harried-looking Secret Service agent. Cam wore only threadbare jeans, a plain cotton shirt, and loafers without socks. She wasn't even wearing her gun, and aside from seeming just one step away from frantic—which was unusual enough—there was a sheen of desperation in her eyes. And that was beyond extraordinary.

"Where are you going?" Blair asked abruptly, one arm holding the doors open as the bell sounded behind her in the car.

"To look for you."

"What made you think I didn't go straight back to the White House?" Blair stepped out of the elevator. Unimpeded now, the doors slid closed, silencing the warning bell. Still facing each other, Cam and Blair were left in the sudden hush of the deserted hallway.

"I knew you wouldn't go there."

Blair leaned one shoulder against the wall and studied Cam's face. Only the pain of imagining Cam in the arms of the alluring blond kept her from reaching out and stroking away the suffering that was etched in her features. "Where did you think I'd go?"

Cam shrugged. "A club, probably." Her voice was pitched low, oddly flat.

"And someone else's bed?"

Cam flinched as if struck. "Blair, please—"

"Stop." Blair took Cam's hand and pulled her across the hall toward the apartment door. "We can't do this out here."

Wordlessly, Cam fitted her key to the lock, unable to stop the faint trembling in her hands. She'd been more than frightened when Blair had disappeared down the stairwell before she could explain what must have looked like an assignation with another woman. She had been terrified that Blair would rush headlong into the night, driven by pain and anger and betrayal into the solace of a stranger's arms. She'd seen her do it before, and it had been agony to watch even the first time—*before* she'd loved her. Now, it would kill her.

Cam opened the door, and the two of them stepped inside. The room was aglow with moonlight and a sliver of illumination that slanted into the room from beyond a partially closed door on the other side of the apartment. There was a faint trace of fragrance lingering in the air.

"She's very beautiful, isn't she," Blair stated unexpectedly, stopping just inside the entrance to the large living room.

"Blair—"

"We met downstairs."

Cam stared, at a loss, her heart hammering as she listened to the hurt ripple beneath Blair's carefully modulated tones.

"Do you love her?"

"No," Cam exclaimed hoarsely, struggling not to touch her. The hard ring of Blair's words, like steel striking stone, warned her to keep her distance. "Let me expl—"

"You've slept with her though, haven't you?"

"Yes. But—"

"Tonight?"

"No! Not for a long time. Will you—"

"Did she make you co—"

"Christ, Blair. *Stop* it."

"It makes me crazy to think about it," Blair whispered almost to herself, her voice breaking. She was shaking now, too, but she wasn't aware of it.

It was the anguish in her voice more than the cold anger that cracked Cam's resolve. She caught Blair around the waist and pulled her hard against her chest. With her face buried in Blair's hair, she murmured, "I know. God, I know."

Blair's arms came around Cam's shoulders, and her cheek, wet with tears she hadn't known she'd shed, moistened her lover's skin.

"Oh Jesus, don't cry," Cam begged, nearly choking on the desperate need to comfort her. "It's not what you think. I swear to God."

"Don't talk anymore," Blair pleaded, her fingers digging into Cam's arms. "Just, please...make it stop hurting."

"I will," Cam pledged fervently. "I promise, I will."

Cam found Blair's hand and led her through the apartment to the bedroom. By the side of the bed, she tenderly kissed first Blair's eyes, then the corner of her mouth, then the smooth skin of her neck. Lightly, she caressed her jaw, then over her shoulders and lower, thumbs brushing across the swell of her breasts and the rise of her nipples.

Blair caught her lower lip between her teeth and swallowed a small cry. Lids fluttering, eyes unfocused, she rested her hands on Cam's shoulders for support as her lover slowly undressed her.

When Cam unzipped Blair's jeans and slipped her hands underneath the bottom of the T-shirt, smoothing her palms across the flat stomach, Blair's muscles flickered, and for an instant, Cam was afraid she would forget herself. Slowly, she drew the shirt over Blair's head and dropped it to the floor. Then, deliberately, she knelt, feeling Blair's hands move from her shoulders and into her hair. Gently, she hooked her fingers over the waistband of Blair's jeans and worked them down over her hips, lowering them until Blair could kick off her boots and step free of her pants.

Blair stood naked, exposed and vulnerable, as Cam rested her cheek against the hollow at the base of Blair's abdomen. She wrapped her arms around Blair's hips, and, eyes closed, listened to the rush of blood through the arteries and veins just beneath the delicate skin where body joined thigh, her own heart quickening to echo the racing pulse. With one hand, she stroked the soft skin on the inside of Blair's leg, moving upward, gently teasing her thighs apart, circling a fingertip between swollen folds, tracing pulsating ridges again and again until Blair swayed in her arms, her breath a tumble of small moans. Finally, she shifted until she could press her mouth to Blair's clitoris, hard and full with need.

"Cam," Blair whispered, her neck arched, the muscles of her jaw tight as her thighs quivered in expectation.

Parting her lips, Cam enclosed her and sucked gently.

"Oh," Blair breathed, her hands fisting in Cam's hair. "Don't. Not like this—I'll come right away."

From far away, Cam registered the edge of urgency in Blair's voice and, against every instinct, pulled her mouth away. She rose rapidly and gathered Blair close once again. Then with her lips against Blair's ear, she rasped, "I love you so damn much."

"Take off your clothes," Blair implored. "I have to feel you... everywhere."

Cam stepped away while Blair stretched out on top of the bed, her body open, inviting. Eyes glued to her lover, Cam feverishly stripped off shirt and jeans, pulling her loafers off with her clothes. She lowered herself, fitting one leg between Blair's thighs, their breasts just touching as she supported herself on her elbows, her palms framing Blair's head. She rocked slowly into the space between her lover's legs, feeling the prominence of her clitoris against her thigh, the slick patina of need along her skin. Their faces were only inches apart, but she did not claim a kiss yet. With each thrust of her hips, she watched Blair's face grow tense with the rising storm.

Staring into Blair's eyes, her dark gaze holding Blair captive, Cam said fiercely, "Being with you makes me forget ever touching another woman. Being with you makes me forget that anyone else ever touched *me*. Being with you is what keeps me alive."

Blair's body tightened with the presence and power of Cam's voice as much as the press of her flesh, and, as if she had been stroked in some essential place, the words tore through her, obliterating a lifetime of loss. She arched beneath Cam's weight, a cry wrenched from her lips. In surrender, with arms wrapped tightly around her lover, she came.

"God, you're beautiful," Cam gasped as Blair shuddered beneath her.

When Blair quieted, Cam collapsed onto the bed and pulled Blair against the length of her body. She kissed her hair, then her forehead. "I love you."

Blair pressed her face to the hollow between Cam's neck and shoulder and breathed in the familiar scent, wanting nothing more than to be surrounded by her, immersed in her, lost to her. After what might have been a moment, or an hour, she murmured, "I wanted you from the minute you walked into my apartment that first day, all rules and regulations and so goddamned untouchable."

"Not so untouchable," Cam confessed lazily, remembering her first vision of Blair, fresh from the shower in a loose robe, radiating sex and danger. "I was hot by the time I'd left you."

"Good," Blair said with soft satisfaction. "At first, I wanted you because I wanted to control you and not have it be the other way around."

Cam laughed faintly. "Didn't you forget the part about me being such a stud?"

"Oh, that. Yeah, that, too." Blair traced Cam's lips with her fingertips. "But then I wanted you because every time I saw you, you made me ache."

"You destroy me," Cam whispered, tightening her grip on the woman in her arms.

"And now," Blair finished shakily, "I want you because the thought of being without you terrifies me."

"I don't have words to tell you what you mean to me," Cam replied, her voice choked with feeling. "I don't think anything will ever make you understand, except the days turning into weeks and then into months and finally into years...and I'll still be here, loving you."

Blair stroked her hand across Cam's shoulder and down her chest, lingering on her breasts before drawing her fingertips down the center of her abdomen. Cam tensed under her touch, her breath catching.

"There's something about touching you that makes me feel like I'm God," Blair said quietly.

"I know."

"The thought of anyone else—"

"Don't think it. It won't happen."

Suddenly revitalized by the feel of Cam's flesh, Blair shifted on the bed and straddled Cam's hips. She leaned down with one hand on either side of Cam's shoulders, her breasts inches from her lover's face, her eyes bright with purpose. "I do have this thing about what is mine. I don't like to share."

"Neither do I."

"Good," Blair said firmly just before she took Cam's mouth, the kiss hard and possessive.

The kiss lasted a long time. It was more than a kiss, it was an assertion of owning and belonging. Cam opened herself to the depth of Blair's desire, letting her have whatever she demanded, giving her willingly all that she needed, reveling in the surrender that felt like nothing but freedom. When Blair pushed down on the bed and placed her hands between Cam's thighs, Cam arched her back and lifted her hips, offering all that she had. When Blair thrust inside her, fast and hard and deep, a light burst behind her eyes, and her fists closed convulsively on the air. The power of Blair's claim struck deep in her bones, and her blood raced beyond her control. Thighs trembling, breath caught between heartbeats, she came soundlessly, throat closed around the cry, suspended for an eternity between heaven and earth.

Sweat-soaked and shaking, Cam lay gasping. Blair sagged against her, weakly moaning her name.

Somewhere between love and desire, they slept.

CHAPTER EIGHTEEN

Shortly after dawn, Blair was awakened by a faint stirring beside her. She opened her eyes to find Cam seated on the side of the bed, naked. Reaching out one hand, she stroked the length of her spine, feeling the muscles tense and hard beneath her touch. "What's the matter?"

"Nothing," Cam said quickly, turning to face her lover in the gray light. Smiling down at her, she brushed a lock of hair from Blair's cheek, then leaned to kiss her softly.

"Couldn't sleep?" At Cam's slight shrug of assent, Blair teased, "I must be slipping."

"Oh no—believe me, you're not." Cam laughed faintly. "I guess I'm just a little restless. I'm used to being up and working by now."

"Lie down," Blair said, taking her lover's hand and drawing her down beside her. Cam stretched out on her back, and Blair raised her weight on one elbow to search her face. "It's about last night, isn't it?"

"A little."

"You want to tell me who she is?"

"I can't."

"Can't or won't?" Surprisingly, her tone held neither anger nor accusation, only the question.

"I don't know precisely who she is. I never have."

"And if you did?"

"Even then, I probably wouldn't tell you," Cam confessed.

"To protect her?"

"Partly," Cam replied carefully, watching Blair's face. "But mostly to protect you."

"I heard a rumor that you were paying for sex. Is that true?"

If Cam was surprised by the bluntness of the question, she didn't show it. Her dark eyes held Blair's steadily. "Yes."

"With her?"

"Yes."

"Why?" Blair ran her hand down the center of Cam's abdomen, tracing the muscles etched below the skin, her eyes following the path of sinew and bone down the length of her thighs. The sight of her lover's body never failed to make her think of art made flesh. "God only knows, you don't need to."

"It was simpler."

"Simpler?" Blair raised an eyebrow. "Than what?"

"It was easy to schedule. There were no complications. There were no repercussions."

"A simple business arrangement, huh?"

"Something like that."

Blair leaned forward and kissed her, a long slow sensuous kiss that held both reminders of passions past and promises of future pleasures. When she drew back, the corner of her full mouth lifted in a satisfied smile at the slightly unfocused look in her lover's eyes. "Cameron, cut the secret agent stuff. Why did you do it?"

For one of the few times Blair could ever remember, Cam broke eye contact. Silently, she waited for Cam to make a decision, one that she knew was more about them and their future than anything that had happened in the past. At length, Cam met her gaze.

"The day my lover Janet was killed, we'd made love in the morning. But we'd fought, too, about things I thought she should have told me. We parted angry. I hadn't known the details of a dangerous assignment she was involved in until, as it turned out, it was too late. That's how we lived—we kept secrets from one another as a matter of routine. It was comfortable, and it was safe, and I don't think either of us really wanted to change. Neither of us wanted to risk too much. After I watched her die, I couldn't bring myself to make love to anyone else."

"Because you still loved her?" Blair was pleased that her voice did not waver on the words.

"No." Cam blew out a breath. "Because I felt guilty for not having loved her more. I keep thinking maybe I could have changed the way it turned out if I had."

"I'm sorry," Blair whispered.

"It's over," Cam said quietly. She smoothed her palm over Blair's thigh. "But thanks."

"The woman last night—*she's* in love with you, you know."

"No," Cam said quickly, her voice adamant. "It wasn't like that."

Blair ran her fingertips along Cam's jaw to the corner of her mouth. "Not for you, maybe. Maybe."

"We never shared anything like this, Blair," Cam insisted.

"I'm glad. It makes me wild to think of you making love with her. I can't even contemplate you sharing more."

Cam brushed her fingers through the hair at the base of Blair's neck, her thumb moving over the skin behind her ear, a caress at once tender and possessive. "I've never shared anything like this with *anyone* before."

"I love you, Cameron Roberts."

"I like the way that sounds."

"Yeah, me, too."

Blair settled down on the bed and rested her head on Cam's shoulder, her hand lying on the arch of Cam's hip, her fingers slowly moving back and forth. As calmly as she could, she asked, "So why was she here last night?"

"It's not something you should know about. For security reasons."

"Fuck security. Just tell me."

"Someone is investigating the organization she works for," Cam disclosed reluctantly. "My name has come up. She wanted to warn me."

"Jesus." Blair pushed away and sat up in bed, brushing her hair back from her face with both hands, suddenly intense and focused. "Who?"

"I don't know. My guess is it's probably an FBI sting operation. I suppose it could be a RICO investigation out of Justice, but I've never heard that this organization has any mob connections. It's hard to know for sure, but everything I was able to find out about them suggested they didn't."

"Can you be hurt with this?"

Cam was silent.

"*Damn* it, Cameron. Tell me."

"I would lose my security clearance at the very least. If that happens, I'll never do this kind of work again."

"God, how ironic," Blair said sharply. "Under any other circumstances, the thought of that would delight me. But not like this. No one is going to do this to you. What else?"

"I don't know how deep this goes. Apparently, there've been questions about your father, too."

"What are you going to do?"

"I don't know yet. If I could find out who's behind this probe, especially if it isn't officially sanctioned, I might be able to turn it around on them."

"I know someone," Blair said absently, thinking about A.J. An FBI agent, but also a friend, A.J. had given her Cam's home address, although admittedly only after an unusual amount of coercion on Blair's part. She didn't like to compromise her friends, but this was a threat to her lover, and she'd do anything. "Someone I might be able to ask about this."

"No." Cam shot straight up in bed. "*You* cannot come anywhere near this thing. I've jeopardized you just by *telling* you what I have. Don't you realize that under oath you'd have to reveal what I told you—and that by knowing, you're complicit in the crime? You have to let this go, Blair. I never would have told you any of this if we weren't lovers."

"You can't expect me to stand by and watch someone ruin you."

"This may not even be *about* me. I may just be a sideline to the main agenda. Until they make their next move, we don't know what any of this means."

"Oh, come on," Blair said deprecatingly. "They're sending *me* pictures of you in a bar with a woman who might have been sent there to entrap you. Who else are they going to send the pictures to, my father's security director?"

"Just promise me you'll stay out of it," Cam tried again, feeling desperate, "and I promise I'll tell you whatever I discover. Please."

"I'm not going to promise anything right now, because I don't want to lie to you."

"God damn it, Blair—"

"You'd do the same in my position."

For a moment, they stared at one another in tense silence until Cam nodded once, still muttering under her breath.

"Is there anything *else* you haven't told me?" Blair's expression was resolute.

"One thing," Cam finally admitted.

"Jesus, there's more?" Blair's heart skipped a beat. "What?"

Cam sighed. "There's going to be a formal inquiry into the operation in New York City."

"An inquiry? Focused on what?"

"Me. My actions are being questioned." She hesitated, then added reluctantly, "I may be suspended until the internal review is finished."

"When did you learn this?" Blair's voice was steel again.

"I met with Stewart Carlisle last night, and he confirmed it."

"Confirmed it? So you knew there was a possibility of this *before* last night?"

"It was just a possibility," Cam said uneasily.

"It came up during the debriefings last week, didn't it?" Blair's anger was quickly escalating. "*That's* why you left here so suddenly in the middle of the night, and why you haven't been sleeping, and why you look like hell half the time. And you didn't tell me."

"There wasn't anything to tell," Cam insisted. "Nothing had been decided then."

"And while I was relaxing in San Francisco—reading, shopping, talking with your mother—you knew that this could happen. But you didn't think it was important enough to tell me. God damn it, how are we going to have a relationship if this is the way you behave with me?"

Cam stared at her, speechless. "I thought we already *had* a relationship."

"That's not what I mean, and you know it. I love you. It's not just about sex and it's not just about common ground. It's about needing to be with you. It's about needing to be in your life. What's so hard to understand about that?" She threw back the sheets and started to get out of bed. Cam stopped her with a hand on her forearm.

"I'm sorry," Cam said. "I've never done this with anyone. The secrecy—it's a habit—it's what I'm used to. That can change."

"I'm sorry for asking," Blair said, her voice pitched low, her eyes averted.

"No. Don't ever apologize for asking me for what you need, especially when it's the right thing for *both* of us. That's part of love, too, right?"

Blair glanced at her but said nothing.

Cam slid her arm around Blair's waist, pulling her back down on the bed. "From the beginning I've needed you to help me see what *I* needed. You never let up—you never gave up. I hope you never do."

Smiling at that, Blair curled against the welcoming warmth and strength of Cam's body, murmuring, "You're going to drive me crazy."

"Yeah, but I love you like crazy."

"I suppose there is that."

"Before you fall asleep, you need to make a call," Cam said quietly.

"To who?"

"The White House detail commander. When you're not there in the morning, he's going to start a manhunt."

Blair sighed and rolled over, reaching for her cell phone on the bedside table. "I'll call one of my friends on the inside. That should take care of it."

"Good," Cam replied. "Because I have plans for you in the morning."

❖

Just after eight the next morning, they stepped into the shower together and kissed while the water cascaded over them. Then, they took turns soaping each other's bodies until Cam wordlessly placed the bar on the small shelf behind her, took Blair's shoulders in both hands, and pressed her against the tiled back wall of the shower. With her mouth covering Blair's, she slid her fingers, wet with water and Blair's arousal, between Blair's thighs, moving slowly, pushing ever deeper, until she felt the walls of Blair's soul fall before her touch.

Cam held her lover upright with the sheer strength of an arm pinioning her to the wall and the pressure of her hips against Blair's. As she moved within her, forcing her ever closer to a precipice from which there was no return, she felt Blair build to orgasm, jerking against her body, convulsing around her hand, and she smiled.

"What was that all about?" Blair gasped a moment later, her eyes still dazed.

"Just this thing I have about what's mine," Cam murmured.

"You made your point quite effectively." Blair slipped her palm to the back of Cam's neck, drawing her close.

"Problem with that?" Cam asked from a breath away.

"Not a one." And then Blair kissed her.

A few minutes later as Blair toweled her hair, admiring Cam's ass in the mirror, her cell phone rang on the counter nearby. She reached for it and listened a second. "All right."

Naked, Cam turned and raised an inquiring eyebrow when she saw the expression on Blair's face. "What?"

"You might want to find your jeans," Blair said in an oddly disembodied voice. "My father is on his way up."

CHAPTER NINETEEN

The two of them scrambled for their clothes and had barely finished zipping and buttoning when a sharp rap sounded on the door. Cam crossed the living room, peered through the peephole, and hastily pulled open the door.

"Good morning, Mr. President."

"Agent Roberts."

He was wearing a navy blue suit, white shirt, and striped tie. On the near side of fifty, he looked collegiate and fit, with a natural tan that was present year-round. Cam could see Blair in his blue eyes, his physical presence, and his intensity. Irrationally, she liked him because of that.

"Please, come in, sir."

"You can wait outside, Tom," Andrew Powell said to the clean-shaven, slender African-American man who stood just behind his right shoulder.

"That would not be advisable, sir," the agent replied in a deep rumbling baritone.

Cam glanced right and then left, noting the positions of three other agents stationed at intervals in the hallway outside her apartment door. She knew there would be at least one additional agent stationed in each of the stairwells at either end of the hallway, another downstairs in the lobby by the elevator, and half a dozen outside in the two or three vehicles idling out front. She also knew it was SOP for the president never to be alone with anyone other than immediate family. It was an immutable rule.

"I believe that Secret Service Agent Roberts and my daughter can be trusted," the president said as Cam stepped aside to let him pass.

As the president disappeared behind her, she looked into the exasperated countenance of the security chief assigned to protect the most powerful man on the planet, but there was nothing to say. She sympathized with him as only she could, because the president, very much like his daughter, eschewed security when it suited him. She closed the door and turned around in time to see Blair hug her father briefly before moving away to face him with a question in her eyes.

"What's going on, Dad?" Blair asked. "What's wrong?"

"I'll just wait in the other room," Cam said quietly, turning to walk across the living room to the small second bedroom, which served as her study and home office.

It occurred to her that both she and Blair looked like they had just stepped from the shower, which of course, they had. Their hair was wet, Blair was without makeup, and both of them were wearing last night's discarded clothing. She glanced surreptitiously around the room, hoping that they hadn't left a trail of undergarments behind. *Jesus, what an impression we must be making.*

"I think you should probably stay, Agent Roberts," Andrew Powell said in a smooth, well-modulated tone that on the surface didn't sound like the order it was. His expression was mild as he regarded first Cam and then his daughter, but his deep-blue eyes were laser-sharp.

"Yes, sir." Cam was not entirely certain what the hell to do with him in her apartment. "Can I get you anything, Mr. President? Coffee, maybe?"

"Fine." He looked from one to the other of them, smiling faintly. "I'd wager that you two are about ready for some. Sorry to arrive before breakfast."

"It'll just take a minute." Cam was trying desperately not to blush.

"Come sit down, Dad." Blair indicated the sofa and nearby matching chairs grouped in front of the windows. When they were seated, she on the sofa, he on the chair across from her, Blair asked again, "What are you doing here?"

"I thought we should talk." Andrew Powell glanced up as Cam joined them.

"About what?"

"About Lucinda Washburn's six a.m. visit to my office this morning."

"Oh," Blair commented. "Well—"

He stopped her with a quick wave of his hand. "First of all, it's not really any of my business. If it weren't for the...unusual circumstances in which we find ourselves, I wouldn't even mention it."

"Well, if it weren't for our *circumstances,* neither would have Lucinda, in all likelihood," Blair rejoined dryly.

"She shouldn't have brought it up with *you* at all." There was a trace of ire in his tone that was reflected in the flash of his eyes. "It's a family matter."

"She was doing her job," Blair pointed out without animosity. "I understand that. Besides, I came down here to talk to her on my own."

Cam wasn't entirely certain what to do, but she decided that since she had been invited, she would sit where she belonged, next to Blair. Blair glanced at her quickly, almost apologetically, and then regarded her father again.

"Luce was concerned about a picture of me in an intimate moment that turned up in the *Post* two days ago," Blair said matter-of-factly. "I was careless. I'm sorry. It wasn't intended."

"I'm the one responsible for that, sir," Cam interjected quickly, ignoring Blair's swift look of displeasure. "I let someone get close enough to take the photo—"

"There's no way to prevent something like that one hundred percent of the time," the president said with no apparent concern. "There's certainly no way to avoid publicity."

"I've tried," Blair murmured.

"I'm sorry that you've had to." Andrew Powell leaned forward to search his daughter's face.

She was silent, and Cam saw her hands tremble where they rested on her thighs.

"At any rate," the president continued, "I saw the photo. It seemed innocent enough to me."

"It wasn't a very good image," Blair said flatly. "Next time it might be clearer."

"Apparently that's what my chief of staff is worried about."
He shrugged. "She says it's a woman with you."

"Yes."

"And you've tried to keep that a secret, too?"

"It seemed the wisest thing to do."

He sighed. "If I had more time, I'd probably be able to do this
a little more diplomatically, but I don't. I'm sorry."

"You don't need to be." Blair's voice was uninflected, her
face impossible to read. "Fire away."

Her father regarded Blair intently, as if trying to delve
beneath the cool veneer to the heat below. "Is it serious...this
relationship?"

Cam cleared her throat. "Sir—"

"Yes," Blair interrupted emphatically. "Very."

"Were you going to tell me about her?"

"Uh—" Cam began.

"Eventually," Blair said hurriedly. "It's complicated."

Cam blew out a breath and leaned forward, meeting the
commander in chief's gaze steadily. "That would be me in the
photo, sir."

"I see." He looked thoughtful for a moment and then nodded,
once. "That further *complicates* the situation, doesn't it?"

"Dad, please." Blair was emphatic. "I want to keep Cam's
name out of things, if I—"

"That's not necessary," Cam interjected. "I have nothing to
hide, sir, nor do I have any regrets."

"The point is," Blair said with the first hint of exasperation,
"this could be misconstrued, considering Cam's official relationship
to me. I don't want there to be any repercus—"

Her voice tight, Cam stated forcefully, "I take full
responsibility—"

"Damn it, Cameron," Blair seethed, forgetting her father for a
moment as she turned to look into Cam's face. "Will you just *once*
let me take care of you?"

Cam stared, words failing her.

The president laughed. "I can see that Lucinda has absolutely
no idea just how complicated this is."

The three of them looked from one to the other, and then they all laughed, the tension in the room noticeably ebbing. To Cam's surprise, Blair reached over and took her hand with a softly muttered, "Sorry," before turning to her father again.

"Lucinda is concerned about backlash and the potential damage to your reelection campaign."

"Yes, I know. She outlined that for me this morning. In detail." He grimaced. "There were graphs involved."

"She has a point," Blair said, her voice subdued. Without realizing it, she closed her fingers tightly around Cam's. "Political reputations have been jeopardized by less, and I'm sure you still need to raise reelection funds. Backers can be fickle."

"It's a very difficult thing to gauge," the president said contemplatively. "There are only so many factors we can control— or spin—at one time. I'm sure that someone on my staff will be doing some kind of poll within the next day or so, carefully disguised so that no one will realize they're really talking about us. Then someone else will draw up a list of possible voter responses, and the director of communications will draft a speech in the event that I need to make a position statement, and Lucinda will advise Aaron on exactly what he should say in the press briefings—all of which means absolutely nothing in the final analysis."

"This is still going to be a volatile topic, Dad," Blair insisted.

"And there's going to be considerable criticism because we were attempting to hide our relationship," Cam said carefully. "Some will call it cowardice; others subterfuge. We're likely to anger people on both sides of the fence."

"Well, I'm not certain that Lucinda's suggestion that you put your relationship on hold for more than a year until the nomination is secured is particularly practical or even useful."

Cam stiffened, feeling as if she'd been struck; she struggled not to look at Blair.

"I'm not going to do that," Blair said, her voice calm.

"And I'm not asking you to," her father said. "That's why I'm here. Mostly, I wanted to tell you to do whatever you choose in terms of discussing or *not* discussing this—or anything else—with the press. Whatever the consequences, we'll deal with them, but we are not about to allow our private lives to be dictated by public opinion. That's not the message I intend to send about this office—or about us."

He glanced at his watch, then at Cam. "I still have a few minutes, Agent Roberts. Any chance for that coffee now?"

"Right away, sir."

"Excellent." Smiling, the president extended his hand. "And when it's just family, I'm Andrew."

Nonplussed, Cam glanced at Blair, who was grinning wickedly. Recovering quickly, she returned his handshake. "Thank you, sir. And please...call me Cam. Sir."

Cam thought she heard Blair's soft laughter as she headed for the kitchen.

❖

Fifteen minutes later, after coffee and a conversation that centered on Blair's plans for her gallery showing in the fall, Blair and Cam walked the president to the door. After it closed behind him, they stood staring at one another, both still slightly stunned.

"He gets to the point, doesn't he?" Cam remarked.

"Well, he surprised me," Blair admitted, her expression pensive. She walked to the sofa and rested her hips against the arm. "We've never exactly been big on personal discussions. I always assumed he knew, because he's never asked about the men in my life. Or absence of them, either. It's just not something we talked about."

"Maybe he was waiting for you to bring it up."

"Maybe. He seemed...okay about us, don't you think?"

Cam thought about the conversation, although it was hard to be objective when the president of the United States was inquiring about her love life. "Yeah. He seemed...fine." She ran a hand through her hair and grinned at Blair. "Jesus."

"Do I want to know how *he* knew I was here?"

"Most likely someone on the White House security detail told him. If they really didn't have a very good idea of where you were, they'd have called Mac, and he would have called me." That had happened before, but she saw no reason to remind Blair that she had very little true freedom, despite appearances.

Blair made a disgusted sound.

"He's the president," Cam pointed out reasonably. "If there's something he wants to know, it's pretty unlikely that he wouldn't be able to find out."

Cam crossed to Blair, took her hand, and drew her around to the front of the sofa, then tugged her down with her. As Blair's fingers laced in hers, she asked quietly, "Why didn't you tell me that Lucinda Washburn doesn't want you to see me anymore?"

"If you'll recall," Blair said pointedly, "we were discussing other matters last evening. And then we weren't *discussing* at all."

Ignoring the evasive answer, Cam persisted. "There was time this morning when we were talking about *my* problems."

Blair said nothing, and for the briefest moment, she looked away.

"It's not just my problems and my life that we have to share," Cam said gently. "This isn't something you should have to face by yourself. It involves both of us."

Suddenly, Blair stood and strode to the opposite side of the room. She turned and faced Cam across the distance. "I wasn't sure what you would say. I was...afraid...that you would agree with her. That you would..."

As Blair's voice trailed off, Cam got to her feet. "You were afraid that I would disappear, weren't you?"

Blair nodded solemnly, the pain swimming in her eyes.

In a heartbeat, Cam closed the space between them and placed both hands on Blair's shoulders. Then she found Blair's eyes and held her gaze steadily. "And you would have been right—a few months ago, that's probably exactly what I would have considered. I don't know that I would've been able to do it—I've never been able to stay away from you." She skimmed her fingers along Blair's rigid jaw. "Never been able to stop wanting you. But, to keep you safe, I might have wanted to try."

Blair's eyes darkened, the blue shading nearly to black. Cam felt Blair stiffen under her hands, sensed her desire to run. Holding onto her, she repeated, "A few months ago...maybe. Definitely not now."

"I don't know what I would do." Blair's voice wavered and she clamped down hard on the old pain. The *old* pain—not Cam's doing, but so hard to remember that. "I don't think I could stand it."

"No—neither could I."

Blair wrapped her arms around Cam's waist and stepped into her embrace, the fear that had coiled around her heart since the moment her father had walked into the room loosening its hold. She pressed her lips to Cam's neck, then leaned back to look at her lover.

"That doesn't mean we've heard the end of this," Blair warned, her voice stronger, the anguish extinguished by the solid reassurance of Cam's body, the certainty of her words. "Just because my father believes that nothing can damage his reputation or hurt his reelection prospects, doesn't necessarily mean it's true. He is an excellent leader, but sometimes he refuses to believe he's not invincible. He forgets to watch his back."

"I have a feeling that's what Lucinda Washburn is for," Cam commented dryly. "And I have a feeling she won't give up easily."

"Most definitely not. I'm sure we'll be hearing from her again."

Cam drew Blair closer and rested her cheek against her lover's. Softly, she murmured, "Let's deal with that when we have to. For the time being, we'll carry on."

"I love you," Blair whispered, so softly Cam could barely hear her.

"Good thing. I love you, too." Then Cam sighed, kissed Blair's temple, and stepped back. "We need to call the team and make plans to go back to New York—unless you're staying down here?"

"Not for a moment longer than I have to," Blair said adamantly. "Although if we *could* stay here..."

"We could," Cam countered, "but we'd still need to call the team."

"I know," Blair said with a sigh of her own, taking her first real opportunity to survey Cam's apartment in daylight. She turned slowly, admiring the clean, modern style of the layout and furnishings, and her eyes stopped on something familiar on the far wall. She gasped involuntarily.

Cam followed her gaze and grinned.

"When did you get those?" Blair asked, clearly astonished.

"At the gallery opening last winter."

"Right after we met?" Blair's eyes held a question. *Did you know?*

"Yes." Cam regarded the series of charcoal nudes, finding them just as beautiful as she had the first time she'd seen them. "I knew they were yours, even though you didn't sign them with your own name."

"How?" Blair's voice was hushed.

"I'd seen the work in your loft the first time I came for a briefing. Your style is distinctive."

Blair stared at her. "Why did you buy them?"

"Because they're very good." After a beat, she added, "And because they're yours. At the time, I thought that was as close to you as I would ever get."

Their eyes caught and held, a flame arcing between them.

"We don't have to call the team right away, do we?" Blair's voice was husky as she moved toward her lover.

Watching the color rise along Blair's throat, Cam swallowed as she tightened inside and throbbed. Thickly, she replied, "I think we might have a little bit of time."

CHAPTER TWENTY

Blair leaned against the dresser in Cam's bedroom, wearing a pair of her lover's chinos that were a little too long and one of her blue button-front shirts that was a tad large. She liked wearing Cam's clothes. *Silly. You're hardly a teenager and this isn't puppy love.* But it felt good just the same. "Do you know what I'd really like to do?"

"What?" Cam looked up from where she sat on the side of the bed pulling on her socks and loafers. The whimsical note in Blair's voice made her smile. A faint blush still colored Blair's skin from their recent lovemaking, and the memory of those moments twisted through her, making her unexpectedly catch her breath. "What would you like, darling?"

For an instant, Blair was speechless. The tone of Cam's voice, almost more than the endearment, shook her with its intimacy. *Oh my God, what you do to me.*

"Blair?" Cam repeated with a quizzical smile.

"I...I'd like to order a pizza, get two or three videos, and spend the day on the sofa watching bad science fiction movies with you."

Cam stopped what she was doing, her smile turning to an expression of regret. Softly, she said, "I know. So would I. I'm sorry that we can't. If I were anyone else—"

"No, not true," Blair said adamantly, crossing the room quickly to nestle between Cam's parted thighs. Looking down, her mouth still bruised with their kisses, she brushed her fingers gently through Cam's hair. "No. If *I* were anyone else we might be able to do that. Even if you weren't my security chief, it would still be very difficult for us to do something that simple. Your position may complicate things for us, but it didn't create my problems."

The thinly veiled pain in Blair's voice ripped at Cam, because she knew it was a pain she could not ease. Resting her forehead against Blair's midsection, her arms lightly clasping her lover's waist, Cam murmured, "It won't always be this way."

"I know. I have to believe that."

Cam looked up, her dark eyes swirling with emotion. "I'd do anything to be able to take you out for a late lunch and then stroll around Dupont Circle holding your hand, just letting whatever happens, happen. I'd give you that if I could."

"Yes, I know you would." Blair knelt and snugged her body between Cam's legs, her eyes meeting her lover's. "And that's what makes *not* being able to do that bearable. Sometimes knowing you understand is the only thing that makes it bearable."

"Christ, I love you," Cam breathed, her fingers lightly tracing Blair's face. Then she kissed Blair's forehead and finally, because she had to, she glanced at her watch. "The team should be downstairs by now. Are you ready?"

Blair lingered for just a moment, her hands slowly caressing Cam's shoulders and chest, loving the heat of her lover through the cloth, unwilling to let her go because she didn't know how long it would be before she could touch her this way again. Then, reluctantly, she pushed herself upright, straightened her shoulders, and said firmly, "Yes. I'm ready."

They didn't stop to kiss at the door of Cam's apartment. Their goodbyes had already been said. Instead, they walked directly to the elevator, waited for the doors to open, and rode down to the lobby in silence. They stood close together, their arms lightly touching.

As they crossed the brightly lit lobby toward the front doors, beyond which Cam could see the Suburban idling at the curb with several agents inside and Stark waiting by the rear door, the building's security guard called out.

"Excuse me. There's a package for you, Ms. Roberts."

At her look of surprise, he added, "The courier said not to phone up but that I should give it to you when you came downstairs."

"Courier?" Reflexively, Cam glanced around the lobby, one hand unbuttoning her blazer, then closing over the grip of her automatic. Other than the security guard, she and Blair were alone. Nevertheless, she spoke quickly into her wrist microphone. "Mac, secure the street. Stark—inside."

Outside, the Suburban's doors flew open and agents piled out, weapons drawn. Cam positioned her body between Blair and the glass front doors, one hand cupped lightly under Blair's right elbow, blocking a direct sightline from the outside to the president's daughter while waiting for Stark to enter the building and back her up.

"What is it?" Blair asked urgently.

"Probably nothing," Cam said in a low, controlled voice. "But it's unusual for anything to be delivered to me here. No one should have this address except for Treasury, and they don't leave *anything* without a signature and ID check."

"What...?"

Stark approached at a near run, and Cam instructed briskly, "Escort Ms. Powell to the vehicle and evacuate to fifteen hundred yards. Do it now."

Looking directly at the guard, she said, "Step away from the desk."

Her tone left no room for question and to his credit, he didn't. He simply slid off his stool and moved hurriedly around the front of the waist-high partition, which enclosed the building's closed-circuit security monitors.

"Cam?" Blair protested, her voice rife with alarm as Stark began to direct her to the door.

"*Evacuate her,* Stark," Cam ordered without turning back, walking around the partition and studying the package sitting on the shelf. It was an oversized manila envelope, the kind that had been delivered to Blair's apartment the day before. Without touching it, she leaned closer and studied her address, hand-printed with bold strokes in magic marker. There was no return address. Outside the vehicles screamed away from the curb and, knowing that Blair was safe, Cam felt the tightness in her chest ease.

She had no reason to suspect that the parcel's contents were incendiary or explosive, especially since the security guard had already handled it with no particular regard for caution. She lifted it by the corner. It was light, and she assumed that it held photographs or documents of some kind.

"Should I call for a bomb squad?" The guard's voice was high with tension.

"No. Thanks. I've got it."

"Yes, ma'am." He was clearly stunned by the rapid evacuation of the remarkably familiar looking blond whose name he couldn't quite place and just as taken aback by 17 B's commanding attitude.

"Someone will be by a bit later to talk to you about the delivery. Write down anything you can remember about it now—exact time of delivery, description of the courier, exactly what he said."

"She."

"What?" Cam asked quickly.

"She—it was a woman."

"Okay. Fine. Get it all down." Cam glanced up to the corner of the room at the slowly panning video camera. "And I want copies of the surveillance tapes—streetside and in here."

"I'll need permission from the managers for that."

She walked over to him and held out her ID. "Get it."

"Yes, ma'am." He swallowed and straightened his shoulders. "Right away."

"Good."

She flashed him a wave as she walked out the door. Once on the street, she began walking north and radioed her location to Mac. Three minutes later, the lead Suburban, Stark at the wheel, appeared from around a corner and pulled up beside her.

Once settled in the back with Blair across from her, Cam swiveled forward and said through the privacy partition, "All clear for the airport, Stark. Nice execution, by the way." When she turned back, she was nearly pinned to her seat by the fire shooting from Blair's blue eyes.

"Was that really necessary?" Blair demanded hotly.

"What?"

"Dragging me out of there like that."

"I could hardly let you stand in harm's way if there was any possibility that someone had delivered a volatile package," Cam said reasonably.

"Oh, I see, but it's okay if you get blown into a few million pieces?" Blair bit off each word as she fisted her hands by her sides to stop the trembling.

"There was very little chance of that, considering that the guard had already handled it—unless someone was watching for me to pick it and planned to trigger the device with a remote detonator. It was highly unlikely that it would pose any real danger."

"But you were careful enough to get *me* out of the building."

"Of course," Cam said with a hint of genuine confusion in her voice. "Even the slightest risk to you is unacceptable."

"You don't have a clue what this does to me, do you?" Blair asked incredulously.

"It was just routine, Blair," Cam began patiently. "I know you dislike being handled, and I wouldn't do it if it weren't absolutely necessary."

"No—that's not what I'm talking about."

"I don't—"

"Do you have *any* idea how I felt watching you get shot that day?" She spoke as if they were no longer in the car but back on the street in front of her apartment building on that beautiful sunny afternoon that had become the setting of her worst nightmare. Her voice was low and tormented. "Do you *know* what that did to me to see you lying on the sidewalk, blood pouring from your chest, certain you were dying? Knowing I couldn't touch you—couldn't stop it? That I was losing you, too?"

Cam's face drained of color. Her voice was hoarse as she whispered, "Yes. I know."

Stunned by the transformation in her usually imperturbable lover, Blair suddenly realized what she had said, and she knew instantly that Cam must have experienced almost the same thing the day Janet had died. "Jesus, Cameron, I'm so sorry. I didn't think."

Cam held up her hand. "No. It's all right." She cleared her throat, chased the demons away. "I never realized something like today would make you feel that way...I'm sorry. I would never want you to go through that again."

"I can't seem to get used to you putting me first." Blair leaned forward, her fingers touching Cam's hand. "Not just physically but the caring—all of it. It will take a little practice."

"I don't put you first just because of the job, Blair," Cam said emphatically. "I do it because I love you, and I know that if the situation called for it, you'd do the same."

Blair nodded. She knew Cam was right. It wasn't so much about who protected whom, but much more about the urgency they both felt to keep the other safe. She would die before she'd let anyone harm Cam.

"Just don't get hurt, okay?" Blair's voice broke.

"I won't. I promise."

As the vehicles turned off the road into the airport, they smiled at each other, peace following softly in the wake of trust.

❖

Cam took Mac aside and spoke to him privately before they boarded. He didn't join them for the flight but, instead, left the airport with the local detail in one of the Suburbans.

Once on the plane, after everyone was situated, Blair asked Cam, "Where did Mac go?"

"I asked him to talk with the guard at my building. He'll catch a later flight."

"Is he inquiring...officially?"

Cam shrugged. "We're skirting the definitions a bit. It involves you peripherally, so I don't mind using official resources to look into it. But the nature of the information is...sensitive."

Thinking of the photos of the two of them kissing and Cam with a strange woman in a bar, Blair snorted. "Rather."

"So I'm not filing any paper on what we find."

"Do they *all* know about us?" Blair asked quietly. She would have thought she'd hate that—relative strangers knowing about her private life—but she found that she didn't. These men and women weren't strangers. Not anymore.

"Mac and Stark do. I needed their help." Cam glanced at Blair, suddenly concerned. "Jesus. I should have asked you before I said anything to them. I'm sorr—"

Blair touched her hand. "It's okay. I don't care. I just wanted to know." She nodded toward the briefcase open on Cam's lap. "Are you going to open that envelope?"

"Not yet." Cam regarded the still-unopened package and shook her head. "If we're lucky, there'll be forensic evidence on the contents. I want to open it somewhere it can be examined properly."

"Do you know someone you can trust to do that for you?"

"Maybe. Savard has been helping out, too." At Blair's raised eyebrow, she clarified, "Stark's suggestion. And a good one. I'll call her when we get to New York City."

"I want to be there."

Cam's first reaction was to say no, and then she realized that she couldn't. It was likely that whatever was inside had something to do with her or Blair or both of them, and she had promised Blair that she would not shut her out. She didn't like it, because her instinct was to keep Blair far away from anything that might potentially endanger her—emotionally *or* physically. But they had come too far for that now.

"All right."

Pleased, Blair rested her fingers on Cam's thigh. "Thank you."

CHAPTER TWENTY-ONE

It was early evening by the time they landed in New York and made the trek to Blair's apartment in Manhattan. As they disembarked in front of the building, Cam said to Stark, "Would you mind staying a bit longer, Agent?"

Stark, who was technically off shift, having already worked twenty-four hours overtime because of Egret's unexpected trip to DC *and* having missed her date with Savard in the bargain, said immediately, "No problem, ma'am. I'll be in the command center."

"Very well."

The agents sorted themselves out, some proceeding upstairs with Stark for the evening shift and others signing out for the night. Finally alone, Cam and Blair took the keyed elevator to Blair's apartment.

Once inside, Cam said, "I need to give Mac a call and see if he's turned up anything."

Blair dropped her overnight bag inside the door. "Are you hungry? I can fix us something."

"That would be great." Cam shed her jacket but kept her shoulder harness on over her blended-silk dress shirt. "I'll give you a hand in a minute."

Smiling, Blair shook her head. "Just do what you need to do."

Cam settled into one of the fabric sling chairs, which, along with the sofa, defined the loft's central living area, and picked up the phone. She dialed and after a minute said, "It's Roberts. Where are you?...Turn up anything?...Do you have the tapes?...Okay, fine. Call me when you get in...yes...right."

With an audible breath, she replaced the receiver and came around the breakfast bar into the kitchen where Blair was slicing mushrooms on a cutting board. A pot of water boiled on the cook top to her right. "Can I do something?"

"Plates. What did he say?" Blair asked as she rinsed several tomatoes under the faucet and then cubed them.

"The security guard didn't have much more to offer than what he'd already told me. The package was dropped off at 7:52 this morning."

"Huh—just before my father arrived. Does that mean anything?"

"I don't know. I doubt it."

"What did he say about the courier?"

"He doesn't remember anything in particular except that it was a woman—Caucasian, medium height, twenty-five, maybe thirty. Mac has the tapes and is bringing them back here. Then we can compare them with our surveillance videos from downstairs when the first envelope was delivered here yesterday. If we get lucky, maybe we'll be able to ID her."

"A woman delivered it?" Blair inquired in surprise. "Like last time?"

"Apparently." Cam shrugged. "That probably doesn't mean anything either. Half the couriers are women these days. Besides, it's doubtful that whoever is behind this would deliver it in person. But we have to check it out."

"I suppose you're right," Blair said contemplatively as she placed a handful of pasta in the boiling water.

"What?" Cam asked, noting Blair's expression.

"It's probably nothing."

"What is it? At this point, we can't afford to overlook anything."

"When I called my friend A.J. to get your home address last night...I thought it was really odd. She was very reluctant to give it to me."

"A.J.? Who's she?"

"An FBI agent stationed at Bureau headquarters in DC. She's an information specialist."

"An FBI agent has been feeding you classified information?" Cam exclaimed incredulously. "Holy Christ. She could lose her job for that—or worse."

"She's discreet, and I don't ask her for much. We're old friends from prep school."

"I never realized you had such an impressive network of insiders," Cam said appreciatively. *That explains a lot about how she's been able to keep such a low profile about her private life all these years. She's had help keeping the information under wraps.*

It was Blair's turn to shrug. Then she grinned sheepishly. "I've had a long time to acquire them."

"So," Cam continued, "just how well do you know her?"

Blair smiled enigmatically.

"Aha," Cam said, arching an eyebrow. "Recently?" There was just a touch of heat in her voice.

Blair laughed. "It's not what you're thinking, surprisingly enough. I covered for her a few times when she was out all night on a date, back when schools actually tried to keep track of such things. She's the daughter of a senator—one who gave my father a run for his money in the primaries, actually. We have a lot in common."

"And you trust her?"

"Absolutely."

"Enough to tell her about this?"

"Yesterday morning I would have said yes." Blair hesitated as she dished out pasta and sautéed vegetables. "Last night she sounded...off. Like she wanted to say something, but didn't."

"Or couldn't," Cam countered.

They carried the plates to the breakfast bar and sat side by side.

"What do you mean?"

"Did you call her at work?"

"Yes. But I was circumspect. I didn't use your name."

"Still," Cam said around bites, "she knows everything going in and out of there is taped. And besides, maybe she's more loyal to the Bureau than to you, especially if she thinks *I'm* dirty. Remember, she doesn't know me at all."

"I hadn't considered that," Blair said softly. The thought of anyone, but especially a friend, thinking ill of Cam bothered her. She was at once angry and saddened. Unconsciously, she dropped her hand onto Cam's thigh, stroking her softly. "Do you think I should try talking to her?"

"Not yet. Maybe we'll know more after we see what's in the newest delivery." Cam covered Blair's hand with hers. "As soon as we're done, I'm going to find out if Savard is available to walk us through the lab."

"Cam, it's almost eight. Do you really think she'll be able to do anything tonight?"

"The Bureau's open twenty-four hours a day. We can always ask."

❖

Twenty minutes later, Cam, perched on a stool at the breakfast bar, used the nearby wall phone to call down to the command center for Stark.

"Yes, Commander?"

"I'd like to arrange a meeting with Special Agent Savard this evening. I'd like you to come along."

"Sure. Absolutely," Stark said, then added hastily, "Yes, ma'am."

"Would you happen to have the number where she's staying?"

"Uh—right here, yes." Stark had just finished talking to Renee moments before. "Would you like me to call, or..."

"Best let me do that. But thanks."

Stark gave her the number and Cam jotted it down. "Fine. Would you get one of the vehicles and wait for us downstairs, please."

Us, Stark thought. *Huh.*

"Also, advise the night shift to stand down. You and I will cover Egret."

"Roger, Commander."

After Cam hung up, Blair asked, "Are you sure we should involve them?"

"No, not really." Cam swiveled around on the stool until her back was to the counter and regarded Blair. Tired, she rubbed her eyes. The headache was back. "But unfortunately, we need to do some digging and some legwork, and I don't see that we have much choice. Hopefully, if things go bad, I can keep them out of it."

"Go bad?" Blair worked to keep her voice casual.

"If I'm wrong, and I really am the primary target of whoever is digging around in DC, then something may break—or leak—anytime. If I go down in a big way, I don't want anyone else going with me."

"That's *not* going to happen," Blair said emphatically, eyes blazing.

"We have to be prepared for that eventuality. And if it happens, you're going to need to get distance from me, too."

"No. Wrong again, Commander."

Softly, Cam said, "It will have to be done. I would want it that way even if you *weren't* the first daughter. If this is some junior reporter's bid for fame, it'll probably turn into an exposition piece on degeneracy in the nation's capitol or security breaches within the Secret Service or God knows what else. The story will be huge...and ugly. If that happens, even the best spin doctors on your father's staff won't be able to fix it. Your name and his can't be linked to it—or to me." Before Blair could object, Cam added, "You know I'm right."

"Define what *exactly* you mean by distance, Cameron," Blair said steadily, her voice sharp-edged and cold. "A week, a month—six goddamned years?"

"Please, Blair," Cam said wearily, sagging perceptibly. "Do you honestly think I'd want that? You can't think it would be easy for me, can you?"

There was no fire in her voice, only a deep sadness. It was one of the few times that Blair had ever seen Cam show even the slightest hint of defeat. It was so unusual, it shocked her free of her anger. With brutal clarity, she saw that Cam was facing the potential destruction of her career as well as the threat to their relationship. Immediately, she slipped her arms around Cam's shoulders and pressed Cam's cheek against her breasts. To her surprise, Cam's arms came around her waist and tightened. Blair could feel her tremble.

"Hey." Tenderly, Blair kissed the top of Cam's head. "It's going to be okay. We'll figure out what this is all about, and we'll find out who's behind it, and we'll put an end to it. Whatever happens, there's no way you're getting rid of me."

"I'd die for you without even thinking about it," Cam murmured hoarsely, her eyes closed, just holding on. "But I can't imagine living without you. Not now."

Listening to Cam's words, Blair pulled her closer still, a strange peace suffusing her.

"You don't have to worry, because you won't ever have to."

❖

Forty-five minutes later, Stark, Cam, and Blair stood outside the rear entrance of a nondescript six-story stone building in midtown Manhattan. Precisely at the designated time, Savard keyed the security lock and opened the door.

"Commander," she said when she saw Cam, her eyes moving over Stark's face with a faint smile, then stopping in surprise when they met Blair's. "Good evening, Ms. Powell."

"Hi, Renee," Blair replied. "How are you feeling?"

"Okay. I'll be better when I can get out of this damn thing," Savard said, indicating the sling tethering her left arm to her chest. "Follow me. The security cameras are timed back here. We've got a few minutes."

Savard led them through a warren of beige hallways that were indistinguishable from one another. All the office doors were closed and the harsh fluorescent lights spaced at intervals overhead cast everything in the same impersonal institutional glare. Opening the door to a stairwell, she said, "The lab's on the third floor. There's a video camera in the main elevators, so I thought we might as well walk."

"Good idea," Cam replied. It was doubtful that anyone would actually review the routine surveillance tapes in the absence of any reason to do so, but the less time their little group was recorded, the better.

The four of them climbed single file and then walked silently through yet another corridor to the last door on the right. Savard pushed it open, and they stepped into a large brightly lit space divided into work stations by laboratory benches and tables containing high-tech analytical equipment.

Most of the technicians who worked in the lab were regular eight-to-fivers, and the vast area was empty save for a lone white-coated figure hunched over a lab bench at the far end of the room. As the group approached, Savard called out, "Hey, Sammy."

A pale, bespectacled young man with a mildly befuddled expression on his face and a thatch of red hair badly in need of a cut glanced in their direction. Then, as if suddenly remembering an appointment, he smiled broadly. "Hey, Renee. You got something for me?"

"Yep." Savard pointed to the manila envelope in Cam's hand. "I need you to take a look at whatever's inside and do your magic. Anything you can give us will be helpful."

His hands were covered by thin latex gloves, which he stripped off and replaced with a new pair from a cardboard box by his right elbow. Despite the fact that he must have realized that dozens of people had already handled the envelope, he took it from Cam with stainless steel tongs and laid it on a nearby glass surface. He bent down to examine the surface with a magnifying glass, pausing a few seconds over the hand-printed address.

Mumbling to himself, he remarked, "Standard indelible marker—black, no postmark, nothing distinctive about the packaging."

He straightened and picked up the envelope. "Give me a few minutes and I'll see what I can turn up. I'll scan it for handwriting analysis in case you need that done later."

"Okay, great. We'll be in the conference room," Savard said, indicating a door in the far corner of the room.

"Uh-huh," he said distractedly, his mind clearly elsewhere already.

The four of them settled into chairs around the small table in the unadorned windowless room in the rear of the forensic analysis lab. The silence as they regarded one another speculatively was broken when Blair said, "How do you know he's not going to make a record of all of this?"

Her tone held no censure, merely curiosity.

"I've known him since we were cadets," Savard replied. "He's a genius with anything that's quantifiable, but he's a lousy marksman and not particularly adept in the physical fitness department either. Somehow, we ended up being workout partners, and I spent a lot of extra time helping him prepare for the things that didn't come easily. We're friends, and he's loyal."

"What about the *contents* of the envelope? They could be... sensitive," Cam pointed out.

"He doesn't care what's in there; he only cares what's *on* it— fingerprints, fiber, bodily fluids. That's what makes an impression on him. If it's a photograph like the first one you gave me yesterday, he won't even notice the subject matter."

"Did he find anything on that one?" Cam inquired, this being the first opportunity she'd had to ask.

Savard shook her head. "No, that's why I didn't bother calling you when I found out the results. You'd already left for DC at that point, and I figured it could wait. It was a computer-generated copy, probably scanned, of the original. It wasn't made from the negative."

"Which means," Cam mused, "that it may have been made by someone who didn't have physical access to the original file."

"Or by someone who was pressed for time," Stark noted. "If you're looking through material that you don't have clearance for, you don't bother doing anything except making quick copies."

"Could be."

"Are you saying we weren't really supposed to get it?" Blair queried.

"Maybe we've been looking at this the wrong way," Cam theorized. "Maybe these packages aren't meant to be threats. Maybe they're warnings."

"Warnings? You mean someone is trying to tell us that we're being...looked at?"

Cam nodded. "Maybe these are friendly messages."

"Yeah," Stark commented darkly. "Another DC Deep Throat."

"Why don't I feel reassured?" Blair said sarcastically. "I'd prefer a straightforward phone call to this."

"You have a point," Cam agreed with a sigh. "Maybe once we see what's in this one, it will make a little more sense."

Thirty minutes later, Sammy returned. He handed Savard the envelope. "I didn't bother with everything this time. The preliminary run-through shows exactly what the other one did—nothing. Whoever sent it knew what they were doing. No saliva, so no DNA. There are no prints; nothing distinguishing about the paper—standard commercial brand; it's printed on an inkjet printer. Computer generated. Just like the other one."

"Can you narrow down the printer?" Stark asked.

He glanced at her, then at Blair, who sat beside her. Quickly, he averted his gaze. If he recognized the president's daughter, he gave no sign of it. He kept his eyes fixed on Savard, the person he was clearly most comfortable addressing. "I analyzed the pixel register on the first print. It's an Epson high-end printer. We've got one down the hall. Standard government issue, as well as the one used by most desktop publishers or almost any other business doing high-quality photo reproductions."

"If you had a sample from the precise printer, could you match them?" Stark persisted.

"Possible. I'm not sure it would hold up in court, though."

"It doesn't have to," Cam said flatly.

Since it was evident that they weren't going to get any more information, Savard held out her hand. "Thanks, Sammy."

"No problem, Renee," he said, blushing as he shook her hand. "Anytime."

Without looking at them, he sketched a small wave in the air, turned, and hurried back to his bench.

"Well," Blair said on a long exhalation. "I guess we can see what it is now."

"Let's get out of here first," Cam suggested. "Before we wear out our welcome."

Cautiously, Savard offered, "I've got my sister's apartment to myself—she's working tonight. We could do it there...unless you're headed back to Command Central?"

"No," Cam said. "I'd like you and Stark to see this. Your sister's apartment sounds fine."

CHAPTER TWENTY-TWO

The four of them had barely settled into the Suburban with Stark behind the wheel when Cam's cell phone rang. "Roberts."

She listened for a moment, then handed the phone to Savard. "It's Mac. Would you give him your sister's address? He's got some information for us, and I want him to be there when we take a look at our latest present."

Nodding, Savard quickly gave Mac the information.

Fifteen minutes later, Savard let them into the small but comfortable living room of an apartment in Chelsea. The furnishings were worn but had once been expensive, and the space beneath the windows and most of the other available niches were filled with plants of all description, adding a sense of warm welcome that was distinctly different from the impersonal apartments and hotel rooms in which most of them were used to spending their time.

With satisfaction, Cam noted a work area in a small alcove adjoining the living room that contained a desk, high-end video equipment, and a state of the art computer system. She indicated the electronic array with a tilt of her head. "You think we can use that if we need to look at the tapes Mac is bringing?"

"Sure," Savard said, her blue eyes sparkling. "As long as it's *your* paycheck guaranteeing against any damage."

Cam smiled, appreciating the brief respite afforded by levity. "I'll put it in writing."

"Deal." Then Savard walked through to a tiny kitchen and called over her shoulder, "Coffee, anybody?" At the chorus of assents, she started setting up the machine. In the midst of the preparations, the buzzer rang. "Paula? Can you get that?"

Stark crossed to the door and pushed the intercom beside it. "Hello?"

"Phillips here."

"Three C," Stark reminded him as she held down the button to release the security lock on the lobby door.

A moment later, she opened the apartment door for Mac. After greetings all around, everyone found seats on the sofa and nearby chairs. A pine coffee table sat in the middle on a brightly colored area rug.

"I guess I'll go first," Cam said grimly from where she sat on the sofa next to Blair.

Savard had cleared a space in the center of the coffee table and, as everyone leaned near, Cam reached into the manila envelope. There were two glossy sheets which she separated and placed on the table for all to see. Everyone shifted so they could look at the images from the proper perspective.

The photos had again been taken from a distance, but the first, shot in broad daylight, was of excellent quality; both her face and Blair's were clearly recognizable.

"How the hell—" Stark exploded.

"That's the deck at the rear of my mother's house," Cam said impassively for Savard's elucidation. Inside, she was raging. "It was taken at approximately 0800 hours the last day of Ms. Powell's stay in San Francisco."

"Bastards," Blair murmured, a cold chill making her shiver. It wasn't so much that someone had been watching; it wasn't even that she and Cam had been captured in a private moment—a moment that she remembered very well.

"I'll be sorry to leave here."
"Being with you makes the entire world look different."
"We don't have to leave that feeling here, do we?"
"No. We don't. Let's make sure we don't."

It was a moment that she would never *want* to forget. What bothered her was that there had been a silent witness to something beautiful—someone who was trying now to turn it into something ugly.

"I wonder where they were?" Blair's tone was as even as she could make it.

"Anywhere," Cam stated flatly. "A nearby rooftop, an apartment on an adjoining street, up a goddamned tree—anywhere with the sightline. If I'd known then what we know now, I would have paid more attention to that avenue of access to you." Unconsciously, she rubbed her temple, annoyed at the pain that was surging again. "I didn't anticipate a photographer stalking us."

Blair caught the movement and heard the self-recrimination in Cam's voice. Regarding her lover with concern, she stifled the urge to touch her. *When this is over, Cam is taking a vacation.*

"What about the other one?" Savard asked quietly, her eyes on Blair, who was now staring at the second photo. It was a grainy night shot, and of poorer quality than the one taken in San Francisco, but the faces of the two women who stood in the circle of light cast by a street lamp in front of Cam's apartment building in Washington, DC were quite clear. "Do you know her?"

"No, not precisely," Blair said steadily.

No one spoke, nor asked for further explanation. Despite the unusual circumstances, their training ruled. Federal agents did not question the private life of the first daughter.

"I think Ms. Powell and I need to speak alone for a few minutes," Cam said into the silence. *It's all going to come out now.*

As everyone began to rise, Blair said, "No, please stay." Glancing at Cam, she smiled wryly. "If you don't mind, I don't."

Cam studied the faces of the three agents sitting shoulder to shoulder across from her. Then she nodded in agreement. "I don't know where all this is going. Maybe nowhere." She lifted the photos and let them fall back to the table. "Maybe straight to the AP hotline and the front page of every newspaper in the country. Before we take this any further, each of you has to decide if helping us is worth your career, because that's what it may come down to. You have my word I'll do what I can to protect you, but if this blows up, I may not be able to. If you leave now, there'll be no har—"

"I'm staying," Stark said with conviction.

"And so am I," Mac seconded.

"I'm in," Savard added quietly.

"Thank you," Blair and Cam said simultaneously.

Cam drew another long breath, then squared the second photo on the table.

"*I* know this woman," she said, pointing to Claire in the photograph. "She's an escort with a highly exclusive service in DC. She and Ms. Powell have no relationship whatsoever."

"That might be difficult to disprove after this photo," Stark pointed out in as nonaccusatory a tone as she could manage.

Blair laughed humorlessly. "I'm certain that's precisely what this is meant to imply."

"Well," Cam said bitterly, "it seems that someone is tightening the noose. First we have a leak to the press about Blair's *secret* relationship. Then, obviously, the picture on the deck puts us together in a position that's hard to explain away." She glanced quickly at Blair. "Whether we wanted to or not. And now," she finished, pointing to the photo of her lover and Claire, "we have the connection between myself, Ms. Powell, and an escort service. All highly inflammatory business in DC."

"I'm sorry," Stark said ingenuously. "What link is there between you and the escort?"

"I know this woman in the photograph because I've been involved with her, professionally."

"Oh." Stark blushed but held Cam's gaze. "Can anyone prove that?"

"I have no idea." Cam tried unsuccessfully to shrug off her anger. "A week ago I would have said no. Now, I'm not so sure."

"Well," Mac said briskly, getting to his feet. "That's one of the things we're going to have to find out. And from the looks of things, pretty quickly."

"I agree," Savard seconded. "We need to narrow down the suspects, devise a strategy, and divide up the work in short order—before this whole thing spins out of control."

"Suspects?" Blair's surprise hung in the air.

"Yes," Cam said, looking at Savard. She and the FBI agent were the only two people in the room with true investigative experience. Stark and Mac had both been part of the protective arm of the Secret Service their entire careers. "Who stands to gain by this?"

"As you mentioned before," Blair offered, "any reporter who uncovers an elite escort service in Washington, DC that caters to government employees and visiting dignitaries would certainly garner quite a reputation. It's a career maker and reason enough."

"That's true," Mac remarked as he returned from the kitchen, balancing cups of coffee in both hands, which he then handed around. "Except it seems unlikely that an investigative reporter would also be interested in impugning *your* reputation, Ms. Powell. That would only piss off the White House."

"The story's more likely to end up on the front page of a rag like the *Star*, don't you think?" Blair countered.

"Exactly—and if that's the case, why release the photo of you and the commander to the newspaper before the whole story breaks? In fact, why involve you at all?"

"Point taken," Blair agreed. "Besides, I have no connection to the service."

"Except through me." Cam's expression was grim. "Guilt by association. And as Stark pointed out, it's difficult to disprove the implications of a photograph."

"I'm not worried about that," Blair replied, her eyes holding Cam's, refusing to allow her lover to shoulder the blame for a sin she hadn't committed.

"What about Patrick Doyle?" Stark offered, careful not to look at Renee Savard. "*He* hasn't been happy since the commander upstaged him in the capture of Loverboy—"

"Before that, really," Mac interjected. "He's always had it in for her."

Stark nodded eagerly. "If he's behind this, it would explain a photograph of her with the woman in the bar. She could have been an FBI agent or just a decoy he used to set up the commander. We all know the Bureau still uses civilian informants."

"I don't disagree with any of that," Savard said calmly, giving Stark a small smile. "And if I weren't willing to clean my own house, I wouldn't be here. But this looks like a much bigger operation than one man could possibly orchestrate. Especially if you're talking about infiltrating and exposing a very well shielded escort service that's obviously been operating undetected for a long time. That takes undercover agents and personnel with computer expertise who can access IRS filings, pull phone records, trace calls—the whole nine yards. Doyle couldn't do that on his own."

"Besides," Blair commented, "none of this explains why Cam and I are getting these cryptic messages. If they're threats, why hasn't something been demanded? Why hasn't someone asked for money or threatened to go public if Cam doesn't resign or put pressure on me to intervene with my father about something?"

"Maybe," Cam muttered, thinking aloud, "maybe it's a little bit of all of the above."

Four sets of questioning eyes stared at her.

"Maybe there is a political *and* a personal agenda at work here. Maybe the FBI or a Justice division or, hell, a *joint* team from both is gathering information for some future political purpose. Maybe Doyle is part of it or knows someone who is." Cam frowned. "If he's privy to what's going on, he may have discovered my involvement with the escort service by chance. Maybe he's taking advantage of that knowledge."

"How?" Mac asked warily.

Cam met his eyes. "Stewart Carlisle confirmed yesterday that Justice has initiated an independent investigation into what happened with Loverboy. They're looking at me, specifically. Carlisle warned me that suspension is imminent."

Mac and Stark exploded simultaneously with a series of expletives and outraged remonstrations.

"If it weren't for you, I'd be dead." Savard was furious. *And she wonders why I'm helping her now.*

Cam finally had to hold up a hand to still the grumbling. "For some reason, Carlisle hasn't put up much of a roadblock, which I find unusual. All I can figure is, if there *is* a large-scale operation accessing personal data, maybe he's in a crunch, too."

"Can something like that really be happening?" Blair asked incredulously. "We're not talking about the Hoover administration here."

Savard shook her head. "It didn't all stop in the mid-70s when Hoover was forced to retire. It's just gotten more subterranean." Her regret was clear. "It's been rumored for some time that the new director—whose appointment President Powell opposed, I might add—has been pushing both Justice *and* the Foreign Intelligence Surveillance Court hard for clearance to use surveillance in the private sector. He's asking for electronic wiretaps and computer investigation into corporate and private accounts, ostensibly under the guise of national security. Could be a splinter group is running some practice trials already."

"All right," Blair acquiesced. "So if there is some covert group of high-level intelligence agents, or politicians, or *both* gathering information, what would be the reason?"

"Almost anything," Cam noted darkly. "Anything from controlling promotions within various departments to influencing who will be the next party nomination for president. That's what's so dangerous about these operations. Information gathered today might be used a decade from now to force someone's vote in a critical congressional decision or to place a candidate sympathetic to more stringent law enforcement and less gun control in a newly created cabinet position. *When, where,* and *how* intelligence is used can't always be projected—which makes it impossible to neutralize. That's also what makes it so potent a weapon."

"For the time being," Savard said emphatically, "we need to concentrate on gathering as much hard evidence as possible about who's behind this." She stared at the opposite wall for a second and then began ticking off points with the fingers of her good hand. "Mac—you've already been looking into the reporter who provided the first photograph to the Associated Press, right?"

He nodded. "I should have a name by midday tomorrow."

"Good. What we need is to work backwards from there. We need his source. There has to be a connection to someone in DC. Whoever leaked the photograph almost certainly used someone he knew and trusted."

"Fine. I've got that," Mac said. "I also have the videotapes of the couriers who delivered the packages."

"Let's view them now," Cam suggested.

Two minutes later, the group crowded around the monitor in the tiny work space while Mac ran the pertinent segments of tape back and forth a half-dozen times.

"Ring any bells for anyone?" Cam wasn't surprised at the chorus of negatives as everyone returned to their seats.

"I'll dig a bit more," Mac said as he collected the tapes and put them back into his briefcase. "I'll scan the images and run them through the DMV, NCIC, and Armed Forces data banks. If I can ID any of them, I'll go ahead and interview."

"Try for a match with the registered courier services in New York and DC, too," Cam added. "These people have to be bonded, so the companies will have photos of all employees. I doubt our Deep Throat used a service, but you never know."

Mac nodded.

"Two," Savard said, regarding Cam evenly. "Stark and I will run background checks on everyone associated with you, Commander. We'll need a list of friends, lovers, professional associates—anyone who could be remotely connected."

At Cam's raised eyebrows, Savard continued, "We have to assume that if there is a personal agenda in addition to a political one, you are the epicenter."

"All right, Savard. You'll get the list."

"We'll need the name of the woman in the photograph, too." Stark blushed, but her voice was steady.

Cam shook her head. "I don't know it. The service took extensive precautions to provide anonymity to both clients and personnel."

"I suppose if we have to, we could run this photo through the national data banks, too." Stark stared at the eight-by-ten glossy still lying on the table.

"She's not involved," Cam said with certainty. "She put herself at risk for me, and I'd like to keep her out of it, if at all possible."

"Understood, Commander." Savard picked up the photographs and returned them to the envelope. "On the other hand, it might become necessary."

"If it does, there's a wine glass in my dishwasher in DC that will have her fingerprints on it." Cam glanced sideways at Blair, concerned about her response to that fact, but Blair just smiled faintly and shook her head. Cam returned a fleeting grin.

"Does she have a key?" Paula Stark studiously avoided looking at Blair.

"No."

"Anyone else have one?"

"Just the maid," Cam said flatly.

"Do we need to worry about her running the washer?"

"Not for two glasses, which is all that's in there."

"Sounds secure then," Stark commented, looking at Savard. "You agree?"

"Yes. If we need to ID her, we'll go get the glass. For now, I'll settle for the phone numbers or mail drop you used to contact her, Commander, and how you identified yourself."

"Done." Cam hesitated. "There's one other thing—we need to run background checks on everyone in Ms. Powell's security detail. The logical place for someone to get sensitive intel is from *inside* the security screen."

"It can't be one of us," Mac exclaimed. "What would be the point? The Secret Service exists to protect the lives, and by extension, the reputations of public figures—not destroy them."

Cam shrugged. "Maybe someone's doing double duty and working for the Bureau or is part of a Justice Department probe."

"That would be unbelievable," Stark said vehemently.

"People are known to do many things for career advancement." Cam didn't believe she had misjudged a team member, but she had to be sure. Too much was riding on it. "It has to be done, but it's not fair to put you two on that. I'll do it myself."

Both Mac and Stark looked glum, but it was Stark who spoke up. "No, I'll do it, Commander. Savard and I are going to be doing background checks anyhow."

Cam appreciated the unwavering tone in her voice. "I'll do the first routine run—if anything jumps out, you two can chase it."

"All right," Stark consented.

"The last thing we need is a computer cracker," Savard said. "We need to get into the FBI and Justice files. And we'll need to break the escort ring, too."

Everyone in the room looked at each other.

"Well, none of us qualifies," Cam remarked dryly.

"Felicia does."

"No way, Mac." Cam was adamant. "I've already involved too many people. Plus, she's new to the group and we don't know her well enough yet."

"I know her," Mac said firmly. "I'll vouch for her, Commander."

Cam studied him seriously for a moment, then shook her head again. "I just can't do it, Mac. I've already endangered all of you by involving you in this operation. I can't bring in anyone else, because I can't offer any kind of protection."

"What if she volunteers?" Mac persisted.

"Besides," Stark pointed out, "if somebody manages to bring you down, it's going to taint all of us—and we'll all be out of a job anyhow."

"I have to agree with both of them, Commander," Savard said. "If we can't get into those files, we're never going to get a complete picture of how deep this goes and who might be behind it. If we don't use our own internal resources, we'll have to go out on a limb and involve an outsider. That's even more dangerous than using someone we've only known for a short time." She paused, then added more softly, "I don't think anyone here doubts that Felicia can be trusted."

Exasperated, Cam rubbed her face with both hands. "It sounds like I'm outvoted, then."

Blair moved a little closer to Cam on the sofa and rested her hand on Cam's knee while leaning softly against her shoulder. "You don't have to worry, Commander. I'm certain it won't happen very often."

That first public, uncensored touch was so simple and spoke of so much—caring, belonging, the rightness of their being together.

Everyone laughed, and for the first time in more than a week, Cam's headache completely vanished.

CHAPTER TWENTY-THREE

"Well," Cam said, surveying her friends and colleagues, "it looks like we've got our work cut out for us. We're running against the clock, only I don't know how much time we have—not much, probably. What we *do* know is that Ms. Powell is due to go abroad in less than a week. I do *not* want this to follow her to Paris."

"Felicia may be the key." Mac was still adamant in her favor. "The files are the only thing that will give us hard evidence, unless we can find a primary witness—someone giving or getting the orders in the covert investigation—who is willing to name names."

"Maybe our Deep Throat?" Blair asked hopefully.

"Possible," Stark commented. "Except he—or she—clearly doesn't want to be found. If he's friendly, and I tend to agree that's the most likely scenario, for some reason he's afraid to approach you directly. It's not going to be easy to draw him—or her—out given our limited time frame."

"It's after midnight," Cam said, unable to hide her bone-deep weariness. "I'll brief Davis personally in the morning, but I'm going to urge her not to touch this."

Her statement was met with vociferous protests, but she shook her head determinedly. "She'll be the one at the most risk. If she can crack their computers, someone on the other end can no doubt track hers back here."

"I don't think so, Commander." Mac spoke with both conviction and an unexpected note of pride. "After all, she was assigned to go after Loverboy because she's one of the best computer hackers in the world. She knows how to cover her tracks when she's breaking down someone's back door."

"Let's hope so," Cam rejoined, still unhappy about involving yet another agent. "We'll see after I've talked with her."

"I'm going to see her tonight. With your permission, Commander, I can brief her," Mac offered. "It will save time."

"Whoa, Mac," Savard jibed, her blue eyes twinkling. "Fast worker."

He blushed, but his grin was pleased. "Not *that* fast—she said no the first six times I asked her out." He cleared his throat, suddenly serious. "Commander?"

Cam glanced at the faces of those around her and knew the decision had already been made. Sighing, she shrugged. "I surrender. Go ahead, Mac. If she's willing, bring her up to date on everything we've got so far."

Mac gathered his briefcase and placed the envelope with the photographs inside along with the surveillance tapes. "I'll speak with you in the morning then, Commander."

"Let's plan on a noon meeting for updates all around." Cam glanced at Blair. "Is it all right if we meet in the Aerie?"

"Of course," Blair said. "And I think it's time that everyone started calling me Blair."

"Yes, ma'am," Stark replied smartly, and once again the group shared a laugh.

"Everyone take some down time tonight," Cam suggested as she signaled good night to Mac, who stood at the door about to leave. She turned to Blair's primary guard, "Ready to go, Stark?"

Stark hesitated, glancing quickly at Savard. Before she could reply, Blair intervened.

"I thought I'd spend the evening at Diane's, Cam. You can take me there, can't you? No need for Stark to come, too."

"Of course. Stark, you're officially off duty now anyhow. I'll call the command center and have someone meet us downstairs to escort Ms. Powell to her destination."

"Don't bother, Commander," Stark said without a second's hesitation. "I can accompany her."

Cam sensed rather than saw Savard stiffen, and the fog cleared enough from her exhausted brain to register Blair's small sigh of disapproval, too.

"That's all right, Agent." Cam was already pulling the cell phone from her belt. "Take what's left of the night off. My orders."

After Cam arranged for the night detail to meet them with the second vehicle downstairs, she and Blair said good night to the other two women and left.

❖

"I can't believe you just volunteered to work *another* night. What is that—three in a row?" Savard definitely had a threatening look in her eye as she crossed the living room to stand in front of Stark.

"Two—well, two and a half, I guess, but I didn't *volunteer* for last night," Stark said in self-defense.

"Getting stood up two nights straight could seriously bruise my ego, you know."

"Well, it's kind of a tricky situation since the commander and Egr—uh, Blair—are trying not to be too obvious about spending time alone together," Stark began seriously. "It's easier if I—"

"Paula, shut up." Then Savard effectively implemented the order by pressing her mouth to Stark's.

Stark's small cry of surprise gave way to a soft moan as Savard's tongue moved gently over her lips, then into her mouth. In surrender, she just closed her eyes and let the warmth and softness of the caress move through her until every cell tingled. When the kiss ended, Stark opened her eyes, amazed to find she couldn't focus. Her head was spinning too much.

"That was awfully nice," she managed, her voice slightly unsteady. The apartment suddenly felt extremely warm, too.

Savard rested her palm against Stark's cheek, then gently swept the dark hair back from her temple with trembling fingers. "Yes, it was. And there's a lot more where that came from."

"There's no quota or anything, is there?" Stark brushed her lips over the fingertips stroking her face.

"None at all." Savard's voice was husky and low. "In fact, I believe there's an endless supply."

"That's good, because I'm going to want a lot."

"Starting now?"

"What about your sister?" Stark rested both hands on Savard's waist and stepped closer until their thighs touched. She was happy to find that Renee was a bit unsteady, too.

"She's a cop—seven to seven. And she won't bother us if we're...asleep...when she comes in."

"Yeah—now would be good then." Stark was a little worried that her legs weren't going to move if they waited much longer, because they were beginning to shake all on their own.

"Sure?" There was nothing teasing in Savard's tone now, only a gentle question, full of patience and tenderness and sweet longing.

"I want to make love with you so much," Stark confessed, her body vibrating with urgency. "I've wanted to touch you for what feels like forever."

The simplicity of her statement struck Savard harder than the force of the explosion the night she'd shot Loverboy. Sharply, she drew in a sharp breath, her blood suddenly racing. "I can't wait."

Stark slipped one arm around her waist. Just before she kissed her, she whispered, "Then let's not."

In the Suburban, Cam leaned forward to relay instructions to Foster, who was at the wheel, and then settled back in the rear seat next to Blair. Rubbing her temple absently, she said, "I ought to be able to run the first-level background checks tonight."

"Cam, you're about ready to fall down. You need some sleep."

"I'm okay."

"Oh, really? How's your head?"

"A few aspirin will take care of it."

"Don't you dare try that with me," Blair countered. "I may be crazy in love, but I'm not brain dead."

Cam smiled and consciously straightened her shoulders, shaking her head to clear her mind. "Not as bad as it was, honest. I can nap between—"

"I want you to stay at Diane's with me tonight." Blair's voice was calm, quieter now, but there was a finality in the way she spoke that suggested she was not going to yield.

Cam was silent, considering her options. It wouldn't be the first time that she and Blair had spent hours, even entire nights, together at some place other than Blair's apartment. Their being alone didn't necessarily imply that they were personally involved—and at this point, it seemed moot what anyone thought about their relationship. In truth, she was too tired to make a good argument. And she *wanted* to be with Blair.

"All right."

"Good." Cam's easy assent only confirmed Blair's suspicions that her lover was teetering on the brink of exhaustion. She had expected more of a fight, but she was happy to have avoided it. She, too, was emotionally and physically drained, and all she really wanted was to see that Cam got some rest.

Fifteen minutes later, she and Cam stood outside Diane Bleeker's apartment door. When it opened, Diane lazily raised one eyebrow as she leaned against the doorjamb in a burgundy dressing down, looking like a siren from a 1940s movie. "Good evening."

"Hi," Blair said, taking Cam's hand as she bent forward to kiss Diane on the cheek. "You have houseguests for the night."

"Goodie. I love a pajama party." Diane stepped aside to allow them entrance, her sharp eyes taking in the Secret Service agent's pale complexion and slightly unsteady step.

"No," Blair threw back over her shoulder, leading Cam determinedly across the living room. "We're going directly to bed."

"Well, you're certainly no fun," Diane declared with an exaggerated frown. Her tone was gentle, however, when she added, "Do you need anything?"

"No, we're all right. We just needed to escape for a while."

Diane settled on the sofa as her friend and her lover disappeared around the corner in the direction of the guest room. *What you both need is a few weeks alone together—away from the news people and the White House both*. She sighed as she picked up a magazine. She knew her wistful thought was unlikely to come true.

❖

"I should shower," Cam said as she eased out of her jacket and worked to shrug the leather weapon harness off her shoulders.

"You're fine." Blair moved to Cam's side, lifted the holster free, and then placed it over a nearby chair. The guest room was large enough for a queen-sized bed, a small dressing table with mirrors, several chairs, and an adjoining bath. The single window was open and the curtains moved desultorily in the weak summer breeze. "Just come to bed."

Stubbornly, Cam shook her head. "It's been a long day, and I don't want to lie naked next to you until I've had a shower."

"Well, I definitely want you naked," Blair conceded. She reached for Cam's hand once again and turned toward the bathroom. "Come along then, Commander."

As they stood together beneath the warm spray, they were almost too tired to talk. Cam leaned forward with both palms against the wall in front of her while the water hit her head and neck. She groaned as Blair began to soap her shoulders and back, the familiar hands finding all her tender places.

"God, that's good."

"Turn around," Blair said softly. When Cam complied, she smoothed her palms, soft and slippery with suds, over Cam's chest and abdomen. "Starting to feel human?" She sensed Cam relaxing beneath her touch.

At another time, the sight of Cam nude with her head thrown back, eyes closed, vulnerable in a way that she allowed with no one else, would have ignited a surge of desire. Tonight, being able to take care of her was satisfying in a way that Blair had barely imagined. The responsibility of loving her was wonderful and terrifying at the same time. Suddenly, she wrapped her arms around Cam's waist and pressed against her, the white froth on Cam's body coating her own.

"What's this?" Cam murmured, feeling Blair tremble.

"Nothing. I just...love you."

Cam smiled and rested her cheek against Blair's. "It feels good that you do."

"Yes," Blair whispered almost to herself.

Another five minutes and they crawled between crisp clean sheets to embrace, face to face. Cam kissed the tip of Blair's nose and sighed.

"For the record, I want to make love," Cam murmured.

"But?" Blair settled her head on Cam's shoulder as she stroked her lover's chest, finally gently cradling a breast in one palm.

"I'm too damned tired."

"Well," Blair said as her lids fluttered closed. "There's always tomorrow."

Cam's last thought before surrendering to sleep was that she hoped that would always be true for them.

CHAPTER TWENTY-FOUR

Good morning," Diane said, surprise apparent in her tone as Cam walked into the kitchen a little after seven the next morning. "I didn't expect to see you up so early. In fact, I expected you to sleep for a week."

"I smelled the coffee." Cam grinned, nodding toward the coffee maker on the counter.

"Ah," Diane said with a smile, lifting her own cup to her lips. She was in the burgundy dressing gown again, but this time she was obviously nude beneath it. The plunging neckline bared a nearly lethal expanse of creamy skin between her full breasts, and the curve of her hip and thigh was tantalizingly outlined in shimmering silk.

When Cam realized she was in danger of staring, she averted her gaze. "Do you mind if I take some to Blair?"

"Not at all. In fact, I'd appreciate it."

"Oh?" Cam raised an eyebrow.

Diane smiled fondly. "She's beastly in the morning before coffee, or haven't you noticed?"

"I can't say as I have," Cam replied mildly. She moved to the counter and took down two cups from a glass-enclosed shelf above the sink.

"Very diplomatic, Commander," Diane said, her voice a low purr. "One could either take that to mean that you've never *seen* her first thing in the morning, or that you've never found her to be cranky at that hour."

Cam turned, leaned her hip against the counter, and regarded Diane solemnly. "I've seen her first thing in the morning, just not often."

"Something tells me that's going to change."

"I hope so."

Cam poured coffee, sensing Diane watching her. "Thanks," she said when she'd finished, "for the coffee, and for putting us up last night."

"She's my best friend, and I love her."

Briefly, Cam wondered if those two things were related or if they were, in fact, separate statements. She had never asked Blair if she and Diane had been lovers and never would. It didn't matter because it didn't affect what was between her and Blair now. "I know, and I'm glad. She needs friends like you."

"Apparently what she needs most of all, Commander," Diane said emphatically, "is you."

"It's Cam. And if it makes you worry any less, I love her, too."

Diane smiled, and this time the smile was sensuous. Her voice dropped a register as she remarked throatily, "She's very fortunate."

"No. I'm the fortunate one."

"Are things going to work out with this latest press brouhaha?" Diane asked suddenly.

Cam was used to keeping her reactions to herself, but the question surprised her. "You know about that?"

"Some. Blair told me about the photograph in the newspaper and the fact that she expects more publicity."

"I doubt that our relationship will remain a secret much longer."

"If I may be so bold...are you ready for that?"

"More than ready."

Diane saluted her with the coffee cup. "As I said, she's very lucky."

At that moment, Blair shuffled into the kitchen, dressed only in a long T-shirt that came to mid thigh. She glanced from her lover to her best friend. "Who's lucky? Is that coffee?"

"Here you go." Cam laughed and held out the cup.

Blair frowned when she realized that Cam was barefoot in old clothes that Blair kept at Diane's for emergencies—tight threadbare jeans that didn't snap at the top and a shirt that was missing buttons in decidedly dangerous places, especially considering Diane's proximity. Crossing quickly to Cam's side, she took the cup and wrapped her free arm around her lover's waist.

"What are you two talking about...or shouldn't I ask?"

Cam kissed Blair's temple lightly and murmured, "Newspaper photographs."

"Oh, that." Blair grimaced. "What else?"

"Don't worry, darlin'," Diane said lightly. "Once they've had their week of fun with you, they'll move on to something else. In six months, no one will care."

"In six months, my father is going to be in the middle of his reelection campaign. *Someone* is going to care."

"He can handle it," Cam asserted.

"I hope so," Blair said, almost to herself.

At noon, Cam, monochromatic in a two-piece charcoal suit and linen shirt, arrived at Blair's door for the scheduled update. She was accompanied by Stark, Savard, Mac, and Felicia.

"Hi," Blair said as she stepped aside to admit them. For an instant, seeing Cam in her professional mode, she remembered how her lover had looked that morning, disheveled and still sleep-tossed, and she wanted to kiss her. Just because.

"Hi," Cam murmured as she passed, the fingers of her right hand brushing the length of Blair's bare forearm.

"There's coffee in the kitchen if anyone wants some," Blair called. "Just help yourself."

Once fortified with caffeine, everyone settled in a loose circle around the low wide coffee table in the sitting area just to the right of the door. Cam sat on the couch next to Blair with Mac on her left. Felicia was next to him in one of the sling-back chairs, while Stark and Savard occupied a small love seat on the other side of the table.

"I ran preliminaries on our team this morning," Cam said. "As expected, the process was fairly nonproductive. I did turn up one interesting fact, however."

Beside her, she felt Mac stiffen and saw Stark's eyes widen with surprise, or maybe alarm. Savard watched her intently. The only person in the room who seemed completely relaxed was Felicia Davis.

"It seems that Fielding was assigned as the FBI liaison in DC three years ago. The Bureau field agent he worked with was Special Agent Patrick Doyle."

"Jesus," Stark exclaimed. "He never said anything about knowing Doyle."

"True, but that doesn't mean anything," Mac hastened to add. "It's not as if they were old friends or anything. Considering what an asshole Doyle turned out to be, John probably wanted to downplay any relationship they might have had."

Reluctantly, Stark recalled, "He was with us in San Francisco. And he'd just gone off duty the night that Ms. Pow—uh, Blair and the commander were photographed on the beach. He could have tipped someone to their location."

"Well, yes, perhaps," Mac agreed grudgingly, "but there are plenty of other explanations for that photograph. The Bureau has agents there, and they'd most likely take pictures of anyone with no questions asked if a DC SAC ordered them to."

"At this point," Cam interjected before Mac and Stark ended up at odds, "I consider this only a coincidental association. It could just be a paper link—Fielding might never even have interfaced with Doyle in person. But it bears follow-up. Right now, we can't discount any potential connections." She had known her agents wouldn't like one of their own being examined, and she didn't blame them. She would have been unhappy if they'd reacted otherwise. But it had to be done. "Savard? Can you run with it?"

"Yes, ma'am."

"Good. How about you two—any progress with *my* background check?" Cam gazed steadily at Stark and Savard.

Savard cleared her throat. "So far, Commander, you're in the clear. We looked at family members and the list of...ah...intimate contacts you provided." To her credit, she neither blushed nor looked away. "Other than your association with the escort service in DC, we don't see anything that could potentially be an avenue for blackmail or future coercion."

"For now, we'll accept that as a dead end," Cam responded evenly. "If something turns up that does lead back to me, we'll look further."

"Yes, ma'am."

Cam turned next to her communications director. "Mac?"

He grimaced, his frustration evident. "I'd hoped to have more. I finally backtracked the photograph of you and Blair in the *Post* through the AP's source files and came up with the name of a freelance reporter—Eric Mitchell out of Chicago."

"Name mean anything to anyone?" Cam addressed the room at large. All the agents shook their heads in the negative. She nodded. "Go ahead, Mac."

"I wish I could." He ran a hand through his blond hair and blew out a breath. "I talked to him an hour ago, and he's unbreakable. I don't think he'd give up a source if President Powell flew out there and confronted him in the news room. The only thing he *would* tell me is that it came to him via an anonymous e-mail."

"I'm looking at that, Commander," Davis said quietly. "Newspapers aren't particularly difficult to hack."

Cam raised an eyebrow but made no comment. "You think there's any value in bracing him in person, Mac?"

Mac shook his head. "Believe me, Commander, I'd be on a plane this afternoon if I thought it would do any good. He's not going to give us anything."

"All right," Cam said with a sigh. "Anything in *his* background?"

"Nothing much, but I haven't looked too hard yet. I just came up with his name right before this meeting."

"Go ahead and dig. There's got to be a reason that the source contacted him specifically. Find it."

"Roger that."

Finally, Cam looked to Felicia, who she knew was their best hope. "Any progress?"

Crossing one elegant calf over the other, Felicia Davis leaned forward, her hands loosely clasped in her lap. She was a stunning combination of composure and intensity. "I've just started, but I can tell you this—there is a concentrated exchange of e-mails and attached files going back and forth between a limited number of Bureau addresses and some offices on the Hill. Ordinarily, I wouldn't even find this kind of traffic unusual, but every single message in this cluster is encrypted, and the source files are limited."

"E-mails?" Stark interjected. "Who would be stupid enough to document an undercover operation in e-mail?"

"You'd be surprised," Felicia responded. "Just because someone is responsible for our nation's security doesn't mean they know a damn thing about technology. Most people think encryption is all they need."

"And remember," Blair pointed out, "Richard Nixon *taped* hundreds of hours of criminal activity that transpired in the Oval Office. Enough to put several key advisors in jail and eventually cost him the presidency. There's something about the air in DC that makes some politicians think they're invincible."

"Specifics, Davis?" Cam's eyes glinted. *This is what we need.*

"Not yet. It will take me a while to pinpoint the origination, but eventually, I ought to be able to give you not only the *who* but also the *what*."

"Excellent. While you're at it," Cam instructed, "see if you can trace a path from those same e-mail addresses to anyone in Justice or Treasury."

"That means a lot of transmissions to sort out, Commander," Felicia advised. "Most intra- and interagency business is conducted electronically these days."

"I know that. But what we need," Cam said, her frustration escalating, "is to find out who is coordinating this operation. These messages have *got* to lead there." She stood, and the others followed. "I'll be in Command Central all day. If anyone gets anything, advise me immediately. I need you all to remain available to meet back here at any time in case something breaks."

Everyone murmured their assent as they gathered papers and moved toward the door. After Blair closed the door behind the small group of supporters, she turned to Cam. "What do you think?"

"I think Davis is onto something." Cam leaned against the back of the sofa, her arms crossed loosely over her chest. "There *has* to be a tie-in to the Hill, because I can't see the Bureau in this all alone, even if it *does* have Hoover-esque overtones." She rubbed both hands briskly over her face and sighed.

"What is it?"

"I've had three calls from Carlisle since eight a.m."

Blair's chest tightened. "What did he want?"

"I don't know." Cam's voice was tight. "I haven't answered."

"What do you *think* he wants?"

"To advise me of my suspension."

Blair started toward the phone. "I'm calling Lucinda."

"Blair, no. This isn't your fight."

"I beg your pardon?" The president's daughter stopped dead and stared stonily at Cam.

"This is internal—something between Carlisle and me and whoever might be squeezing him on this." Cam held out her hands. "Come here."

After a second's hesitation, Blair crossed the room. She fit her hips between Cam's parted thighs, loosely wrapping her arms around her lover's shoulders, one hand going to the back of Cam's neck. She stroked her gently. "Don't shut me out."

"I won't," Cam promised, encircling Blair's waist. "But let's wait to pull out the big guns."

Blair laughed. "Lucinda would love to know you called her that."

"Speaking of the formidable chief of staff," Cam said, "what have you decided about making a statement to the press—about us?"

"I believe I'm at the point that if asked, I will acknowledge. In fact, I'm thinking maybe I shouldn't even *wait* to be asked."

"If you make a statement," Cam murmured as she kissed Blair's forehead, "you're going to catapult yourself into the spotlight. Every talk show host in the country will be looking to book you."

"They'll be disappointed."

"And every right-wing fanatic will make you their poster child for moral corruption."

"I know." Blair had indeed thought about that. "We'll be a hot topic for a while."

"Well, I can't see that there's much choice."

Blair studied Cam's eyes, looking for any sign of worry. "Are you sure you're okay with it if I do? You're going to get most of the heat initially. Someone is bound to insinuate that you took advantage of your position or that your effectiveness has been compromised."

"I'm fine with it." Cam brushed her thumb against the corner of Blair's mouth, smiling when Blair quickly turned her head and kissed it. "I love you."

Those words never failed to pierce Blair to the core. Sighing softly, she pressed closer, her lips finding Cam's neck before she rested her cheek on Cam's shoulder. "Well, I can testify to the fact that your effectiveness has not been diminished in the least."

"Good to know," Cam murmured.

Closing her eyes, Blair breathed her lover's scent and felt her heartbeat strong beneath her palm. Feeling inexplicably at peace, she whispered, "I love you, too, Commander."

CHAPTER TWENTY-FIVE

As the afternoon dragged on, Blair tried to occupy her mind with work. Usually, once she began applying paint to canvas, her focus was so intense that everything else receded from her consciousness. To her chagrin and even greater frustration, it wasn't working this time. She finally set her palette and brushes aside and pushed both hands through her hair. Then she glanced at the clock for the fifth time in as many minutes—seven p.m.

I'm going crazy up here. Maybe I can call Cam, discreetly, for an upda—

A knock interrupted her thoughts.

As soon as she had the door open, she grasped Cam's hand and pulled her inside, then kissed her swiftly on the mouth. "Tell me you've got something."

Cam shook her head, shedding her jacket to the back of a nearby chair and shrugging out of her shoulder holster. "Not yet, but Davis is hopeful that it won't be too long. I've got to believe we'll turn up something soon." *We have to, because the clock is ticking faster than I thought.*

"Maybe this really *will* be over soon," Blair said wearily. "At least we haven't gotten any more envelopes with surveillance photographs of us inside."

"No, and I don't think we will either." Cam sat on the sofa, leaned back, and relaxed into the cushions. She'd been hunched over a computer in the command center for hours.

"What makes you think that?" Blair followed and settled next to Cam.

"Because I think our theory that these came from a friendly source is correct," Cam said as she took Blair's hand, intertwined their fingers, and rested them on her thigh. "I think they were meant to warn us—or at least *you*—of the scope of the investigation and perhaps to give a hint of the intent. The first photograph that went out on the wire was of you and me together, letting you know that our relationship wasn't a secret. But it told us a lot more than it revealed to the public. It wasn't nearly as damaging as it might have been, because it wasn't clear that you were with a woman, and I wasn't identifiable. Plus, there's been no follow-up to that. A reporter wouldn't be likely to sit on that kind of juicy tidbit for long."

"I agree," Blair mused. "That photo told *us* a lot but didn't reveal much to anyone else. In fact, this reporter in Chicago, Eric Mitchell, is probably dying for a follow-up. Obviously he hasn't gotten anything further or he would have run with it."

"Exactly." Cam circled her thumb in Blair's palm as she spoke. "Then we have a photograph of me in a bar with a woman in a compromising position. As a result, *we* know that there's an active covert investigation of me. *And* it points to the kind of surveillance that only professionals can carry out—a link to the Bureau or Justice."

"And finally," Blair said emphatically, "there's a picture of the woman with whom you've been having a clandestine affair."

"Hardly an affair," Cam objected.

Blair raised an eyebrow. "Cameron, let's not split hairs."

"Point taken."

"Regardless of what you call it," Blair continued unperturbed, "the third photograph warned us that the escort service was under investigation, suggesting that the operation extended to personal lives—possibly not just yours but also those of influential people as well."

"Including the president," Cam added. "I'd say that someone managed to draw us a pretty clear picture of what was going on without actually naming names—or risking personal exposure."

"I suppose he thought the follow-up photos would scare me enough to stop seeing you."

"Thereby giving you credible distance and keeping you clear of any scandal." Cam's stomach tightened. "Everything points to a DC insider."

"Right—the Deep Throat theory again," Blair said. "I suppose it would seem like a favor to anyone who doesn't know how serious

I am about you already."

"Does anyone know?"

Blair shook her head. "Only Diane. And your mother."

Cam stared blankly for a second, then grinned for the first time in what felt like days. "I think we can safely rule them out. What about your friends—your contacts? You seem to have a pretty well positioned circle of insiders at the White House and other handy places."

"Believe me, I've thought of that. I can think of one or two who might stumble onto a conspiracy like this, but I can't imagine why they wouldn't just pick up the phone and call me."

Cam frowned. "I agree—that angle makes no sense."

Blair drew her legs under her and curled against Cam's side, threading a free arm around her waist. "Well, I'm grateful to whoever was responsible, but there's nothing that could keep me away from you."

Yes, there is.

When Cam stiffened but didn't reply, Blair sat up, her heart suddenly pounding. "Cam? What is it?"

"As of 0900 tomorrow morning, I'll no longer be your security chief. Mac will be interi—"

"No," Blair cried, jumping to her feet, her eyes slightly wild. "No. That's not how this is going to go. No way."

Startled, Cam stood also and reached for her hands. "Blair—"

"Don't," Blair said sharply, stepping back, avoiding Cam's touch. "I *know* what will happen. They'll replace you, and I'll never see you again."

"No, that's not true," Cam vowed, moving tentatively toward her lover.

Blair looked as if she was ready to bolt. Cam couldn't remember ever having seen her so frantic, not even when Loverboy was stalking her. This wasn't just about them; this was something else, an old terror of loss and abandonment come back to haunt her. Heart aching, Cam said again, "I won't disappear. I promised I wouldn't."

Blair's eyes stung with tears, and a cold hard fear blossomed in her chest. "What if you can't help it?"

"I *can* help it," Cam said with conviction. "I *will* help it. Even if I'm not on your detail, I'll still see you. No one's going to stop me—stop us."

"What if—" Blair blinked as Cam's arms came around her, and then she shuddered. Despite the urge to flee, she let herself be held. Cam was warm, her body solid, her hands tender. The shadow of the past slipped away and the world righted itself. She took a deep breath. "I'm sorry. I panicked. I—"

"It's okay." Cam kissed her tenderly, and in that moment, holding one another, they found strength in the certainty of their love.

When Blair eased out of the embrace, her eyes were hot, but this time with fury. "God damn it, Cameron—I'm not letting this happen to you. I'm not letting someone tear us apart. And I'm not letting Capitol Hill run my life any longer." She started across the loft toward her sleeping alcove.

"What are you doing?"

"I'm going to Washington."

"We don't know enough—"

"Then I'll find out," Blair seethed.

Cam swore as her cell phone rang. She snatched it off her belt and snapped, "Roberts."

Her face grew still, her eyes fiercely intent as she listened. "Come upstairs, and bring what you have."

As she closed the phone, she met Blair's questioning gaze. "Stark says they've got something. She's on her way up with Mac and Savard."

❖

"Okay, let's hear it," Cam said, looking from Stark to Savard. Both of them were unusually subdued, and she had a distinct sensation that Stark was trying not to fidget. "Agent Stark?"

"We've been running everyone we could think of who had any connection to you, Commander, past or present, testing the theory that the exposure of your involvement with the...uh...escort service might be a payback of some kind." Stark took a breath, seemed to be gathering herself. "You know, a grudge kind of thing—someone passed over for promotion, someone who resents a woman heading the security team, someone who might be jealous of—"

"I think we all follow your reasoning, Stark," Cam said dryly. "Where are you going with this?"

"Right. Well, naturally, it made more sense to start with recent contacts, so we prioritized known personal and professional associates. Obviously, we dug deeper on a few people and—"

"You're rambling," Cam said brusquely. "Just spit it out."

Her nerves were fraying, and she was losing the battle not to show it. Despite what she'd told Blair earlier, she knew that once a formal investigation was launched into her conduct in the Loverboy operation, she wouldn't be able to see Blair. At least not until she was cleared—*if* she was cleared. The thought of being separated from Blair, even for a few weeks, made her ache.

"We don't have time for the long version." She was surprised to feel Blair's hand move over to rest lightly on her knee. Drawing a breath, settling herself, she said, "Sorry. Continue."

Stark sat up straighter and reported smartly. "It came to our attention that Detective Sergeant Janet Aronson of the DC Metropolitan Police was married at one time."

"Yes, I know that." Cam's eyes never left Stark's, but her pulse rate jumped at the mention of Janet's name. "It was well before I knew her, and she'd been divorced a number of years by the time she and I were involved. It wasn't something we spent any time talking about."

"Yes, ma'am, I understand. She was married to—"

"Another cop. I *know* all this," Cam said impatiently, but she felt a tightening in her chest—a foreboding—as if there was something she should know, but didn't. Something she had missed. God, there were so many things she had done wrong in her relationship with Janet.

Blair's fingers tightened briefly on Cam's leg and then stroked softly in a small circle. The touch brought Cam back to the present, and she slid her own fingers fleetingly over her lover's. "I'm sorry. I...just go ahead."

"She wasn't married to another *cop,* Commander. She was married to a federal agent. Patrick Doyle."

"Jesus." Cam stood abruptly and walked to the far side of the room. Her back to the group, she looked out over Gramercy Park, remembering Janet's face, and the look in her eyes the day she'd died. Without turning, her voice rough with memory, she said, "Maybe she said law enforcement, and I just assumed it was another cop. I never asked...it didn't seem important, but..."

Nothing personal seemed important between us. We shared a bed and not much more. God, she deserved better.

From across the room, Blair watched Cam's back stiffen and her hands clench at her sides. She wanted to go to her, to put her arms around her, to rest her cheek against her back. To hold her until the memories faded and the pain diminished. She couldn't, not because the people in the room were not her friends, but because this was the pain that Cam guarded and was not ready to share. *But you'll tell me someday, won't you? When you're ready to forgive yourself. And when that day comes, I'll be here to help.*

After a minute, Cam returned to her seat. Her face was expressionless, her voice steady. "Well, if Doyle had been keeping any kind of track of her, he might have known about us. It's hard to keep anything secret in a cop shop. I'm sure he has friends on the DC police force."

"That would certainly explain why he's always had it in for you," Mac noted.

"He wouldn't be alone," Cam said quietly. "A lot of people thought I should have been able to prevent what happened to her."

"It also explains why if he stumbled across something incidental about you in an investigative file, he would try to use it against you," Savard pointed out, her tone calm and matter-of-fact. She'd seen the pain flicker through Cameron Roberts's eyes, and she'd almost *felt* Blair Powell's desperate desire to comfort her. She hurt for both women, imaging how hard it would be to have her own deepest secrets laid bare like this.

"Yes." Cam reached for Blair's hand without realizing it. "I suppose it would explain the photograph of me and the redhead in the bar—and possibly the one of Blair and me as well. If he's working to sabotage my career, he's made a good start."

Mac swore and Cam gave him a quick smile.

"It doesn't, however, explain the photograph of Blair and Cl—my previous companion."

"It does if he was going to hold it over your head," Stark asserted indignantly. "If he threatened to implicate Blair in something illegal or even just...unsavory, he'd have a pretty good screw in you."

"I suppose you're right." Cam rubbed her face with her free hand, the other loosely linked with Blair's on the sofa between them. "Anything else?"

Stark and Savard shook their heads.

"Felicia's still working—she says she's getting closer," Mac offered in a desperate attempt to infuse some hope. When Cam had told him about the call from Carlisle and her imminent suspension, he'd wanted to punch something. "I've got some stuff on the reporter. Nothing much there, though."

"Can you guys give us a while, and then we'll regroup and see where we are?" Blair asked quietly. "I'll call you when we're ready."

"It's okay," Cam murmured as her agents hastened to leave.

"No, it's not," Blair answered just as softly. "But it will be."

Chapter Twenty-Six

When the door closed behind her team members, Cam, still seated on the couch, dropped her head into her hands, elbows braced on her knees. "Ah, fuck," she said wearily. "What a mess. Christ, I'm sorry."

Blair went to her side, sat close, and rested her left hand gently on the small of Cam's back. The shirt was soaked with sweat even though the loft was cool. The anguish in Cam's voice was so rare, and so raw, she felt the edges of her own soul bleed.

"Cam?" Blair's fingers made small gentle circles over the tense muscles. "What are you sorry for?"

Without lifting her head, without turning toward her lover's soothing voice, Cam replied dully, "I'm sorry my past is causing trouble for you now. I had no idea...I can't believe Doyle and Janet...Jesus Christ."

"It's not your fault that Doyle is doing this."

"If I'd been there for her, she might be alive." Cam straightened, anger whipping through her frame, making her tremble. "If I'd asked about her assignment, *cared* about what she was doing...if I'd done more than *drop around* when I needed...oh fuck, you don't need to hear this."

Cam got abruptly to her feet, seeking desperately to regain control. She was tired, and the goddamn headache had returned with a vengeance, and she was having trouble pushing the memories back where they belonged, behind the door that she kept locked and barricaded.

"Sit back down, Cameron," Blair said firmly and reached for her lover's hand.

For a second, Cam resisted, and then, almost against her will, she sat. She met Blair's eyes, her own clouded with regret. "I've made so many mistakes. With Janet, with you. It's bad enough that I got involved with you while I was on the detail. I never thought anyone would find out about the escort service, and before, when it was just me at risk, I didn't care. I didn't care about much of anything. Now, I've pulled you into this...and I'm sorry."

Blair's gaze never wavered. "I know you're tired, because I am, too. I have a feeling your concussion was a lot worse than we thought, because I can tell the pain is back again. I know you're worried about me. I know what it will mean to you if there's an inquiry and your competence is questioned. I *know* all those things, Cam." Blair paused a beat and then said in a strong, resolute voice, "But if you *ever* apologize to me again for loving me, I'm going to tell you to leave...and not come back."

Cam's eyes widened and she jerked, feeling the invisible blow as surely as a fist. "Blair," she breathed and lifted her fingers to stroke the rigid line of Blair's tense jaw. "I'm *not* sorry for loving you. I never will be. Loving you is the best thing I've ever done in my life. I'm only sorry that my loving you has brought you pain."

"It hasn't—not once—not the way you think. You've hurt me when you didn't tell me things, and you've hurt me when you let false issues come between us. I'm guilty of those things, too," Blair said softly, lifting her hand to close her fingers over Cam's. "But you've never hurt me in any way that threatened the trust between us. You've never lied to me."

"I won't. I promise."

Blair drew Cam's hand to her lips and kissed it tenderly. "You're not to blame for Janet's death, and you're not at fault for having been unable to prevent it. You're not always responsible, Cam, for what happens to other people. I know that's what makes you who you are, and I love you for it. But sometimes you have to let it go. If you don't, it's going to destroy you...or us."

"Ah, God." Cam's intake of breath was sharp. "I'd do anything not to lose you."

"Well, good." Blair drew her first full breath in many minutes, then smiled a bit tremulously. "Because I need you so very much."

Leaning forward, Cam kissed her mouth, gently at first and then with increasing urgency, a kiss heavy with possession and need. Blair's hands came to Cam's chest, then moved upward inside the collar of her shirt, to the back of her neck. She insinuated her fingers in the thick dark hair, pulling Cam's head closer, hungry for her. When they edged away from each other, both gasping, Blair moaned. "God, you make me ache inside."

"I want you now." The feel of Blair, the want in her voice, the urgency in her words made Cam's head swim. All she could think of was the heat of Blair's flesh and the sound of her cries and the beating of her heart beneath her own fingers and tongue. "Right now."

"I know...I can feel it. I can see it your eyes. I love the way you want me."

When Cam lifted shaking hands to Blair's shirt, Blair stopped her, closing her fingers around Cam's wrists. "We've got a lot to do before tomorrow morning," she barely managed through a throat thick with need.

"I'll be able to think better when all my blood isn't pooling between my legs," Cam insisted, sliding her palms under the material and over the bare breasts beneath. Blair's sigh of pleasure was all the permission she needed to continue.

Once she had Blair's shirt open, Cam pressed Blair back against the pillows on the sofa and fit herself between her lover's thighs. Forcing her hips hard into Blair's, Cam braced herself on her extended arms and lowered her head to work her lips and tongue over Blair's nipples and the sides of her breasts and down the center of her belly. By the time she reached Blair's navel and tugged at the small gold ring with her teeth, Blair was moaning, eyes closed, head rocking from side to side. Sitting back on her knees, Cam freed the buttons on Blair's jeans and jerked the zipper down, then switched her hands to the waistband and pulled.

"I'm so damn hot," Blair muttered anxiously as she lifted her hips to help push.

Once the jeans were below Blair's knees, Cam ran her fingers up the inside of Blair's legs, teasing them apart, making room for her mouth. Blair was ready, the way Cam knew she would be, already swollen, pulsating, heavy and dark with urgency and blood. Cam inhaled her arousal and felt the answering beat between her own thighs.

"Ah, God...when I touch you, I can feel it inside, like you're touching me back. I could come from making you come."

"Try," Blair whispered hoarsely.

Cam laughed and lowered her head. She didn't rush; she didn't tease; she took Blair steadily and certainly and unerringly. She knew when to tug and when to suck and when to slowly work her tongue around the pounding, quivering nerve center, following the rise of Blair's hips, riding the crescendo of her cries.

Together, their blood soared. And when their passion surged, it flowed as one, anointing them both.

❖

Cam turned on her side, her cheek resting on Blair's lower abdomen. Drowsily, she murmured, "Why is it that I can't remember what I was so worried about a few minutes ago?"

"Sex does that." Blair threaded her fingers through Cam's hair and drew the damp strands over her palm. "It melts your synapses, at least it does when we do it."

"Well, I'd better get my brain reconnected." Cam pushed herself upright, her hand trailing lightly up and down Blair's bare thigh. "I need to review the Paris itinerary with Mac tonight and be sure everything is in place since I won't be go—"

"If you don't go, I don't go." Blair's words were said with absolute finality and brooked no argument.

Cam turned her head and studied her lover, who still reclined among the displaced cushions, her clothes disheveled, her color still high with their lingering passion. She was beautiful and strong and everything that mattered in Cam's life.

"You have to go."

"No, I don't. It's a public relations trip, and there are plenty of other people my father—or, rather, Lucinda—can tap to make nice to the French president and whoever else needs to be stroked. It doesn't have to be me, and it's not *going* to be me—unless you go as my security chief."

Cam raised an eyebrow. "Correct me if I'm wrong, but didn't you nearly freeze me out a month ago after I took the reassignment as your security chief?"

"That was different," Blair said calmly. "That was your choice, and you made it without my input. You were wrong."

Momentarily, Cam was silent. "You're right. You were right then, too. I'm sorry."

"I know. And it's over." Blair found Cam's hand and squeezed it. "This is something entirely different. You're being targeted, and by someone who has a personal agenda—if not Doyle directly, then someone who Doyle or one his cronies is twisting, too. It's wrong, and I won't let that happen. I won't be a willing party to this kind of political terrorism."

"Have I mentioned lately that I love you?" Cam's throat was tight again, not with want this time but with gratitude and wonder.

"You've mentioned it, occasionally. In fact, you just showed me."

Through a grin, Cam said, "I don't know at this point that there's anything we can do to stop my suspension."

"Doesn't this new information about Doyle help at all?"

Cam shook her head. "It explains some things, but I don't think it gives us any particular ammunition. Now we know why Doyle has always had it in for me, and in all likelihood he's the one who ordered the surveillance of you and me in San Francisco. That's got Bureau written all over it. I doubt that he's the one behind the investigation of the escort service, though. And if we're going to fight back, we need to know the power behind the entire operation."

"I want to come with you tomorrow when you go to Treasur—"

The ringing phone interrupted her.

Leaning on her side, Blair fumbled with one hand on the end table until she found the receiver. "Blair Powell." After a second, she continued, "Yes...no, it's fine...come up now."

She set down the phone and sat up on the sofa, rapidly buttoning her shirt. Reaching for her jeans, she said, "Time to get yourself together, Commander. The troops are returning."

CHAPTER TWENTY-SEVEN

"Felicia caught a break," Mac said before the door had closed fully.

Felicia, who managed to retain her composed, elegant appearance despite having worked more than fifteen hours without a break, smiled at his obvious excitement. "I've narrowed down the origin of the e-mails," she explained as she and Mac walked to the sofas and the four of them sat down. Mac and Felicia faced Cam and Blair across the coffee table.

"Where?" Cam asked, ignoring the first flutter of hope in her chest.

"I've got bundled transmissions to and from the Bureau director, the deputy attorney general's office in Justice, and two Senate subcommittees. Much higher density than anywhere else."

"Which committees?" Blair asked sharply.

"Intelligence and Arms."

"Specifics?" Cam probed. *The power centers. This is bigger than I thought.*

"Unfortunately, no," Felicia replied. "I can't trace the link to individuals until I search every file."

"How long?" Cam was somber, thinking of time running out.

"I don't know. I might get lucky and hit right away, or it could take...days."

It's over. Cam straightened, slapping her palms on her thighs briskly. "Well, that's it then. I'd say you've done about all you can do. I appreciate your efforts."

Looking to Mac, studiously avoiding Blair's piercing gaze, she said, "I'll need to review the details of the transition with you, Mac, before you take over in the morning."

"Commander," he protested.

"It's got to be done." Cam glanced at her watch. It was 11:15 p.m. "We're out of time."

"What about Stark and Savard?" Blair struggled to keep her growing desperation from showing in her voice. "Have they turned up anything new in the background checks?"

"No, and neither have I." Mac shook his head dispiritedly. "They've pretty much cleared Fielding, which we expected. I ran down everything I could think of on the reporter in Chicago. I can't find a link."

"There must be something there, Mac," Blair insisted. "What about Mitchell's friends or associates?"

"It would take too long to run that kind of search, and I calculated the yield would be low." He slipped his PDA from his shirt pocket and tapped through several items. "The guy's clean— married, couple of little kids. Finances unremarkable. Freelances out of Chicago."

"What about his wife?" Cam asked reflexively. Her investigative training made it impossible for her to leave any avenue unexamined. "Anything there?"

Mac shook his head, reading from the small screen. "Not that I can see. They were married four years ago. Wife Patricia, maiden name Carpenter, educated—"

"Patty Carpenter? College at Amherst?" Blair's voice shook with sudden intensity.

Mac's head snapped up. "That's right."

"God," Blair breathed. It was her turn to stand and pace. She walked from the group gathered around the coffee table to the windows, needing some semblance of space and air. Even the huge loft seemed suddenly too close. As she considered the new information, she ran her fingers over the double-paned bulletproof glass. She was beginning to see how all of this had been engineered, but what to do about it wasn't as simple as she had imagined it would be. Knowing the source did not make the solution any easier. Far from it.

She jumped, startled, when Cam came to her side.

"What is it?" Cam spoke too quietly for the others to hear.

"I know her. I think I know how her husband came to have that photograph of us. And I know who's been sending us the warnings."

"But?" Cam was gentle, sensing Blair's struggle. With anyone else, she would have pushed. But this wasn't a suspect; this was her lover. And she knew Blair would tell her, if she could. "Blair?"

Blair took a deep breath and turned to search Cam's eyes. Those dark eyes were tender, patient, giving her time to decide. And in the deep, uncompromising love she found there, she also found her answers.

"But nothing, really. Your reputation, your career, is at risk here. And our relationship is in danger of being interrupted by negative publicity and pressure from any number of quarters...at the very least. I can't let that happen."

"It's a friend, isn't it?"

"Yes." Blair rested her palm on Cam's chest, her fingers gently stroking. "It's a friend. And you're my lover."

"Blair, we can find another way through this. I don't want you to betray—"

"Cameron," Blair said with a fond shake of her head. "When are you going to learn that you are the one and only person who matters to me? You—more than anyone or anything in this world."

Without waiting for Cam's answer, she walked back to Felicia and Mac, who were conspicuously not looking in their direction.

"Mac, try cross-referencing those two committees with the name Gerald Wallace."

Mac's eyebrows flew up, and even Felicia's normally calm countenance registered surprise. "*Senator* Wallace?"

"Yes, that's the one."

"With a name to follow," Felicia commented as she stood, "I might have something for you within a few hours."

"If he's the link." Mac was dubious.

"He is," Blair stated with absolute certainty.

"Senator Wallace," Mac repeated, almost to himself. "There's been a low-level hum for months that he'll challenge your father for the nomination. Jesus Christ, this is going to get ugly."

Cam moved to Blair's side and rested her fingers on the back of Blair's hand. "Let's try to see that it doesn't. Keep this totally under wraps. Advise Stark and Savard, but nothing gets written down and only one hard copy to me along with all the disks."

"I can guarantee our security here," Felicia said without hesitation. "I'll reformat the hard drives when I'm done."

"Good. I'll be here when you have something."

The two agents nodded and departed. Cam turned to Blair and said, "Can you tell me now what's going on?"

Blair sat heavily on the sofa and patted the cushion for Cam to join her. When they were both settled, she said quietly, "Gerald Wallace is A.J.'s father."

"Ah—and how did you make the connection?"

"Patty and A.J. were roommates at Amherst. They were close, but I never knew Patty all that well. That's why A.J. used Patty's husband—because he would hold off on a follow-up story if she asked him to, whereas any other reporter would have kept digging or just fabricated something."

"It fits," Cam mused. "That explains why the media coverage hasn't escalated, despite that one photo in the *Post*. There hasn't been anything else to chase because A.J. didn't leak anything else." She grimaced. "Of course, they'll still want their story sooner or later."

"And they'll get it," Blair responded acerbically. "But when *I'm* ready, and the way *I* say."

"I love you." Cam grinned.

Blair smiled, but her eyes were sad. "This explains why A.J. was so strange on the phone. She's our Deep Throat. She warned me in the only way she could without betraying her father. I doubt that she ever thought we would uncover his involvement."

"Christ," Cam said. "Justice and the Bureau and Wallace, all colluding to covertly investigate political figures on the Hill, including the president? It'll be to be a scandal of major proportions if this gets out."

"And if it comes out that A.J. was the leak, she's going to lose her job, to say nothing of what it will do to her relationship with her father." Blair tightened her grip on Cam's hand. "I don't want that to happen, Cam. She was trying to *help* me. I can imagine how hard it must've been for her to send me information when it endangered her father's career. I can't turn around and destroy hers."

"When we get hard facts—and we *will*, eventually—we can shut this operation down," Cam said, thinking aloud. "But we can't go public to do it. Too many people could get hurt, including A.J. There's nothing we can do right now to stop the inquiry."

"You mean...just keep quiet, when they're coming after you *tomorrow*?"

"I can weather a Justice inquiry."

"Not if the cards are stacked against you," Blair protested. "You know and I know and everyone involved knows that your actions were perfectly appropriate during the entire Loverboy operation, up to and *including* the endgame. But if Doyle has enough pull to get you investigated in the first place, who knows how the outcome of the inquiry might be rigged? We can't chance that."

"True, but if it means we can avoid creating a public scandal that might extend even further than we already know, I'll chance it." Cam scrubbed at her face with her free hand. "I have a responsibility to the Agency—to the entire system—and I don't want to put that system on public trial for my own personal benefit. I'm willing to risk the inquiry."

"Well, I'm not. Not when it's you. Besides, Cam, it's not just a Justice inquiry. God knows what they're going to do with the information about you and the escort service, or how they might try to link me to it."

"I know, and we won't let that happen. We just need time for Felicia and Mac to get us the ammunition. Then we can plan our attack."

"I might have some ideas," Blair said.

"I don't suppose there's any chance that I can talk you into staying out of this, is there?"

Blair smiled softly and kissed her. When she drew back, eyes bright, she said, "Not a chance in hell."

"That's what I thought." With a faint grin, Cam reached for the phone, called down to Mac, and asked him to set up a five a.m. flight for two to DC. "You know," she turned to Blair, "we should try to get some rest. Think you can sleep?"

Blair threaded her arms around Cam's neck and molded her body to her lover's. With her lips close to Cam's ear, she whispered throatily, "I know some great relaxation techniques."

"So do I. Let's compare."

❖

Blair's bed faced the floor-to-ceiling windows, and from the top floor, Cam could only see the moon and the shadows of buildings across the square. Blair was curled around her, head pillowed on Cam's shoulder, one arm and leg thrown over her body. Resting her cheek against the silken softness of Blair's hair, Cam breathed the familiar scent, softly stroked the curve of her hip, and listened to her even breathing as she slept.

They'd made love quickly, not because of time, but because of need. Their kisses had been ferocious, their hands greedy, their bodies aflame. When they'd climaxed, it had been as much with urgency as release.

Lying there with Blair, Cam realized it was one of the very few times they had ever spent even part of the night together, and she struggled with the anguish of knowing that it might be a long time before she would hold her lover again. Despite the hope that her colleagues and friends would find some concrete evidence that she could use as a bargaining chip with Carlisle, she despaired that she would be able to change what had already been set in motion.

She thought about Doyle, his deeply harbored animosity over a relationship that was long dead and his jealousy over a woman who had left him long before she had died as well, and strived to keep her regrets and remorse over Janet's death at bay. She knew Blair was right—neither Janet's death nor Doyle's fanaticism were her fault or even her responsibility—but she couldn't stop remembering the disappointment that had flickered in Janet's eyes just before she died. Now she might lose another woman, the woman whom she knew she couldn't live without, and she felt the dam of her fortitude crack.

Blair stirred and whispered, "What's wrong?"

"I'm sorry, I...I didn't mean to wake you." Cam wondered why her throat was so tight.

Blair ran her fingers over Cam's face and drew a sharp breath as her hand came away wet with tears. Stunned, heart aching, she pushed herself up in bed and gathered Cam into her arms. "It's all right," she murmured, holding Cam tightly, rocking her without even thinking about it. "Tell me?"

When Cam tried to answer, her voice caught on a sob. For so many months, she had kept the pain buried, immersing herself in work and detached sex. Then she had found Blair. Now that special peace was threatened by forces she did not know how to fight. She was breaking, and she didn't know how to stop it. Desperate, she clung to Blair and struggled for breath.

Holding Cam, wanting nothing so much as to protect her, Blair understood, for the first time in her life, that the essence of love is the solace given in the dark of the night when terror and uncertainty and the ghosts of old heartache are the strongest. With a grip so firm it might have been painful if it hadn't been so essential, she pulled her lover close and whispered fiercely, "I love you, baby. I love you."

Eventually, Cam's head cleared, and the fist that had squeezed the air from her lungs and threatened to stop the blood in her veins relinquished its hold. She pushed away onto her back, gasping. "God, I'm...sorry. I have no idea what happened."

"Are you all right?" Blair's own breath contracted in her chest. Blindly, she found Cam's hand and squeezed.

"Yes. Just a nightmare—the kind you have when you're awake."

"I've had them," Blair said quietly. "For me, you make them stop."

"So do you." Cam turned on her side and brushed her fingers over Blair's face, stroking her neck and shoulders. "Thank you."

When they kissed, the kiss spoke of gratitude as well as desire. Cam shifted until her thigh nestled between Blair's legs and groaned faintly as Blair pressed into her. "I need you, Blair."

As she leaned down to kiss Blair again, the phone rang. Cam pulled away, cursing.

"Easy, lover." Blair patted Cam's cheek and laughed a little unsteadily. "Ordinarily, I'd ignore it, but I think we'd better answer that."

"I'll take a rain check then," Cam whispered and kissed her quickly.

"You bet you will."

Reluctantly, Cam moved away, and Blair reached for the phone.

"Blair Powell...okay, give us ten minutes. We'll be down." Suddenly wide awake, she hung up and pushed back the sheets.

"Time for a shower, Commander. Felicia says she has what we need."

CHAPTER TWENTY-EIGHT

Lucinda Washburn looked up from the stack of papers and studied Blair unblinkingly. "How many people know about this?"

"Five federal agents." Across from her, Blair was settled in the comfortable office chair, dressed in jeans and the light cotton sweater in which she had traveled.

"Jesus," Lucinda muttered. "That's a security nightmare."

"No, it isn't," Blair assured her. "No one is going to say anything to anyone."

"You trust them *all?*"

Blair laughed at the irony, thinking of all they'd been through together. "With my life."

"As I understand it," Lucinda rifled through the pages, "a three-term United States senator has been gathering intelligence on both private citizens and fellow politicians, including the president of the United States, ostensibly to plan campaign strategy and possibly influence lobbyists, voters, and party officials—and he's using federal agents and resources. Is *that* what you're telling me?"

"Pretty much." Blair shrugged. "I don't really know *what* his intentions were, but the transmissions we intercepted clearly indicate unsanctioned surveillance being carried out by FBI agents, with that information being routed to Senator Wallace and at least one person at Justice."

"And who tipped you to this?"

"Anonymous." She would not reveal A.J.'s role. She wasn't certain that her old friend hadn't been an active part of the operation herself, and, if she had been, Blair had no desire to torpedo her career. "When the photo of Cam and me leaked to the press, we started digging, and this is what we found."

"Pretty lucky." Lucinda's wry tone made it clear that she knew there was more to these documents than Blair had revealed. "As it stands, the use of wiretaps and electronic surveillance in the investigation of private citizens who are not suspected of *anything* violates any number of federal statutes, not to mention the campaign irregularities if Wallace tries to capitalize on any of this."

"That's why I brought it to you." Blair looked directly at the chief of staff. "If it doesn't involve Dad now, it might next year. And there are plenty of other names in that file who are on his reelection team or who are big supporters."

"That's not all." Lucinda had something close to distaste in her voice as she slid one of the pages from the pile and held it up. "Here we have the clients list of an escort service. This looks suspiciously like the basis for blackmail, and that's getting a little far afield from simple campaign violations."

"We don't know that anyone has actually been blackmailed. *Coerced* might be a better word."

"That's a fine distinction."

"I know—but if we...uh, you...put an end to this situation now, it won't ever reach that point."

"The only good thing," Lucinda remarked dryly, "is that they weren't particularly selective in their surveillance—liberals and conservatives, Democrats and Republicans; they were indiscriminate in their violation of privacy. We've got one DC circuit judge, two congressmen, and a member of your father's cabinet—with a nice mix of affiliations. That will give me leverage on both sides of the fence."

Lucinda pushed the papers away and watched Blair carefully as she spoke. "This is serious, but it can all be handled without going public—and I think that's for the best."

"*I* certainly don't have any desire to air Washington's soiled linens on prime-time TV."

"But you brought this to me for a reason." She held up a hand when Blair started to explain. "Oh, I know—you're concerned about your father's political future. I believe you. So am I. What else do you want?"

"I want the Justice investigation of my security chief called off. It never should have gotten as far as it has, but someone is pushing buttons in Treasury or Justice—or both—and I know that at least *one* of those people is involved in this illicit operation."

Lucinda's eyes flicked to the stack of documents. "Your *chief's* name is on the escort list."

"I know that." Blair never blinked, although the image of the beautiful blond who had been Cam's lover crossed her mind. "It has nothing to do with her job performance, and it has nothing to do with our relationship. The Justice inquiry was instigated by someone with a personal ax to grind with her. I want it to stop."

Leaning back in her chair, Lucinda gazed at some point across the room, clearly mentally sorting options. "You know," she contemplated aloud, "most people believe that the currency of government is the almighty dollar, but it isn't. It's favors. I hold IOUs on a lot of people. I don't mind using some of them to clear this up. It will save me a lot of trouble down the road if I shut this down right now." She smiled, a feral smile. "And letting Wallace know *I* know what's he's been up to will make the bastard think twice about challenging a sitting president for the nomination."

The anxiety that had churned in Blair's stomach since she had called Lucinda from the plane on the way to DC to ask for an emergency early morning briefing began to abate. "It will have to be done soon in order to help Cam."

"Oh, it will be," Lucinda said. "But I'll expect something in return."

Blair's eyes narrowed. "And what would that be?"

"That you keep a lid on your relationship with Agent Roberts—at least until after the nominations. No statements, no public acknowledgements, and no more public displays of affection."

Blair shook her head. "No. You said it yourself—if I hadn't brought this information to you, you might have found yourself in a very difficult nomination race against Wallace next year. I'd say we're even."

"You should consider politics."

"Not in this lifetime. I'll tell you what, though," Blair conceded. "I promise that if I do make any public statement about my personal life, I'll give you fair warning so Aaron will be prepared to handle the press corps."

"It sounds like you're already planning something. I'd like the details now."

"Actually, that's something I'd rather discuss with my father first."

Blair rose and walked toward the door. As she reached for the handle, she turned back. "Thanks for the help."

"Don't mention it," Lucinda called dryly as the door slowly closed behind the president's daughter.

❖

When Cam opened the door to her apartment, Blair's heart lurched with sudden worry. Her lover was still in the same jeans and polo shirt that she'd worn on the plane.

"I thought you had an appointment at Justice?" Blair entered and curled her fingers around Cam's bare forearm. "Why aren't you dressed? It's almost nine."

"It seems I don't have anywhere to be this morning after all," Cam replied.

"Damn, if they've suspended you alre—"

"Quite the opposite." Cam grinned and shook her head. "Carlisle's secretary called at 0803 to advise me that the scheduled meeting with him had been canceled. He had also instructed her to inform me that the matter of Loverboy was closed."

Blair slipped her arms around Cam's waist and sighed with relief. "Thank God."

"What *exactly* did you do?"

"Not much, really," Blair replied. "Lucinda and I traded favors."

"Thank you for that...for everything."

"It feels good to be able to do something for you." Blair ran her hand across Cam's chest, seeing the scars again in her mind's eye. Every time they made love, she saw them—felt them with her fingers and her lips. Remembered the moment the bullet struck. She shook her head, letting the memory go, savoring her lover's solid embrace. "You don't need to thank me."

"I still do, though," Cam whispered and kissed her.

"Yes, well," Blair managed when she caught her breath, "Lucinda will be sure to remind me of this when she needs something done on short notice, I'm sure."

"She's a very fast worker," Cam noted admiringly. "Whatever strings she pulled, it didn't take long."

"Lucinda Washburn probably holds more power than anyone in this country, next to my father. If she wants something done, it gets done."

"You have some very interesting contacts." Cam's grin widened. "You're a very handy woman to know."

"You think so, Commander?" Blair ran her hands lightly up and down Cam's back. "Impressed?"

Cam nuzzled Blair's neck, kissing the tender skin beneath her earlobe which Cam knew was a trigger point for her sensitive lover. "Uh-huh. *Very* impressed."

With her lips very close to Cam's ear, Blair whispered throatily, "Then you'll probably be especially excited to learn that we have an appointment with the president of the United States this morning."

Cam stiffened, then straightened suddenly. "Excuse me?"

"He's got a busy day, so we've been sandwiched in between the morning briefing with the national security advisors and a meeting with a representative from the People's Republic of China."

"Christ, I've got to change my clothes!"

"You look fine. It's a family visit, Cam, not a briefing."

"That may be," Cam replied, turning toward the bedroom. "But I'm not going to pay a visit to the president in blue jeans."

"You're going to have to get over that eventually. I expect you'll be seeing quite a lot of him in the future. You know, birthdays, holidays—that sort of thing."

"That's going to take some getting used to," Cam called back over her shoulder and disappeared around the corner.

Blair smiled and followed after her. *Better get started then, lover.*

❖

President Andrew Powell looked up from the report he had been reading as Blair and Cam walked into the Oval Office. He set the papers aside and gestured at the small seating area across from his desk as he moved to join them. "Sit down, please. Coffee?"

"No, sir," Cam said crisply.

"I'll take some." Blair moved to the far side of the room where a small service set of cups and utensils were arranged with a coffee urn on a credenza. "Dad?"

When he shook his head no, she poured herself a cup and returned to sit next to Cam on the sofa, facing her father, who was in his customary wingback chair. "I'm sorry to spring this on you so suddenly. Thanks for seeing us."

"It's all right. Is there a problem?"

"Not exactly." Blair unconsciously rested her hand on Cam's knee. "There's something I wanted to tell you before you heard about it anywhere else."

He nodded and waited.

"I've decided to make a public statement about my relationship with Cam."

His expression didn't change as he looked from his daughter to her lover. "All right."

"Lucinda is going to be unhappy about it." Blair watched his face intently.

"She'll deal with it." His smile was fond, but his tone was flat, uncompromising. "Is there any reason that you've chosen this time, if I might ask? Has something else happened?"

Blair shrugged. She had no intention of telling him about recent developments. That was Lucinda's call.

"I don't want to worry every day about hiding our relationship from the press. Sooner or later, they're going to get the story anyway, somehow. I'd prefer to bring it out into the open honestly, rather than have some reporter sensationalize it." She glanced at Cam. "And we both thought the timing would be better now instead of next year when you're in the midst of your reelection campaign."

"I appreciate that, but, as I said, it's not of particular concern to me. On the other hand, if you want to control the issue, I suggest you fire the first volley."

Cam nodded, thinking how like her father Blair was. Neither of them waited for the fight to come to them.

"That was our thought, too," Blair took a deep breath and carefully avoided Cam's eyes. "There's one other thing. There's the problem of Cam continuing as my security chief once it becomes public knowledge that we're lovers."

Cam tried to hide her surprise. *Well, it's her father. And her show.*

The president shifted his attention from his daughter and fixed it on Cam. "Does your relationship with my daughter affect the way you do your job?"

"Yes, sir, it does," Cam said evenly as she steadily returned his gaze.

"How?" His eyebrow quirked but he gave no other sign of surprise.

"Ordinarily, sir, the only concern of the Secret Service is to ensure the physical safety of the protectee. I find that occasionally my judgment is affected by my concern for Blair's...happiness."

A fleeting smile twitched at the corner of his mouth. "Does this endanger her?"

Cam blew out a breath and considered the very issue that had troubled her from the moment she first realized that she was falling in love with Blair Powell. "I don't think so, sir. It does provoke me to bend the rules on occasion, but in terms of her physical safety, my reactions are instinctual."

"And I'd be happier if they were a little *less* instinctual," Blair interjected. "I was hoping you'd tell her she had to resign, Dad."

"Yes, I gathered that somehow." She had rarely asked him for anything, even when she was a child. He thought about the intense wash of fear that had flooded through him the day he had been informed that shots had been fired at his only child. He had been grateful to the core that a Secret Service agent had taken the bullet meant for her. On the other hand, he could only imagine how his daughter must feel—having someone she loved nearly die in her place.

Carefully, he asked, "Agent Roberts, if you were no longer providing security for my daughter, would your reactions be any different if she were endangered?"

"Absolutely not, sir," Cam responded instantly. "Whether I am officially assigned to her or not, I'm still going to read the terrain with an eye toward her security. That's instinctual, too. If someone threatens her, I'll respond in the manner I've been trained to respond."

The president glanced at Blair, sensing that this was not the answer that would please her. "Well, it seems to me, Blair, that if she's going to behave the same way whether she's officially assigned to you or not, we might as well let her do her job." *And I'll feel a hell of a lot better.*

"Okay, I give up. I can't argue the point with both of you," Blair replied. She glanced from her lover to her father. "I certainly hope this isn't a harbinger of future alliances, because if you two gang up on me like this very often, I'm going to be seriously pissed."

"I wouldn't dream of it," the president said gravely, and both Cam and Blair laughed.

When her father leaned to kiss Blair's cheek at the door of the Oval Office, he whispered, "Good luck."

❖

As Blair and Cam moved through the hallways of the White House, Cam murmured, "That was a very tricky maneuver back there, Ms. Powell—trying to get your father to fire me."

Blair grinned. "It was a long shot, but I figured if he *ordered* you to resign, you wouldn't resist." She hesitated. "Are you angry?"

"No." Cam laughed. "I know you had to try. Are *you* going to be able to live with it?"

"I'll have to."

Suddenly serious, Cam said, "Because if you don't think you can, I'll—"

"He's right. You're right. I surrender," Blair said with only a mild hint of annoyance. "You're going to do the same thing whether you're my security chief or not. At least if you *are* in charge of my team, once in a while we'll be able to pretend we have a normal life."

Cam relaxed. "That sounds very good to me."

"Well, we have one more thing to do, and then I suggest we take advantage of your day off."

"What's on our agenda, Ms. Powell?"

"I'm going to call Eric Mitchell and arrange an exclusive interview. I think he'll be willing to handle it tastefully. Are you ready?"

"Any time you say." Cam reached down and briefly squeezed Blair's hand.

CHAPTER TWENTY-NINE

On their third night in Paris, Cam and Blair stood close together in a minuscule park on the tiny island in the middle of the Seine, the silhouette of Notre Dame looming upward in the night sky behind them. Their hands were linked where they rested on the top of the wrought-iron railing, while the river flowed slowly a few feet below. Thirty feet behind them in the shadow of the trees, a Secret Service agent stood guard.

The night was close around them as the darkness offered its silent shield. They were about as alone as it was possible for them to be.

"What are you thinking about?" Cam asked quietly, marveling at the beauty of Blair's profile in the moonlight.

"Patrick Doyle."

"How unfortunate." Cam grimaced. "Why?"

"Because it pisses me off that nothing's going to happen to him despite all the trouble that he caused you. I want him to suffer, somehow."

"Actually, something *has* happened to him. I noticed in the briefings today that there's been a change of command at the Bureau office in DC. Patrick Doyle is no longer the special agent in charge. He's been posted to a field office in Waukegan."

"Where is that?"

"Exactly."

"Good," Blair said vehemently. "I hope he rots there."

Cam thought of her brief encounter with Doyle the morning after she and Blair had given the interview to Eric Mitchell acknowledging their relationship. She'd gone to see Carlisle, because she'd needed to know where things stood between them. He was still her superior, and she still took orders from him. His only remark had been, "The president has complete confidence in you, and that's good enough for the director. Just try to keep your picture off the front page."

When she left the office after assuring him that she had every intention of doing just that, Doyle was walking toward her. They approached each other from opposite ends of the hallway, their eyes riveted on one another, their bodies tensed and ready for a fight.

As he drew near, Doyle hissed through clenched teeth, "You got lucky this time, Roberts, but I'd watch my back if I were you. You won't be able to hide behind Blair Powell forever."

It grated on her to even hear him say Blair's name, but she just smiled. "You still trying to scare me, Doyle? I thought by now even you would be smart enough to figure out that doesn't work."

He lifted a fist and rocked forward on the balls of his feet, his jaw muscles bulging, but he stopped before he touched her. She remained motionless, her hands open and loose by her sides. She wanted nothing more at that moment than to jam her fist in his face, but she wouldn't give him the satisfaction of goading her into it.

"You weren't good enough for her, Roberts." His face was flushed, his eyes hot with hatred. "She deserved better than you."

Cam's face never changed, but her eyes hardened. When she spoke, her voice was level and edged with flint. "You know, Doyle, that may be true. But I know she was too good for you, and so did she."

And then she stepped around him and walked away, leaving him staring speechless at her back.

Relieved, Cam reached for Blair's hand and drew it to her lips. Softly, she kissed her palm. "I'd say Doyle has paid a high price for revenge."

"I don't think so," Blair grumbled, but the night was gorgeous and so was her lover, and she couldn't hold on to the anger any longer. Moving closer, she rested her head against Cam's shoulder. "I love you."

"I love to hear you say that," Cam murmured. She kissed Blair's temple, then laughed softly. "Do you think the ambassador will be terminally insulted that you stole away early from his gala?"

"I doubt he even noticed. I'm sure he was too busy glad-handing to care what I was doing."

"Well, the *ambassador* might not have noticed, but the ambassador's *wife* certainly did."

Blair chuckled and slid her arm underneath Cam's dinner jacket and encircled her waist. "Why, I can't imagine what you mean, Commander."

"I *mean* that if she had looked at you much longer with that exceptionally eager expression in her eyes, I was going to have to create an international incident."

"You can't seriously be jealous?" Blair laughed out loud.

"You think not?" Cam turned and rested one hip against the railing, pulling Blair into her arms. Bending close, her mouth against Blair's ear, she murmured, "You are a very beautiful woman, Ms. Powell. And in this dress, I might add, a spectacularly sexy one. She wasn't the only one watching you tonight."

"The only person's attention I'm interested in is yours." Blair's voice was husky as she linked her hands behind Cam's neck. They fit together seamlessly, and she felt the heat of Cam's body through the sheer material of her dress. "And at the moment, I'd like quite a bit more of your attention."

"Unfortunately, you're going to have to wait," Cam whispered, but her own voice shook with a swift surge of desire. "I don't think even Stark could pretend to ignore us if I did what I'm thinking of doing right here."

Blair pulled her close and kissed her, a fierce, demanding kiss that deepened as their bodies molded to one another. When she drew back, she gasped, "Patience is not my long suit."

Cam brushed her thumb along the line of Blair's jaw. "I like you hungry."

"I'm hungry now." Blair slid her hand down Cam's chest, over her abdomen, and pressed her fingers fleetingly between her lover's thighs, smiling inwardly when Cam stiffened and bit back a groan.

"Let's walk for a while," Cam whispered, her blood racing. "Then we'll stop at the first little hotel we find and get a room for the night."

"What about Stark and Fielding?" Blair inclined her head toward the darkness behind them.

"Once we're settled, I'll tell them to take the rest of the night off." Cam laughed. "I seem to recall that Renee Savard took a week's vacation and just *happened* to decide to spend it in Paris. I doubt very much that Stark will complain about working a short shift tonight."

"You know," Blair mused, linking her fingers once again with her lover's. "There *are* some real advantages to your position, Commander."

As they walked beneath the stars in the city made for lovers, Cam replied softly, "I love my work."

Blair laughed, embracing the woman—and the love—that had taught her that freedom is a matter of the heart.

The End

About the Author

Radclyffe is a member of the Golden Crown Literary Society, Pink Ink, the Romance Writers of America, and a two-time recipient of the Alice B. award for lesbian fiction. She has written numerous best-selling lesbian romances (*Safe Harbor* and its sequel *Beyond the Breakwater, Innocent Hearts, Love's Melody Lost, Love's Tender Warriors, Tomorrow's Promise, Passion's Bright Fury, Love's Masquerade, shadowland,* and *Fated Love*), two romance/intrigue series: the Honor series *(Above All, Honor, Honor Bound, Love & Honor,* and *Honor Guards)* and the Justice series (*Shield of Justice,* the prequel *A Matter of Trust, In Pursuit of Justice,* and *Justice in the Shadows)*, as well as an erotica collection: *Change of Pace – Erotic Interludes*.

She lives with her partner, Lee, in Philadelphia, PA where she both writes and practices surgery full-time. She is also the president of Bold Strokes Books, a lesbian publishing company.

Her upcoming works include: *Justice Served* (June 2005); *Stolen Moments: Erotic Interludes 2*, ed. with Stacia Seaman (September 2005), and *Honor Reclaimed* (December 2005)

Look for information about these works at www.radfic.com and www.boldstrokesbooks.com.

Other Books Available From
Bold Strokes Books

Distant Shores, Silent Thunder by Radclyffe. Ex-lovers, would-be lovers, and old rivals find their paths unwillingly entwined when Doctors KT O'Bannon and Tory King-and the women who love them-are forced to examine the boundaries of love, friendship, and the ties that transcend time. (1-933110-08-2)

Hunter's Pursuit by Kim Baldwin. A raging blizzard, a remote mountain hideaway, and more than one killer-for hire set a scene for disaster-or desire-when reluctant assassin Katarzyna Demetrious rescues a stranger and unwittingly exposes her heart. (1-933110-09-0)

The Walls of Westernfort by Jane Fletcher. All Temple Guard Natasha Ionadis wants is to serve the Goddess, and she volunteers eagerly for a dangerous mission to infiltrate a band of rebels. But once away from the temple, the issues are no longer so simple, especially in light of her attraction to one of the rebels. Is it too late to work out what she really wants from life? (1-933110-24-4)

Change Of Pace: *Erotic Interludes* by Radclyffe. Twenty-five hot-wired encounters guaranteed to spark more than just your imagination. Erotica as you've always dreamed of it. (1-933110-07-4)

Fated Love by Radclyffe. Amidst the chaos and drama of a busy emergency room, two women must contend not only with the fragile nature of life, but also with the mysteries of the heart and the irresistible forces of fate. (1-933110-05-8)

Justice in the Shadows by Radclyffe. In a shadow world of secrets, lies, and hidden agendas, Detective Sergeant Rebecca Frye and her lover, Dr. Catherine Rawlings, join forces once again in the elusive search for justice. (1-933110-03-1)

shadowland by Radclyffe. In a world on the far edge of desire, two women are drawn together by power, passion, and dark pleasures. An erotic romance. (1-933110-11-2)

Love's Masquerade by Radclyffe. Plunged into the often indistinguishable realms of fiction, fantasy, and hidden desires, Auden Frost discovers a shifting landscape that will force her to question everything she has believed to be true about herself and the nature of love. (1-933110-14-7)

Beyond the Breakwater by Radclyffe. One Province-town summer three women learn the true meaning of love, friendship, and family. Second in the Provincetown Tales. (1-933110-06-6)

Tomorrow's Promise by Radclyffe. One timeless summer, two very different women discover the power of passion to heal and the promise of hope that only love can bestow. (1-933110-12-0)

Love's Tender Warriors by Radclyffe. Two women who have accepted loneliness as a way of life learn that love is worth fighting for and a battle they cannot afford to lose. (1-933110-02-3)

Love's Melody Lost by Radclyffe. A secretive artist with a haunted past and a young woman escaping a life that proved to be a lie find their destinies entwined. (1-933110-00-7)

Safe Harbor by Radclyffe. A mysterious newcomer, a reclusive doctor, and a troubled gay teenager learn about love, friendship, and trust during one tumultuous summer in Provincetown. First in the Provincetown Tales. (1-933110-13-9)

Above All, Honor by Radclyffe. The first in the Honor series introduces single-minded Secret Service Agent Cameron Roberts and the woman she is sworn to protect—Blair Powell, the daughter of the president of the United States. First in the Honor series. (1-933110-04-X)

Love & Honor by Radclyffe. The president's daughter and her security chief are faced with difficult choices as they battle a tangled web of Washington intrigue for...love and honor. Third in the Honor series. (1-933110-10-4)

Honor Guards by Radclyffe. In a journey that begins on the streets of Paris's Left Bank and culminates in a wild flight for their lives, the president's daughter and those who are sworn to protect her wage a desperate struggle for survival. Fourth in the Honor series. (1-933110-01-5)